Praise for Opal Wei
and *Wild Life*

"Opal Wei takes small town romance one step further in this delightful tiny island screwball romance...an absolutely charming opposites attract story that will have you swooning for Davy, feeling for Zoey, and swearing to stay away from geese."

— Lily Chu, author of *The Stand-In* and *The Comeback*

"Creative, compelling, and so witty."

— Kate Clayborn, author of *Georgie, All Along*

"I am utterly enchanted by Opal Wei's voice. This book was a magical blend of humor, heartache and romance. Wei sure knows her way around a beautiful sentence and a human heart."

— Yulin Kuang, author of *How to End a Love Story*

"*Wild Life* somehow manages to combine a delightful homage to *Bringing Up Baby*'s screwball antics with a thoroughly modern romance—one remarkable for its warm intelligence, wit, and complexity. Zoey and Davy are an incredibly charming central couple."

— Olivia Dade, author of *Spoiler Alert* and *Ship Wrecked*

"*Wild Life* is a delightful romp of a romance that will win readers' hearts. As the characters look for a missing slide and deal with disasters of all types, Opal Wei handles their personal struggles with a sensitive touch."

— Jackie Lau, author of *The Stand-Up Groomsman*

**Also available from Opal Wei
(as Ruby Lang)**

OPAL WEI

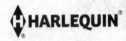

ISBN-13: 978-1-335-47595-4

Wild Life

Copyright © 2024 by Mindy Hung

Recycling programs
for this product may
not exist in your area.

This is a work of fiction. Names, characters, places and incidents are either
the product of the author's imagination or are used fictitiously. Any resemblance
to actual persons, living or dead, businesses, companies, events or locales is
entirely coincidental.

For questions and comments about the quality of this book, please contact us
at CustomerService@Harlequin.com.

® is a trademark of Harlequin Enterprises ULC.

Harlequin Enterprises ULC
22 Adelaide St. West, 41st Floor
Toronto, Ontario M5H 4E3, Canada
www.Harlequin.com

Printed in U.S.A.

For Kristin, Trina, Julie, Gloria and Bernhard.
Thank you for helping me and my family
through our big life change.

Some readers may find topics discussed in this book difficult. These include cancer and terminal illness, anxiety and mental illness, flawed family relationships and the mistreatment of animals.

You only have to let the soft animal of your body
love what it loves.

From "Wild Geese" by Mary Oliver

CHAPTER 1

ZOEY FONG MEETS THE HANDSOME

She was a doll. An adorable, frowning, thunder-browed doll in a spotless white shirt. With round, pink cheeks. The color likely came from anger, but the wrath wasn't directed at Davy so he chose to admire and enjoy rather than be terrified.

Although dolls could be really scary when bent on vengeance.

But the object of her ire seemed to exist safely in the device— a microscope?—she was peering into. And after some colorful but not particularly creative cursing, she glanced up and saw him.

"May I help you?"

When people asked if they could help you in that tone of voice, they weren't really looking to come to your aid. Then again, he *was* intruding.

He smiled apologetically. "I'm a little lost. I'm looking for Dr. Hisanaga."

Davy had never been in university buildings, and he hadn't darkened the halls of any place of learning in a long time, and despite the fact he presented a genial face to the world, he felt a trace of anxiety.

This smelled and looked like a hospital.

He'd been in hospitals.

The woman got up with a sigh and came out into the hall, shutting the door. She crossed her arms.

He tried to look like he enjoyed wandering through the underground caverns of a building at Musqueam University, looking for people named Dr. Hisanaga. As it was, the good professor had only grudgingly extended him an appointment. Which he was now late for.

No use in worrying about that now.

"I don't know a Dr. Hisanaga."

"Well, I don't either, yet. Is there, like, a directory or a kiosk somewhere?"

"Do I look like an information desk?"

He took in her snapping dark eyes and the soft body under the crisp shirt. She was fluffy and angry, like a delicious cake that would give him violent heartburn. He still wanted a bite.

"You're much prettier," he said truthfully.

He turned on his best smile.

"Why do *cis men* think I'm the happy helper booth around here? Tell me this? I mean, I'm working. I've got a microscope. I've got this whole—" she waved her arms at the empty hall "—I've got this whole setup. And these men, these men are forever wandering in asking me for things."

"I apologize."

"You do?"

"I really do."

A pause.

Davy ventured, "It's just—"

"I knew it. You're going to apologize. You're going to make puppy eyes at me. And then you're going to ask me for something. What? What do you want? A moment of my time? A tour? Fix the printer? *Can I borrow one of your mugs, Zoey? I don't have any clean ones.*"

She marched off and half terrified, half intrigued, he followed her.

"Directions. Just directions. My phone isn't charged."

"Can't you ask someone else?"

"No one else seems to be here."

The woman got to what appeared to be a kitchen or lounge of some sort and barged inside. "What do you mean no one else is here?"

She spun slowly as if noticing for the first time they were the only people around.

Davy started into the doorway and then backed out of it. Better to stay clear in case of doll attack—she did seem a little bit more like the haunted, violent type despite the round, rosy cheeks.

"What time is it?"

She pulled out her phone. "Shit, shit, shit. I am so late."

In an unexpected move, she ran to the sink and began scrubbing out mugs.

"I'm sorry," Davy said again, because it was an appropriate thing to say in Canada for all occasions.

"It's not your fault," she muttered.

"At least let me help you do something."

He was already late. And although he hated disappointing people, he got the distinct feeling Dr. Hisanaga would rather he flaked out.

Besides, he had no idea what this woman was going to ask him next. It was invigorating.

"Can you—can you wash these for me?"

He could do that. She dashed out, then back in again.

"My name's Davy," he said. "Davy Hsieh."

He might as well give her his name since he was helping her

and all. She sat down with a laptop and began typing madly into the computer. Papers she'd dumped on a table beside her fluttered to the ground, but when he stepped forward to pick them up, she held up one imperious hand while turning to riffle through her bag with another and coming up with— lip balm?

All right, then.

He began drying. "You have a lot of mugs."

"I have a lot of people borrowing them."

More furious typing.

"Why do you keep them if people borrow them, and you have to wash them, and it makes you angry?"

"I just—people keep giving them to me. Once people think, *Oh, here's the person with the mugs*, then people assume things about you. They start giving you ones with dogs or kittens on them for your birthday, or themed ones for the holidays. Or ones that say, *Don't Peer Review Me Until I've Had My Caffeine*. Or they just pop in and say, *I saw this and thought of you*, and then you're supposed to *thank* them. For a mug. And before you know it, you agree to babysit their experiment for the weekend. Because they were so nice to me for giving me a gift, and since I'm here—yeah, since I'm here and I'm washing mugs for the rest of my natural life."

Davy did not think this was the time to point out that he was cleaning them.

She banged the laptop shut for emphasis.

He sprayed a gentle shower of water over the hated collection.

She said, "Now you're going to ask why I keep them if I dislike them so much. It isn't easy, you know. I can get rid of some at a time, but God forbid I get rid of the one my supervisor gives me. Like, he can't remember if he reordered supplies or that it's his daughter's birthday but can remember he gave me a plastic Scooby Doo travel mug from a year ago. And then there's the ones I do get rid of."

"Okay."

"Like, I took some to the thrift store, but I used to be able to put stuff on the curb in Toronto and someone would take it for sure. A kitchen chair, books, lamps. Even broken things. But in Vancouver—"

"I don't live here most of the time, but I can imagine."

He dried the mugs one by one and, not knowing what else to do, stacked them in a place that looked sort of out of the way.

"I think people just leave them in my space in the lounge at this point hoping they'll be taken care of. *Leave your orphan mugs to Zoey Fong.*"

"I'm guessing you're Zoey Fong."

"I don't have time to make conversation. I need to meet my boss before he leaves."

"Can't you talk to him Monday?"

He opened a cupboard and found a shelf labeled with her name. No one else seemed to have one. Worse, it was already half full. He started putting the ones he'd cleaned away.

"He's going away for a conference. He told everyone he wouldn't be answering emails."

"So that's a no. Listen, I'm sorry. I didn't mean to assume you should help me."

"What about your appointment? With Dr.—"

"Hisanaga. Oh, she's been sort of avoiding me. She thinks I'm a weird amateur playing at philanthropy."

To be honest, he sort of was.

"I'm trying to start an animal sanctuary thing," he added, trying to clear things up.

It didn't.

She was shooing him out now, despite the fact that papers had drifted down from the table again. But she caught them, stuffed them into her bag, and started shutting off the lights. "Hold this," she said, handing him a white envelope.

She added, "That's a big project. Did you describe it that way, as an animal *sanctuary thing*?"

The words were sharp, but she glanced up at him from under a lock of dark hair. Her eyes were brown, like a rich velvet. For a moment he lost his train of thought.

He cleared his throat. "Well, no. I sent her a detailed letter."

In it, he'd outlined the steps he'd already taken, saying he'd set aside some land and money and described the cat he was already sheltering. He supposed that to a scientist he sounded pretty naive. But he figured once he got to talk to Dr. Hisanaga in person she'd see he was in earnest. He would exude seriousness from his pores. People didn't think he was particularly deep, especially his family. He'd disappointed all of them—father, mother, sisters, grandmother, and George— for so long. The failure to finish school, the abortive music career, the anxiety, the rehab. But he'd gotten his life in order in the last ten years. This animal sanctuary was his idea from start to finish. He'd put careful planning into it, and it would be a lasting contribution to society and the environment. Too bad they couldn't see past his youthful mistakes to understand he'd see this through.

Davy glanced at his phone. To his secret relief he was already too late to meet Dr. Hisanaga. He'd email her again and drop the fact that he was ready to give up a large chunk of land and money. Maybe he wouldn't have to work on a pitch much as long as he had cash. Or would he?

He looked to Zoey Fong for an answer, but she'd pushed him out the door and unzipped her backpack. Zoey strode to her lab door and took out an enormous key ring jangling with keys, frowned at it, then produced another ring, just as big and full. Apparently that wasn't the one, either.

Davy was impressed. The bag wasn't small. Was it all keys? If so, it probably weighed Zoey—Ms. Fong—down hugely. She groped around in the backpack once more and pulled out a tiny key ring, and then promptly dropped all the other keys to the floor with a clatter.

More cursing.

Davy bent and picked them up and handed the keys back while Zoey locked her door.

"Well, good luck finding your boss."

"Thanks," she yelled over her shoulder, speeding down the hall.

He stood watching the tidy movement of her limbs in jeans and a white shirt. Her hair swirled as she flew around the corner.

She was kind of exhilarating.

But it wasn't until a couple of minutes later that Davy noticed he was still hanging on to the envelope that Ms. Zoey Fong had given him to hold.

Should he run after her? But he wasn't sure if she'd gone up or down the stairs. And she'd been moving so fast he felt almost dizzy. Should he slip it back under the door? He looked at the envelope and then the solid length of steel door dubiously. Not a crack. You had to admire the craftsmanship.

Well, too late to chase her, and he didn't really think he should just leave it propped up in the hallway. He'd try to find out her email from the university website and let her know he had it. Maybe they could meet, drink some coffee. Have a conversation.

The idea of the pair of *them* making conversation like normal people almost made him laugh out loud in this abandoned university hall.

He tucked the envelope in his jacket pocket. Whatever was in it, he hoped it wasn't important.

★ ★ ★

Zoey Fong breathed a sigh of relief as she exited the Agate Building and walked into the cool Vancouver air. It hadn't been the best day, but she'd managed to grab her supervisor before he hauled off for parts unknown and phone connections unreliable.

It was her own fault. She'd lost track of time and Dr. Smerek was in a different building. She could've just locked up and stepped out, but she had to finish her report, and couldn't leave anything important because her lab mate Alec had a talent—a highly annoying and extremely well-honed talent—of coming in when she wasn't there. And if things weren't in place, he'd leave his little notes everywhere.

If you need help cleaning up your mugs all you have to do is ask. :-)
Or
I can show you a trick to shutting that cabinet.
Or
Must be going well because I couldn't find the cassettes because they weren't in their "usual" spot. ;-)

He unfailingly used her Post-its, too! Even after she'd deliberately given him his own packet. She'd even picked a color that she didn't use—green—so that his notes would be distinctive. And she'd pointed this out to him so he'd feel special.

Well, Alec didn't need Post-its to feel special, and he never used them. He'd taken the gift—her rather pointed present, she'd thought—as a token of the respect he expected.

The jerk.

At least he wouldn't have an excuse to leave her a note about the mugs today. Thanks to that guy—what was his name? Blandly handsome, seemingly agreeable, flashing her a smile when he needed something, as if the smile made up for all his demands. He hadn't fled the first time she snapped at him. He even seemed to care, his unlined forehead wrinkling in confusion as she talked at him, unlike the million other expensively but casually dressed West Coast dudes like him, with their tousled hair and their grins, and their lean surf and ski bodies. They abounded on this campus, and only paid attention to her when they were trying to pick her up.

Well, the Handsome sure hadn't tried to pick her up. Maybe that was the difference.

He was probably intent on bothering that Dr. Hisanaga.

She frowned. In fact, Handsome... Davy—was that it? A ridiculously boyish name—*had* helped her clean the mug flock, her mug gaggle—what was a good collective noun?—her *bane* of mugs. So at least he wasn't a completely useless handsome. Then again, he'd only washed some dishes. That shouldn't earn her undying gratitude, or even some sort of mild, hardly there attraction from her.

The bar was low.

She biked home in the light spring rain, willing the liquid to wash away her tension. When she got back to the garden-floor apartment that she rented in Kitsilano, near the beach she never got to walk on, she found her roommate at the open door flapping a dishcloth while the smoke detector screamed. Zoey grabbed the towel on her way in and fastened it around her ears—not that it helped—and stood on a kitchen stool to take out the batteries.

Her roommate, Li-leng, was even shorter than she.

"If our ears go out in the next five years, it's because of this oversensitive detector," Li-leng said.

Zoey's roommate pushed at the sash of the kitchen window to open it wider but it was open as far as it would go. She fanned the air glumly.

"So, did you get to talk to Smerek? What did he say about your research so far?"

"He was in a rush. He was mentally pretty checked out of it."

But he was not so distracted that he hadn't sighed about what a disappointment her experiments had been—what a disappointment *she'd* proved—thus far. The MD/PhD program was for top-level people, he kept reminding her as if she wasn't told that every single day by every single top-level person in the program.

"He essentially blew off your meeting. Again."

Zoey tried to look unbothered. "It's not a big deal. I just need a little more guidance about what he wants."

She'd never needed her hand held before. *So independent*, her teachers always said. Little Zoey cutting out snowflakes with the sharp scissors, winning science fairs, getting into top-level programs with top-level people.

Li-leng glared at her perfectly roasted chicken. She was probably imagining it was Smerek. Or maybe her own supervisor. She shoved another pan in the oven and shut it defiantly.

Zoey took the tea towel off her head—not that it had helped—and got out some plates. "I'll try him again in a few weeks. When he's not preparing for a conference."

He was *always* traveling, though.

Li-leng started cutting up the chicken. They'd met in the dorms in first year and had been roommates ever since. She was technically in graduate school, too, although she'd seemed to put her dissertation on fan culture on hold to wait tables, procrastibake, and educate herself on theories of hair care.

Zoey shrugged. They sat down side by side at the small breakfast bar.

"You don't have to stay in school, you know. You have skills."

"Setting off smoke detectors."

"Disarming them."

"Collecting and herding mugs."

"Going thirty days without shampoo."

"Hey, my hair has never looked better."

"Thanks, but I like washing my hair. I like showering. It's relaxing."

"You need hobbies, Zoey. Knitting, karaoke, kite flying, taiko drumming. All you do is work, or stuff around work."

It was an old argument. "I did promise myself I wouldn't toil away all weekend. I didn't go back to Toronto for the holidays, and I've been in the lab every weekend for the last four months. I'm going to take naps. I'm going to clean my room. I'm going to go stand in line at that restaurant Phnom Penh so I can eat an entire plate of Cambodian chicken wings by myself. I'm going to read a…a fiction book."

"They're called novels."

"Right. Whatever. You know, one of those books that people who know how to relax read. I'm going to—"

"Zoey."

"Yeah?"

"School sounds like a drag."

Zoey tried to deny it. She liked being a grad student. Didn't she? So why couldn't she offer a retort to her roommate.

"You don't have to do this program, you know. I mean, you're clearly miserable. You'd do just fine being a goddamn doctor."

Zoey swallowed. "I'd still have to do my clerkship and residency. And I can't give up The Plan."

"Right. To become a medical researcher. Find a cure for bone cancer."

"At least put us on the right path."

"But is it the right path for *you*? Because it's not going so well."

"Plans are always a bit difficult when you're in the middle of them."

"But they're supposed to have rewards eventually. You're close to burning out."

"I feel very rewarded."

Although she had to admit, she was maybe a little exhausted from trying to please Smerek and never succeeding. Luckily—or unluckily—there was no time for Zoey's roommate to call her on the lie. Li-leng had started sniffing the air. "Oh no, the clafoutis!"

She hopped toward the oven.

"The what?"

"There were all these cherries on sale!"

Smoke wasn't quite pouring out but there was a definite smell of burning. Luckily the window was still wide open, and the detector batteries were sitting on the kitchen counter—although maybe if either of them had remembered to put them back in they'd have had a little warning. As it was, Li-leng, forgetting an oven mitt in her hurry, tried to take the dessert out of the oven and promptly dropped a pan and two ramekins full of berry and cake at her feet.

In Zoey's expert opinion as a med student, Li-leng had to go to the ER. They spent the rest of the night at the hospital taking in some of that good ole Canadian health care. Luckily Li-leng only sustained minor burns to one hand, and after a long evening in the waiting room at Vancouver General, Zoey was able to bring Li-leng back home in a cab, cherry-batter-splattered and bandaged. Zoey sent her roommate off to bed, she scraped up the dessert from the floor and put away the leftovers, went upstairs to shower dessert and dinner and hospital-people smell off of her, and dropped into bed.

Not the beginning to the weekend that she'd been hoping

for, she thought as she was falling asleep, but at least her room-mate would be all right.

It wasn't until the middle of the night that Zoey sat up bolt upright in bed and remembered.

The slide with the bone sample. What had she done with it?

He'd taken it and forgotten to give it back to her.

The Handsome had taken the slide.

CHAPTER 2

WHERE THE BEEVES ARE

Davy was getting pretty good at navigating the university website's directory. He found Zoey Fong's email that night, sent off a quick note with his phone number, worked on a song, slept two hours, and woke up to three replies and a pile of text messages.

The woman had no chill. He truly admired it.

But he had a lot to do that day, which was too bad, because the song was still drifting at the edges of his consciousness, refusing to coalesce. He couldn't wait to get back to his own home. It was always easier to write on the island. Safer.

After slinging some green tea into a travel mug, he got into the car and was parking at the hardware store when he got yet another phone call.

"Hi! You have the slide? When can I pick it up from you?"

Zoey Fong's voice, already familiar, came out in a rush. She was like an instrument, pure and clear, her urgency coming through like an alarm bell. He could almost envision the quick movements of her hands, poised to grab the envelope from him across the phone lines.

"Ms. Fong. How are you? Yeah, sorry. I guess we both forgot about the thingy you handed me in all the excitement. I was going to pop the envelope in, well, another envelope and send it to you. How does that sound?"

"No! No other envelope! No mailing. It requires delicate handling."

Davy paused as he thought about how he'd crinkled the thing when he shoved it in his jacket pocket, how he'd leaned back on the jacket when he was driving, how it had ended up on the floor.

"How about I slip it in a bubble mailer?"

"No!"

He winced and adjusted his headset. Maybe her voice was a little *too* clear.

"Do you have it now? Stop handling it. Just put it down."

"Well, I…it's a slide, right? It's hard, not very bendy."

"You took it out of the envelope? *Did you try to bend it?*"

"Uh, no," he answered truthfully.

It had fallen out of its envelope when he picked his jacket up off the floor. He'd stared at the little glass rectangle before putting it back in and returning it to his pocket. If it was so important, why hadn't she sealed it in? Why had she let him hold it? It didn't seem like a terribly politic time to ask her these questions, though. At least he hadn't stepped on the thing.

"Never mind. Where are you?"

"I'm at Sun Wah. It's the grocery wholesaler in—"

A rapid clatter of keyboard. "Burnaby. The suburbs. Jesus. I'll be there in thirty."

She clicked off. When he called her back to tell her that he didn't have the jacket, or the envelope, or the slide with him, it went straight to voice mail.

Right. Well, no point in worrying over her wasted trip. Besides, although he probably shouldn't admit it, he was excited to see her again. She was better than caffeine. Prettier, too. He grimaced at the green tea in his mug and left it in the car as he got out.

He had shopping to do.

Handsome was eyeing some big haunches when Zoey arrived.

"Do you have anything more...lively looking?" he was asking in English.

The butcher—was he a butcher?—seemed slightly perplexed. Handsome had this effect on people, probably because he was confusingly attractive with those soft lips and dark eyes. He wore a fleece and yet his shoulders still seemed broad and defined. The butcher had on some kind of coat. Zoey did not. She'd gotten a Lyft and rushed out of the house after leaving a bowl of food and some washed fruit and a drink with a straw in it and some pain pills and a detailed note for her roommate. She'd worn only a thin cardigan. Everyone was dressed for the meat locker except her.

Zoey saw the moment Handsome spotted her. His face lit up. She did not remember the last time anyone had been so happy to see her. He actually glowed. His eyes were brighter, his smile was a shining sun. He had dimples. He was radiant. All of this was for the sight of *her*. For *her*.

Because she could not recall the last time her arrival meant such joy for someone, of course she forgot the reason why she'd rushed out.

She stood there, stunned by the light of him.

Then he stepped forward. "Maybe you have an opinion. You always seem to. Sammy," he said, turning to the butcher, "this is Ms. Fong."

"It's just Zoey."

Handsome turned back to her. "Ms. Just Zoey, do you think

you'd prefer something fattier? Or something a little lean? Or maybe I should get a variety pack."

"I beg your pardon?"

"Meat," Handsome said patiently. "Do you have an opinion?"

Zoey looked around her and shivered. She felt somewhat out of her depth. "Why—why do you need so much meat?"

"It's for my big cat."

He looked very serious. But she didn't know him well enough to tell if his earnestness was real.

"Is that a euphemism or something?"

"No."

He looked puzzled again. Maybe he didn't know the word *euphemism*. Pretty but not bright, she reminded herself. No, that wasn't true. He was radiant. But she didn't need to be thinking about how attractive he was when they were clearly very different. She worked in a lab, and he apparently stood in meat lockers in the suburbs looking at beef—no, there was so much more than one beef in this place. They were looking at *beeves*.

He peered at her again, this time concerned. "You seem cold. Would you like this?"

He unzipped his jacket and held it out.

"I—" She hesitated.

"I have layers," he added, lifting up one corner of his dark blue Henley to reveal another T-shirt. And a flash of skin right above the waistband of his jeans.

She stared at that for a moment.

He had layers. Right.

She nodded and he lent her a hand in putting on the jacket, helped her zip it up, because for some reason, maybe it was the chill, she seemed to be having trouble moving. And thinking. And talking. But that was probably because she was now muffled under a big, warm blanket of fleece. "Fank you," she said, huddling into the warmth.

The fleece smelled faintly of aftershave.

He gave her another one of those luminescent smiles—seriously, was it his toothpaste?—and turned back to the butcher.

"Let's get a variety pack," he said. "Now c'mon, Ms. Zoey, you can help me pick out nonperishables."

Davy sure knew how to show a girl a good time. Well, judging by the way she was studying the niblets label, at least she wasn't bored.

"About that slide—" she began to say at one point. Then, distracted, "A whole box full of jarred artichoke hearts. And half the price at the store!"

She put an entire case of artichoke hearts in his enormous cart. He tried to help but she'd already lowered it in gently.

"What can I do with artichoke hearts?"

She blinked. "You can put them in pastas, add them to stew, make a dip."

"A dip."

"For when you entertain. You seem to do things on a grand scale."

She waved at his many cans of food.

It was unfair of him to laugh if she didn't know. But at the same time, the thought of him having a dinner party was pretty funny.

"I don't do that much." He made a sweeping gesture with an imaginary plumed hat at the case of SpaghettiOs. "Unless you consider this fine dining…"

"Maybe for a nursery school. But with, like, a lot of huge, meat-eating toddlers. Or maybe a wizard academy with, like, a herd of dragons."

He moved a little closer to her. She was smiling at him, and he couldn't remember to be cautious of her when she was bundled in his jacket. "No giant carnivorous children. And all the beasts are decidedly unmagical. SpaghettiOs happens to be easy for me to heat up."

She put her hands on her hips. "You can do better."

Davy had a feeling she said this a lot.

"Maybe I should put some artichoke hearts in the SpaghettiOs?"

She shuddered, picked up a jar, and cradled it. "Please don't do that to them."

"The thing is—"

"Yes?"

"I live on an island. I can take my motorboat to the nearest town, Narrow Falls, and get stuff at the general store, but every couple of months, I come down here, visit my grandma, and do a big shop. Plus, with spring storms coming, I want to stock up in case I get stranded out there."

He could tell that she was thinking very hard about his problem, and he loved it—he enjoyed that little furrow in her otherwise smooth brow, a dog-ear in a book he'd like to study.

"Are you some kind of loner survivalist?" Zoey asked him.

"No. I really am not."

Or was he? He paused to consider. "I mean, I like society, and I really don't like writing manifestos."

"You seem like a people person."

This did not sound like a compliment coming from her lips. Although he didn't mind watching her talk at all.

"But you still live on this remote island. Are there any neighbors at all?"

"There aren't...many."

There were none.

"So it's remote and largely unpopulated."

"Except by wildlife. And my big cat."

She studied him, and he wished suddenly he was a fascinating person. "I decided I wanted something quieter. I haven't always lived here year-round. But I've had some commitments I had to keep lately, so I've been spending more and more time up there."

"Commitments?" she asked sharply. "Are you married?" She immediately blushed. "I don't know why I asked you that."

He liked the fact that she'd asked him. "I'm not married. Or engaged. I have a grandma. And two sisters. One perfect older sister. One cute younger one."

"You're the spoiled middle boy."

"Something like that. Are you married? Or engaged? Or anything?"

"Nope. One younger sister. Mimi."

Her voice softened when she spoke her sister's name. Zoey Fong was beautiful. He probably had a dopey smile on his face as they stood there, staring at each other over a cart full of canned foods.

She looked away first. "I don't know if I'd be able to live so far away from everything," she said.

"Like what?"

"My studies. My friends. You know, city *life*."

The mention of her job made her rouse herself. "I can't believe I've spent this much time talking to you. I was so desperate to get to the slide that I took a car I couldn't afford."

Now he felt guilty.

"I would've dropped it off, but I didn't know how urgent it was, and I have a full day."

She waved her arms around. "It was important! I called you, like, twenty times!"

They both tactfully avoided the fact that it had been more times than that. "That just seems to be your personality, though."

She glowered but didn't argue with his assessment. "What else do you have to do?"

"I have to go to the electronics store and pick up some doodads and make sure they get packed safely. And then I have an appointment to go pick up my piano."

She'd looked a little impatient with him up until that point. But now she was distracted again. "Your what?"

"I'm getting a piano refurbished and I have to pick it up—well, I have to inspect it and have it moved to the dock and inspect it again and make sure it's loaded onto the boat correctly."

"You're transporting a piano across the water?"

"A small piano. Tiny."

He held up a finger and a thumb to indicate how big the piano would look—if it were a block away.

"Like a fun-sized piano?"

"It's a baby grand—the smallest kind of grand piano."

"That's still—"

"Yeah, it's big for something that will be seaworthy. Well, I guess it doesn't have to float. It's going on a big boat."

"Along with the meat."

"Ye-es."

"And some electronic doodads."

"Right."

"And the SpaghettiOs. And these artichokes. That you don't know how to use."

"Well."

She removed the artichokes from the cart.

When she looked up again, her face was wary. "I'd like to go get my slide now."

He blinked. *Right.* The slide. "Why don't I buy you breakfast?"

He didn't have the slide on him.

The Handsome could have led with that. Well, okay, he'd left her two considerate messages saying exactly that, which she didn't check until now. But Zoey had been busy putting together a lunch for her bandaged roommate and rushing out of the house without a coat. Davy had wanted to save her an expensive trip out to the suburbs, and when she arrived she'd gotten swept up in meat and canned goods and…and *dimples* and she hadn't given one thought to her precious fucking slide that he didn't even have on him, and that was still in his jacket pocket up in his grandma's house in a different part of Burnaby.

Well, the slide *was* at least nearby. She didn't need it *right this minute* and nothing ever happened in the suburbs. It was safe. Plus she was starving. She hadn't eaten anything since the Clafoutis Incident last night.

She should definitely have breakfast. On a full stomach she wouldn't be so easily distracted. She blushed thinking of how easily he'd managed to throw her off course each time he smiled. Plus she'd be able to better convince him to skip the doodads and drive her to his grandma's if they sat down for a meal. Because he might do that. She was beginning to think that he was a soft touch, considering he'd decided to stop part-way through his busy day to get her breakfast—and not just any breakfast. He'd let her pick. In fact, she was beginning to suspect he was the kind of person who might get saddled with his own mug flock—a *murder* of mugs—if he wasn't careful. And although she didn't want to take advantage, she did need her slide. It wasn't like a talisman or anything, even though it was a sample of the same kind of cancer that had struck Mimi when she was young.

Okay, maybe it was a little personal.

But this is fine, she thought, eyeing the enormous bowl of pho that arrived at her table. Eating a mess of good food had been on her list. She surveyed the table. Plastic chopsticks, a bunch of other diners slurping their noodles. A plate of soft shrimp rolls and a tall glass of cold-brewed iced coffee thick with sweetened condensed milk. Good by her! She could cross relaxing off her list. Even if it was in pursuit of work.

Davy was blowing into his bowl of vegetarian pho, pho chay, and sighing appreciatively at the piles of vegetables, herbs, fresh chilies, and limes.

"This was such a good idea," he said. "If you hadn't been able to pick, I would've suggested Cafe Biothèque. Not exactly original."

He grimaced.

She almost snorted. Cafe Biothèque had lines stretching down the block—even for brunch. Li-leng had worked there for six days. She'd worn a spotless white uniform, and she said the menu consisted mostly of different kinds of carefully cultivated sprouts. Maybe that was Davy's typical hangout, she thought, as she watched him lift a pile of fragrant basil and noodles to his mouth.

But wait! Was he trying to impress her? She shook her head, trying to clear it. "This is another thing I'd miss," she said. "You know, living in the middle of nowhere. Try getting a bowl of pho, or bibimbap, or a decent dosa in...wherever you live."

"The middle of the water. Are you attempting to lure me back to civilization?"

His eyes crinkled and she had to stop and gaze at his face for a moment. She was blushing. Oh God, was she flirting with him?

Handsome Davy, she reminded herself. A rich boy, obviously, who lived with his grandma—okay, well he lived with her when he came to visit the mainland from his remote, luxurious private island?—a rich boy who ate SpaghettiOs and trundled pianos over the Strait of Georgia.

She was not allowed to get *interested* in people from completely different worlds and who could afford to buy haunches of meat and cases of groceries and who didn't care about the pleasures of cheap takeout, and who clearly didn't worry about jobs and friends. He wasn't her type. She said, "After this do you think we can—"

Her phone rang.

Terrible timing. "I'm sorry. Do you mind if I get this?"

"Of course not, I—"

His phone rang, too, and he smiled at her as if they were sharing something.

Wow.

She returned somewhat dazedly to her phone. It was Li-leng. "While you're out could you pick me up some ChapStick?"

"ChapStick. Check."

She made a little checking-off gesture with her hand and noticed Davy eyeing her. Was he amused by this? She glared.

"Not mint, though. I don't want my lips to tingle."

"Gotcha. No mint. Are you doing okay? How is the hand?"

"I'm fine. It doesn't hurt that much as long as I don't think about it. But I may go back to bed. Thanks for the food and for cleaning up. Where are you, anyway?"

"I'm out to breakfast."

She glanced at Davy again, and found he was still watching her. She looked away.

"Wow, you were not kidding about wanting an entire plate of chicken wings."

She put her hand over her mouth and resisted the urge to gaze at Davy again. "I'm not exactly out on my own."

"You're on a date?"

She muttered, "His name is Davy Hsieh. And it's not a date, per se. It's complicated. I'm just supposed to pick something up from him."

"Sounds like he's already picked you up," Li-leng chortled.

"Stop it. He's right at the table—" She couldn't help herself. She slid her eyes to him. Finally, he wasn't watching her. But was she disappointed? Definitely not. She'd just eaten too much. That was all. Indigestion.

He was speaking in Mandarin to someone and still smiling a little goofily.

"I can't talk right now. But I'll be back by noon."

She'd better be. She hung up to the sound of Li-leng still chuckling over her own very unfunny joke and realized that now was the time to ask Davy if they could go to his house to pick up the slide. Then she could figure out a way to get out of Burnaby and back to Vancouver. They had buses, right? There was the SkyTrain. Maybe he could drop her off at Metrotown. She heard one of those Japanese cheesecake places had opened there. She could buy one for Li-leng—

"There's been a slight change of plans," Davy said.

CHAPTER 3

THE MOST MUSICAL FISH IS A PIANO TUNA

Zoey Fong did not get swept up. She was grounded. It was one of her better qualities as a physician-scientist. She was a bulwark against unreasonable hopes and disappointing results. She plowed on until there was no more earth to turn.

Yet, here she was, in a work studio in North Vancouver with two strange men and a gorgeous, softly glowing piano.

"I do not think you should take it on this journey," Mr. Shu was saying.

He drew a bandanna from his back pocket and swiped at his forehead, as if he himself were going on a long, hot voyage of a thousand miles, instrument strapped to his back.

"It's just half an hour in a truck, maybe forty-five minutes depending on traffic. Then an hour in a boat."

"A rocking boat."

Mr. Shu swayed on his feet as if he couldn't manage to get his sea legs. Zoey sincerely hoped there were no more parts to this journey.

"Well, the forecast says—"

"Never trust the forecast. I don't want you to arrive in—in the wilderness with a cracked soundboard."

"I'm sure it will be fine."

"*Fine* is not good enough."

"Most pianos are okay even with a cracked soundboard."

"Aha. You think you know so much. Who is the expert here? Pah. Musicians."

"You're a musician?" Zoey asked.

"Oh, you aren't aware. How does she not know—?"

Mr. Shu's sunken eyes suddenly gleamed, and he seemed less fragile. She turned to Davy. Was it her imagination or had he gone rigid? But then he interrupted a little *too* smoothly. "Mr. Shu. I know you haven't had the piano for enough time, and I'm sorry it took so long to get here to you—"

"You should have brought it sooner."

"But I'm going to be out there for months. And I don't have anything worthwhile to play."

The thought of Davy alone and without an instrument seemed to melt Mr. Shu's wizened heart.

"I will see what I have in the back," Mr. Shu said, grudgingly.

When Davy made a move as if toward the door, Mr. Shu barked, "Stay here!"

Davy nodded, still serene. Then he rounded the piano and strode to Zoey's side.

"It's my childhood piano," he said. "There's something about the sound of it that I love."

Davy did touch it this time. He had beautiful hands, or maybe it was the way they moved across the dark surface of the lid, the delicate curl of his fingers as they stroked gently across the wood and opened up the keyboard.

She felt herself shivering and he drew closer to her—and

to the piano. "I just want to feel it. I won't make a sound," he murmured, brushing his fingers over the keys.

Zoey could see one black key bobbing, just a tiny bit, under the pressure of his thumb. She heard the click of his fingernail before he took her hand and guided it over the surface he'd made warm. "I can tell you want to do this, too," he whispered again, the words lifting the small hairs near her ears.

She swallowed and allowed him to move her hand. She could feel it, the smoothness of it. She knew it would just yield to her if she pressed down.

So, of course, she did.

They both jumped at the clear note, and Mr. Shu came running.

"No touching!"

"But pianos are meant to be touched," Davy said mildly.

He hadn't let go of her hand.

"You can do that later."

Why was she blushing?

Mr. Shu clapped. "Come back in two hours. Maybe you will change your mind by then about making it seaworthy."

"It's not really going in the ocean—"

"Two hours!"

Hand in hand, they scrambled out of the studio.

"This calls for pastries," Davy said, and he was glad to see Zoey perk up.

He'd needed a peace offering for his grandmother before they went to retrieve the slide. She was already upset with him because he was leaving again so soon.

But his mind was racing. He'd never brought anyone home with him before—technically he and Zoey weren't together, of course, but he was enjoying the hand-holding and the shy, sly glances passing between them too much. It felt like the beginning of something. Of course, he wasn't going to be here tomorrow and who knew when he'd be back, so there was no use thinking that way *even though he was clearly thinking that way*. He started a lot of things he never finished. This could almost be another. Driving was good. It meant he could no longer keep touching her.

Zoey seemed to realize their journey was coming to an end, too. He didn't know her well enough to read her, but she'd turned inward since he said they might as well go and get the slide back. Well, thoughtful except for expressing a few vociferous opinions on bakery goods. Chinese-style hot dogs in a bun were a yes; ham and cheese were no. Custard, almond cream, and red bean were definite yeses. Roll cake was over the top. "I was just thinking how different we are," she said after a few minutes of silence in the car. "My childhood piano was a used Acrosonic. I don't know if it was made from real wood or not—maybe some kind of veneer. A couple of notes didn't quite play and we couldn't afford a piano tuner. Someone from my parents' church gave the piano to us."

"Do you still play?" Davy asked.

"Not really. I was never very musical."

It was hard to believe with a voice like hers, expressive and clear. She was turned to the window, so Davy couldn't read her face, but he could hear the note of thoughtfulness in her tones.

"It just seems very different from my life, is all," Zoey said.

"What is?"

"You're bringing a baby grand to some remote place. For all I know it could be an island you own."

He stared at the red light, willing it to turn. He really shouldn't care about this, that she was thinking about what separate worlds they lived in as if wishing they didn't. Or maybe he was reading too much into it.

"Oh my God, you do own it, don't you? You own an island."

"Technically, it's my father that bought it. But I took the place off his hands."

He was aware that perhaps this didn't make him sound much better. "At the time it cost less than a house in West Van," he added.

She started laughing. Was that good? "West Vancouver real estate prices aren't exactly a low bar. But whatever. It's not my life. Not my luxurious island. Not my grand piano."

"Baby grand."

"The tiniest of grands," she said imitating his voice, or at least trying to.

It was kind of adorable.

"What would a *grand* grand piano be like anyway? Are they huge like aircraft carriers? Encrusted in diamonds? Or gold? I don't even know what a big, expensive piano would be."

"A Bosendorfer."

"Oh. Right. One of those."

"Bosendorfer means evil villager."

"Wow, still more learning to do."

He glanced at her to see if she liked that, but she was still staring out the window. But her voice had changed. She sounded a little defensive, maybe brittle.

"I don't have a Bosendorfer," Davy said.

"There's a mercy."

"Does it bother you that I have money?"

This time she frowned. He could see that clearly in the reflection of the car window.

"Why should it? I hardly know you," she said.

Her tone said she knew enough.

Davy risked another glance at her. Her fingers drummed impatiently on her thighs.

Then she said, "Maybe it bugs me that I don't have a lot. Does that bother you?"

"Of course not," he said uncomfortably.

How could it? He rarely had to think about money, and maybe that was her point. He considered what he'd been doing this morning: carting pianos around, buying large amounts of meat, and how hard it was to figure out ways to supply himself on his (admittedly sparse but she didn't know that) private island—and he felt like an ass.

She was a smart woman. Hell, she worked in a lab at a university studying slides he had no idea about. But smart didn't mean she had cash. Judging by the scant words she'd spoken about her childhood, that probably meant she hadn't grown up with much. His type of immigrant was one thing. Parents jetting to and from China and Taiwan, leaving the kids to live in Canada while they were off in Asia making the wealth that kept them able to maintain households all over the world. Her type was probably the kind that came here with nothing or degrees they couldn't use, who worked in restaurants, or started small businesses, whose kids clawed their way into schools and earned those doctorates.

Davy hadn't considered those differences between them, either. And again, that was because he'd never had to.

After this you won't see her again.

He would probably think about her, though. The thing about living on a secluded island was that there was a lot of time to brood.

They arrived at the quiet cul-de-sac where his grandma lived, where he'd grown up. He tried to look at the house from her eyes. It wasn't ridiculous, was it? It was a house, not, like, a McMansion. Okay, so his parents had torn the other house down and built this new one with the door and face of it edging to the front of the property line. But that was nearly twenty years ago and now it wasn't gleaming and new. It was just a house, his house.

They took off their shoes and both ignored the slippers lined up neatly for visitors. They swept past the living room with the stiff, dark furniture that only got perched on when company came over, the silent, unused dining room, and over to the slightly worn kitchen. "Sit down," he said. "Would you like some coffee? Tea? Water? I think we have orange juice, or some sort of chia seed thing."

He busied himself emptying the paper bag full of pastries onto a plate and offered her one. "Also, we have fruit."

She declined. It was probably a bad sign that she'd stopped eating. And talking.

He continued, "I'm going to leave these here for my A-mà. And make some coffee for her. If you're sure you don't want any. She's probably still asleep or I'd introduce you. She's not a morning person."

"It's 12:30."

"She's not an early afternoon person," he amended. "I'd like you to meet her, actually. But it might be best to sneak up—"

"The slide?" Zoey said.

"Right. Sorry. It's probably up in my room."

He hesitated. Inviting her upstairs seemed awfully forward. At the same time, he was at his *grandma's*. What was he really going to try?

It occurred to him that he hadn't thought of attempting anything on anyone in a long time. But she'd risen and was clearly expecting to take the envelope and bolt from his house and his life forever.

Although he planned to offer her a ride back to the city, at least. He wasn't sure quite where he'd gone off track, but now everything was wrong.

Davy was expecting his room to be a mess. And it sort of still was with uncovered crates everywhere filled with old CDs he hadn't bothered to transfer to the cloud, snarls of wires, and books. But the bed was made and the clothes he'd dropped on the floor were…gone?

Davy opened his closet. "I left it in my jacket. It must be in here."

He opened the seldom-used closet and rummaged through. "I was wearing the—"

"It was black."

He paged through a series of identical sleeves. Why did he have so many black jackets? They all looked exactly the same from the side.

She watched for a minute as he got more frantic and stood up. "No, it wasn't that one. It was more like—" She made a diagonal zipping motion.

"Oh, it was that sort of architectural one. High-tech."

Zoey raised a single eyebrow. "Exactly."

Davy pulled one out and winced. Another statement jacket. The collar was a huge lightning zigzag. Hideous. Clearly it was from his old pop music life. He'd never be able to fit into that again, not that he wanted to. He'd been trying to give the clothing away slowly over the years.

"Uh, not quite like that. How about this one?"

The one she pulled out was more of a costume coat, with long tails, and a splash of glitter that ended in a starburst right over his nipple. He'd always worn that one without a shirt. Honestly, most of them were made for shirtlessness. "Uh."

"What *is* this stuff?"

Luckily—or unluckily—his door burst open right at that moment. And his grandma, very much awake, strode into the room. "Hsieh Da-wei," she thundered in Mandarin. "You have a girl in your room."

"A-mà! I'm twenty-seven years old."

"There is no age limit on bad behavior," she intoned, her back straight.

She was clad, as was her wont, head to toe in logos from the ages. Her eyebrows were plucked to a thin line, her hair dyed dark and cut in a sharp pixie. She was wearing a Gucci sweater with fringe and the interlocking G label prominently across her thin chest, and cigarette jeans spattered in Fendi Fs. And she had on a pair of purple, fuzzy slippers.

Zoey stepped up to her. She was, he noticed, still draped in his fleece. His grandma noticed, too.

Zoey gave a slightly awkward bow. "I'm Zoey Fong. I'm so sorry, ma'am. Davy has something very important of mine, and I was up here helping him find it."

Her Mandarin was okay, kind of cute and kiddie-ish. She probably only ever spoke it to family. His grandma looked slightly less enamored of it. She acknowledged her with a nod.

"I bought pastries from Tai Pan," Davy added helpfully.

"Fine. Find your very important item and come downstairs and visit properly."

"Well, I—" Zoey began. He could tell she was going to say that she had to leave, which wasn't the tack to take with A-mà and wasn't what he wanted her to do, either.

"A-mà," he interrupted, wincing while doing so. "What happened to all my clothes?"

Zoey snorted and glanced incredulously at his very full closet and then back at him. He was not helping his case. "I mean, the ones I had in the room."

"They're outside the door right now—"

Oh, shit. Did that mean—?

Zoey had already stepped to the door and she was staring down at a basket full of freshly washed, folded black clothing. Unerringly, she reached for the diagonally-zippered jacket that he'd worn yesterday and shook it open.

She stood completely still and stared at it for a long, silent moment. Then one by one, she checked all the other items in the basket, her arms growing jerkier with each movement.

There was no way the slide could have survived the laundry.

Then she shot a hot look right at him that almost had him staggering back. In English, she choked, "I can't believe you made your *grandma* do your laundry."

And she marched out of his house.

It turned out there were buses in Burnaby. One right outside his grandmother's house's cul-de-sac that arrived as soon as she turned the corner. It bore her to Metrotown, where she was too tired—and feeling too poor—to buy a Japanese cheesecake. There was a line for that, anyway. So she got on the SkyTrain and made her way home, minus several dollars and one slide.

How was she going to keep getting herself to the lab without the slide?

Of course, she had backed up the images on her laptop, in the cloud, on one of those geek-stick thumb drives that was at the bottom of a drawer somewhere in her lab. Hopefully she'd labeled it properly. But the slide itself was the actual bone tissue, the real sample. It was the thing she went back to when she despaired of her work, and she'd let it out of her hands in one careless moment, in several careless moments, she had to admit to herself. Now it was destroyed. Misplacing the original wasn't quite the end of the world, but its loss wouldn't endear her to Smerek, if he noticed. She shouldn't have been carrying the slide around to begin with. But most of all, it was important to *her*.

How could she have gotten swept up in pastries and pianos and beeves?

The answer, of course, was her own personal slab of beef: Davy.

He'd done that, with his easy looks and easier money. But

the answer came back to her again. Because she'd wanted it. It had been good flying around in a nice car, looking at expensive instruments, eating pho and shopping for artichokes, and chatting and forgetting for a moment that this wasn't her life. She'd even imagined for a few seconds that she might be invited out to his *island*.

Fuck, the man owned an actual island. He'd chartered a boat to bring supplies and a fucking piano that he'd had restored probably at great expense to *an island that he owned*, and he was riding around town casually picking up cases of SpaghettiOs and…and her. And she'd enjoyed it. She'd had a good time for the first time in what seemed like forever.

She should have been thinking of her sister. About important research, not that hers amounted to anything. But *future* discoveries. Instead she'd been living a version of the high life.

Davy had decided so readily to drive back to his house and pick up the slide, despite the fact he had a busy day ahead, and she'd had a sick moment wondering at how quickly he'd changed his plans, wondering if maybe he was tired of her. Because she'd been so agreeable (well, for *her*), so eager to offer her opinions on meats, and the kinds of things he should eat, and Bosen-whatevers, and like, *everything*. Because he seemed to respect and listened to her, she'd been too quick to be impressed, too easy for him.

She'd known him for, what, five hours?

She was never easy. Not for anyone.

Zoey's family was nothing like Davy's. They were gentle, hardworking. They weren't rich. Her much younger sister's brush with osteosarcoma had changed their lives completely.

Zoey herself had taken on a lot of responsibility as a teen, translating between her parents and the doctors, keeping Mimi's appointments on schedule, keeping it all *together*. Or that's how it seemed sometimes. When her father cried, she stepped in and cooked the meals. When her mother needed to take a week off work to stay with Mimi, Zoey made the phone call.

Osteoblastic osteosarcoma. The slide was a specimen taken from someone who had been Mimi's age. It was a reminder of the person Zoey had been and the one she had to be.

Zoey had decided long ago to devote herself to cancer research. She'd made herself The Plan. Get into the MD/PhD program. Dedicate herself to studying the kind of cancer that had caused her family so much grief. She'd finished her first two years of med school, and now she was working on research. When it wasn't going well, the slide helped her remember why she was doing this. Especially now that Mimi was recovered and doing her first year of university, now that Zoey didn't have her sister close by as a reminder of what they'd almost lost. But today, Zoey had completely forgotten about The Plan.

She got off at her stop and dragged herself home where the door was open once again and Li-leng was batting fruitlessly at the smoke with her good hand. Zoey walked right in through it and picked up the toaster and held it upside down out the window.

A chunk of the bread that had been stuck in it fell out.

"Hey," Li-leng said good-naturedly, "I was going to eat that."

"I'll make you another in a second."

"Are you okay?" Li-leng called down the hall as Zoey went to wash the SkyTrain off her hands. "How was your *da-ate?*"

"It wasn't a date," Zoey muttered, scrubbing her hands savagely.

She looked in the bathroom mirror. "It wasn't anything."

He'd messed that up completely, hadn't he?

Zoey had dashed out so quickly, hardly pausing to mutter a

goodbye to his grandma. A-mà had demanded to know what that was about. By the time Davy had gotten A-mà to sit, then found his car keys and put on his shoes, Zoey was…gone.

He would have at least given her a ride back to Vancouver. He would have offered to reimburse her for the slide, which might only make her dislike him (dislike him more?) because there he was throwing his money at a problem. That wasn't even the worst part, was it? The slide was obviously important, but he'd been so full of his projects, full of *himself*, he hadn't even asked her about her work, why the slide was important. He hadn't asked her about herself.

Now it seemed like he'd never know.

Not that anything could have happened.

Davy drove over town picking up the various unimportant things he'd bought to fill the boat, to fill his place. He decided against hauling the piano with him after all, maybe not ever. It felt too extravagant, and Davy really didn't need it. Mr. Shu was certainly happy about this change of plans. Davy *wanted* the piano, yes, but he had a feeling that even that wouldn't make the hollowness inside him go away.

Otherwise, the trip back to town had been relatively productive, on balance. He hadn't met Dr. Hisanaga, but he'd spent time with his grandmother. He'd met Zoey. He wasn't planning on coming back for a long time partly because the weather got trickier this time of year. Although, he told himself, if this thing with Zoey had ended on a better note—wasn't that the understatement of the decade? He had quite possibly ruined her research and her job, and… Well, if it had ended on a better note, he might have been persuaded to return more often. If he thought there was a chance with her.

He laughed at himself. He was such an island hermit. Already crushing on a girl because he'd spent, what, three hours with her?

It wasn't that he was lonely out there. But although he hadn't known her long, for those moments she'd made him feel exhilarated. Seen. *Alive.*

No, too late for that.

He didn't always like looking facts in the eye. He didn't like pinning things down. But he had to do it in this case. He hadn't been the one to throw the clothing in the wash. And no, he hadn't made his grandma do his laundry. Tilda, the housekeeper, whirled through his room *as he'd asked her to* and picked up his clothing to ready it for his trip. He'd left everything in the room, all his *stuff.* He hadn't thought about Zoey's slide. He hadn't thought about the harm he could have done her.

He was going to make it up to her. He'd find another slide just like that one. He'd find her supervisor, who was on a conference in Antarctica, or wherever it was that he couldn't answer email. He'd argue with the man if it turned out she got in trouble at school about it. He'd pay for her degree, endow a chair in her department and install her in it, if he had to.

Of course, he wasn't sure what that all meant but he'd heard people talking about it, so he googled "funding a chair" while he waited for his Wi-Fi boosters to be brought out to him, and again he caught the edges of that song he'd been working on.

It wasn't like songs to be so recalcitrant. He produced a lot of them when he had to. He composed music for Chinese commercials, occasionally for TV shows, sometimes he still wrote for bands but he didn't like collaborating with people he didn't trust. But this song was different, the way everything was different this weekend.

Davy picked up his things. He returned home. He packed through the night, and the next morning, he was ready to set out.

His grandma came out to say goodbye to him. So did Tilda. "Your grandma says you were upset I did the laundry."

"I'm not upset with you, Tilda. It was my fault. I let you wash that black jacket with the important envelope inside."

She pursed her lips. "I took the envelope out, David."

"You…took it out?"

"Your clothes don't end up neat and still black if I leave your receipts and tissues and breath mints and *envelopes* in your pockets."

He stared at her blankly.

"You don't do laundry, do you, Davy?"

His grandmother sniffed.

Well, he did do laundry on the island. Sometimes. But he had a lot of clothing. And his personality changed whenever he was back with his grandma. He became a sheltered, spoiled kid again. But now was not the time to be ashamed of yet another thing.

"Where's the envelope, Tilda?"

"I put it in your box."

"I have a lot of boxes."

Tilda rolled her eyes. "I know."

"Which one?"

But even as he said it, he knew it was no use. His boxes were in crates. They'd been loaded up this morning and driven down to the dock. It would take days to figure out where it was.

Well, Davy thought, as he said his goodbyes and drove down to the waiting boat. There were a few bright sides in this situation: the slide was *alive* (or not ruined, at least) and Zoey would not have her research destroyed (provided nothing happened to the crate or the boat), and that meant that there was a slightly higher chance that she would speak to him again.

Plus, he wouldn't have to endow a chair. Whatever that meant.

CHAPTER 4

AN UNEXPECTED VOYAGE

Zoey had really been planning on ignoring Davy's calls. Correction. She'd been planning on sleeping in this Sunday morning. "Sleeping forever" was in fact what she'd told Li-leng last evening when her roommate had pressed her for details about what had happened.

But it was 7:30 a.m. and Davy had called six times in the last few minutes.

Did that mean he had news? What kind of news could he possibly have that she would care about? Had he magically reconstituted the slide last night using an advanced scientific slide-restoration machine available only to the super rich? Was even he rich enough to afford a scientific slide-restoring machine, if such a thing even existed?

He did own an island after all. An island that cost less than a house in West Vancouver, but again, that wasn't saying much.

Knowing how happy-go-lucky that Handsome-but-not-handsome-to-her-anymore-okay-still-a-little-handsome was, it was far more likely that he'd forgotten everything that happened yesterday. Like a Labrador. "He probably wants me to help him shop for a tuba," she grumbled. "The shiniest baby grand tuba."

Or maybe a sad trombone. Oh, who was she kidding? She was the sad trombone.

She stared at the phone.

She was going to call him back. If only to tell him that her instrument-viewing services were not available to him. Ever.

"The slide!" Davy yelled before she could say anything.

There was a lot of background noise. Maybe he had reconstituted it! Maybe he was super rich and such scientific advances were possible.

She was getting ahead of herself.

"What happened to the slide, Davy?"

"It wasn't washed. No one laundered it. It's here, in my crates."

"Tell me where you are."

"But, Zoey, it's *argha Garble grabble*!"

"Tell. Me. Where. You. Are."

"I'm at the Burrard Civic Marina."

It wasn't far away.

"I'll be there. Do not depart without me, Davy."

"But Zoey—"

"No leaving!"

She scrubbed her face, threw on some clothing, including the fleece he'd given her, and grabbed her backpack and her helmet. Within minutes she was pedaling furiously toward the piers.

It was pretty easy to see which boat was his. It was the one with the hive of activity around it on an otherwise lazy Sunday morning. Cargo was being loaded by men shouting good-naturedly to each other. But the first person who caught her eye was Davy. He was checking the straps around one of his crates and, it seemed, glancing up every now and then as if looking for someone.

To find her.

When Zoey reached him, he turned fully around. God, that glowing smile again. But mixed in with the dazzle was an expression of relief and trepidation and—something else. He put his arms out carefully, checking to see if she was all right with him moving into her space, put his hands on her shoulders, and said, "You *are* impulsive."

"I am not."

Except she really had been ever since she'd met him. But that wasn't their main problem right now.

"The slide. You have it," she reminded him.

"Yes, I do, but if you'd stopped to listen to me—"

"There's always a *but*—"

"This time it's you!" Davy snapped.

A silence. She started laughing. She couldn't help it. Maybe it was the stress, maybe it was the adrenaline, maybe it was because she was sweating from all the frantic biking. Maybe it was because Handsome Davy, boyish Davy, bringer of pastries, shipper of pianos, looked worried. About *her*. She really was a butt for never letting him finish.

"Okay, I don't know why you're cracking up but here's the problem. The slide wasn't washed but Tilda, the housekeeper, put it in one of my boxes. Because that's what I told her to do with the random stuff she finds in my pockets. But, of course, I buried the box in one of those big plastic shipping containers when I was packing. And I don't know where it is."

She was still gasping with laughter. "Of course you don't."

"Listen, I'm really, really sorry about this. I don't think I got a chance to tell you that yesterday—"

"I didn't give you a chance."

A slight hysteria still burbled around her edges. She tried

to slap a mental lid on herself to contain it, but it *leaked*. She ought to be relieved they'd sort of found the slide. *Why didn't she feel better?*

Davy's hands dropped and he stepped back. "I know the slide was important. Maybe someday you can tell me what it means to you and your work. But I don't have time to unpack everything. It could be a few days. I will make every effort to mail it to you when I find it. If I don't, I'll try my best to make it up to you. If you forgive me, maybe someday you'll tell me about yourself, what you're working on, and why you love it."

The wind was whipping through his dark hair. The sky was gray behind him. Davy looked very serious, very noble. It was a good speech, and it stopped her laughter.

Zoey took a deep, calming breath, reached up and took his collar. She pulled him down toward her and said, very clearly, very slowly, "*Davy Hsieh*, we've been through this before. *You are not mailing it.*"

He glanced at her hand gripping him. He looked at her face, so close to his. He stared at her mouth.

Davy whispered hoarsely, "Like, technically, *I* wouldn't be. I'd be handing it off to someone at the general store and then *they'd* pop it in the box."

She said nothing.

"Or I could pay them to courier it to you. That's fine, too."

Still, she said nothing.

"Drone drop?" he asked.

She loosened her hold a bit. "You have a drone?"

"Yes."

"One of those electronic doodads you picked up yesterday?"

"Yeah."

She let go of him.

"You'll forgive me if I don't quite trust you right now," she said.

There, that came out steady and calm. Very professional. Not at all like a woman who was terrified she wouldn't be able to go back to work, and also that she would have to.

"I—I can accept that."

"Technically you haven't really done anything wrong..."

"But."

A snort escaped her. "Yeah, I'm a butt."

It was his turn to laugh—weakly. It wasn't the best joke, she had to admit.

She swallowed and tried to be as logical as she could be in her current state of mind. Which wasn't very. "You know what this means, though, don't you?"

"I—no, actually I don't know what this means."

She stared at him steadily. "I'm going to have to come with you."

His eyes widened. "Okay, what?"

"I'm coming with you. I'm going to this island of yours. I'm going to help you carefully unpack every box, every crate that every strapping man is loading onto the boat right now. I'm going to sit in the sea air and I'm going to paw through your doodads and gizmos. I'm going to touch your baby grand."

"About that—"

"I'm going to page through your extensive and gaudy jacket collection and read your teen diary if I have to. We, together, are going to find that slide, and then I am going to strap it to my person, and then you can drop *me* off at the general store and go, I don't know, buy some artichoke hearts and mix them with your canned noodles. I don't care what you do after I'm back on the mainland. Then you will go back to your fortress of solitude, and I will go back to my lab and pick up where I left off."

She swallowed thickly. Why did the idea of going back make her want to choke? "My supervisor won't notice anything went awry, I will pretend this never happened and pick up my work like I never experienced one glitch or moment of self-doubt about my fitness to be a cancer researcher, or if I even want to, and *everything will be fine.*"

He considered this.

While he was pondering, Zoey also tried to think. Because, she had to admit, she was not really doing that too clearly.

Too soon, he nodded.

"Okay," he said. He held up his hand as she jumped eagerly.

"Buuut," he added soberly, "the weather is unpredictable on the strait so I can't guarantee you'll be able to leave as soon as we find the slide."

"I'm sure it'll be fine."

Her voice careened upward again. It was not going to be fine. She was demanding to get on a boat with a near stranger. She didn't know where she was going or how long it would take to get there! But if she didn't recover the slide and get back to the lab, she wasn't going to be able to keep her head in her work. That was *not* part of The Plan.

Then again, none of this weekend was.

Davy added, "I'm paying for the rest of your passage home. I insist."

She wasn't going to fight *that*, especially from Mr. Private Island. "Sure."

"And maybe you want to let someone know that you're doing this? I can give them my details if it makes you feel safer."

That helped ease her mind a little. She thought of Li-leng and her hand, and of how her roommate might react. She winced. "I'll do all that when we get on the boat."

Davy still looked pretty serious. "All right, then. If you're positive."

"I'm absolutely, completely dead certain."

"Maybe let's not bring death into it."

"My certainty is immortal, okay?"

He took in a deep breath, and she almost felt it herself. She hadn't realized how close she was standing to him. He held out his hand. "Welcome aboard."

She gripped it, and she tried very hard to avoid asking herself what the hell she was doing.

Especially when Davy murmured, almost too quietly for her to hear, "I sure hope you like SpaghettiOs."

Davy Hsieh did not often know what he was doing. He didn't operate with a plan—it was more a set of loose guidelines. And even then, he usually forgot about them.

This—this situation—however, seemed to call for some sort of forethought. While Zoey stood on the deck of the boat, talking on her phone, he jotted down a quick list.

1. *Don't screw up Zoey Fong's life*
2. *Don't screw up MY life*
3. *Help Zoey get the slide back*
4. *Win Zoey's forgiveness*
5. *Get to know Zoey better*
6. *Let Zoey get to know me*
7. *That's kind of scary that most of this list is about Zoey*

But he had to make sure of a few things. She had to be protected and safe at all times. So even if she insisted on doing something foolhardy, *like getting on a boat with a stranger* (this plan was already going well), then he was going to object and stand his ground and not let her dark eyes bore into him until he couldn't think straight.

Although that was heady and exhilarating in its own way.

This was why he was a hermit. He liked people, but trying to consider their needs made him tense. He already had enough of a hard time dealing with his own anxiety. But it was too late now.

Davy pulled a device out of his jacket pocket and handed it to Zoey.

"What is this?" she asked.

"Satellite phone. That's yours. There's internet in the house, but the rest of the island isn't very connected. If you ever feel scared or uncomfortable or whatever, even around me, you can use it. Um, you don't know me very well and you're going to be spending a lot of time with me."

"A lot more time, you mean."

"I'd feel better, and I'm sure you'd feel more secure if you had it. Overall, the island is safe, but I'm also used to living there and some parts of it are wild, and I have all these work-arounds for some of the issues. Anyway, this is something you should have. Just in case."

She peered at it suspiciously. "This isn't some roundabout way of telling me you're a vampire or a shifter or something, is it?"

"You lost me a little bit there."

"Like, you're nice and perfectly human-seeming now, and you've learned to curb your impulses, but maybe your control over your powers is hanging by a thread, so you're giving me a phone to protect myself."

"Uh, I don't have powers. I think."

"Not supernatural ones. Not that you know of."

She shivered.

"Would you like my fleece?" he asked.

"I'm already wearing one of your fleeces."

"I have several."

She took it without another word and put it on over the other fleece.

"I'm trying to be practical," he explained into the silence of their conversation, which was something he'd never expected to come out of his mouth. But here they were.

"Also, I was trying to put myself in your shoes for a bit and think of what would be the best thing to do."

She nodded. "Maybe the best thing would be for you to talk to me about where we're going."

He agreed. "Let me tell you over breakfast."

"That's the second-best thing I've heard all morning."

Zoey's conversation with Li-leng did not go well.

"You got on a boat with him? You don't even know him. He could try to make a barbecue out of you."

"Honestly, Li-leng, I think he has enough meats that he doesn't need me slathered in sauce and strung up over a pit."

That sounded kind of dirty.

Zoey really couldn't think this way about Davy. She had barely forgiven him. Even though technically it was her fault for handing him the slide to begin with. And for not listening to the many messages he left in which he told her he didn't have the slide on him.

"This isn't like you to be so impulsive," Li-leng was saying. "You should never, ever go to a second location with some stranger. Haven't you read *The Gift of Fear*?"

"Strictly speaking, it's only the first location this morning." Okay, so the location was a boat. That was moving through the water. To a remote island. But he wasn't a supernatural creature. His teeth *were* dazzling, though. "And it was my idea. You were fine with my tooling around with a stranger through all of yesterday."

"Yesterday you were in *Burnaby*. Nothing ever happens in the suburbs."

Zoey couldn't argue with that. "It's fine. He's fine. I feel okay with him—" *Okay* was not quite the word, because *the handsome* hadn't quite worn off through proximity as well as she'd hoped. And in addition to the handsome there were also the strong, hot fingers to think of now, and the lips. The shivery voice that asked for her opinions and warmed her with its concern.

She left that out of the conversation, too. "Technically all this is kind of my fault anyway—"

"No."

"Well, the upshot is that we both feel guilty about what happened, and I know what I'm looking for and what to do with it and how to protect it. Basically, it'll be like I'm going through his things. Maybe I'm even helping him by unpacking."

"You're *helping*?"

"Yes! Sort of."

She was proud of herself for coming up with that one.

"You say he's sort of a charming laid-back dude?"

"You know the kind. Has an easygoing drawl and developed, uh, musculature through the arms and shoulders. And chest. That was my first impression."

"And rich, too, you thought. Everything comes easy to him?"

"I—well, yes."

"Zoey, no, no! You've fallen for it again. Himbo in Distress! We've talked about this. You keep saying you don't like coming to people's aid and acting all grumpy, but you end up doing it anyway, and then before you know it you've taken over everything."

Zoey's stomach tightened.

"This isn't like...those other times."

She'd helped many people who weren't himbos. In fact, she wasn't even quite sure what the word meant.

"Zoey, you think a medical degree is only step one on a path to curing your younger sister's cancer *that's she already recovered from years ago.* You aren't responsible for everything despite the fact your parents put you in charge of a lot when you were still a kid! You certainly don't need to come to the rescue of people like him, because life will always help them."

The hysteria was going to bubble up again. Zoey hoped that Li-leng was having as much trouble hearing Zoey as Zoey had hearing her because another short giggle was threatening to escape.

"He's not a himbo. He has not done anything himbo-y. I mean, he's all about pianos and pastries."

"Baby grand pianos, the most himbo of the pianos—"

"And he's not really in distress. In fact, when you look at it one way, he's actually pretty resourceful. He lives on this remote island, and he organizes these shipments. He cooks for himself."

"Yeah, he's a regular Robinson Fucking Crusoe."

Zoey squeezed her eyes shut. Now that she thought about it, she realized she couldn't remember if Davy had mentioned other people on the island. He said his dad had once owned it, but he hadn't dropped anything about a loyal retainer or how big the house was—although if there were all of these electronic doodads and room for a baby grand, it must be big enough.

"Anyway," Zoey said, "he let me take a picture of his license, gave me his address, and his grandma's address. I'm texting them to you before we get out of range—"

"Zoey—"

"I'll be fine. Byeeee."

She ended the call feeling relieved that she wouldn't have to listen to Li-leng being insightful for at least twenty-four hours, sent the information, and put her phone to silent before she could receive any more texts from her roommate. Hopefully the hand injury would slow her friend down.

Then Davy approached, still serious—still handsome. She patted her backpack absently. She wasn't sure why she'd decided to chatter nervously with him about werewolves and vampires. Maybe it was because Li-leng was right. She didn't know him and she would be alone on an island with him—plus or minus a family retainer who was probably extremely loyal.

Maybe Davy made a habit of this, she thought as he led her downstairs to the galley. Maybe he semi-regularly got women to entrust their bone histology slides to him, then wooed them with pho and pastries, and compelled them to come to his island, and then he fed them to his big cat, which was not a euphemism. Or maybe it was.

Wasn't that the real reason she was nervous?

Zoey was going to be alone with him and she found him attractive. *Sexy.* Judging by the way he'd been looking into her eyes when she had him by the collar, he found her compelling enough.

Sex island, she thought. Fling island. In the midst of all that unpacking, she could at least find out what he was packing. It was a perfect setup. He was handsome and pliable. He lived on an island in the middle of nowhere and didn't like to leave it. There would be no awkward meeting as long as he stayed off the mainland.

Plus, if something did go wrong, he had already given her his very large phone.

He'd introduced her to the crew members and led her to a narrow room that she supposed was kind of a break room/kitchen. A bright red cooler was tucked away in a small cupboard under a table. "Tomato avocado or sprouts and vegan cream cheese?"

"Tomato avocado, thanks."

He pulled out two sandwiches, and a couple of apples, and

produced a stainless steel water bottle. "I hope you don't mind sharing," he said.

"That's great," Zoey said brightly. Maybe a little too brightly.

Because now of course the idea was in her head, and she couldn't act naturally. The sandwich tasted like glue and although she tried to take tiny bites, she was still having trouble swallowing and thinking up conversation and sitting elbow to elbow with him.

What experience did she have seducing attractive island owners? Most of her encounters had been with her fellow schlubby graduate students. Her last relationship with a guy from the microbiology department had lasted three weeks until she was thrown over so he could "devote more energy to crypto markets."

"So what is it about this slide that's so important?"

"It's a specimen taken from the bones of someone with osteosarcoma, the kind of cancer that starts in your bones. It's the most common type of bone cancer to affect children and adolescents."

"That's your research? Bone cancer? And helping kids? That sounds pretty important."

"I hope it is," she muttered. "I've always wanted to heal people, but it's hard knowing the right way to do it."

"What do you mean?"

His voice was gentle, and for some reason it made her turn away. "I remembered the pediatric oncologists who worked with my sister, Mimi. I loved the med school portion of the MD/PhD program I'm in, but I told myself you help more people in the long run through research. Anyway, the sample in the slide is taken from a kid who wasn't much older than Mimi when she was diagnosed."

She heard Davy's intake of breath even above the sound of the boat's engines.

Talking about her sister's illness had gotten easier over the years. She'd mentioned it enough when people asked her why she wanted to take on such a heavy program. But for some reason, telling Davy made her words come slow.

"Mimi had cancer in her bones. She was eleven. It always seemed so strange and unfair to me that something like this could grow in the deepest, hardest, strongest part of yourself.

"So the slide is important. To me. Smerek might eventually notice it was gone, and I'd be dinged for being careless, which I really don't need right now. But *I* need it. It reminds me why I keep going on this path. Why I've put in so many years. That it's the right thing to do.

"I don't know why I'm talking like this. Mimi, my sister, she's alive. She's fine. She has an Instagram account where she posts pictures of miniature knitting projects."

Another sound, this one puzzled. "Miniature knitting?"

Zoey wiped her eyes. The salt air stung even though she was inside. "You know, scarves and hats for dolls and figurines."

"Of course."

"She likes to take care of little things."

They were quiet for another minute. Davy seemed to understand that she didn't know how to speak about it anymore. She couldn't.

He touched her elbow gently with one finger, and that small point of contact warmed her.

Zoey was grateful when he cleared his throat. "So on the island, you'll probably have to stay overnight at least because I don't really want to risk coming back in the dark—and who knows how long it'll take to find the slide. But there's a bedroom for you if it comes to that, and we get some electricity from solar panels. There's plumbing."

She took a deep breath and focused on that. It was good to know. She'd assumed it would be luxurious considering he was bringing a piano out there. She was usually five steps ahead, but she'd had to do so much of her thinking on the fly this weekend. She also realized that she hadn't brought much clothing with her. She maybe had an extra T-shirt in her backpack, and if she was lucky, a pair of shorts. Maybe that was enough, but still, they'd be unpacking and if he had a lot, then it was bound to be heavy work.

Priorities, she reminded herself sternly. The slide. *The Plan.*

"It's a long but narrow island. Most of it is kept fenced off. I'd really prefer that you stayed within the fence and keep a safe distance from the wildlife. Even if you're an experienced trekker, it's an hour ride to emergency help on the mainland, and there is the possibility that I won't even know if something's happened to you if you're knocked unconscious or if you break a limb or get stuck. I am trained in first aid, though."

Why was that sexy to her?

"But who takes care of you if something happens to you?" she asked.

"Me?"

"Yes. You."

Was the Handsome blushing? He gazed at her searchingly. "Oh. Well."

"No loyal retainers, then?"

His brow knitted.

"I mean, something might happen. You're alone. Equipment can malfunction sometimes. Something could fall on your head, like a branch, or a big rock, or—or a drone that you were trying to figure out. You know I have my training as a physician, too. In case something happens to us." Maybe she sounded a little overeager for an emergency. "Not that I can do much without equipment."

"Well, in case I fall ill or get hurt, I have some contacts. My old friend on the mainland runs a bed-and-breakfast, and

I check in with her and with the store in Narrow Falls that I get supplies from. And there's a guy, Rudy, who lives on one of the nearby islands."

He paused for a second. "We radio each other, and we've met a couple of times in Narrow Falls."

"Like a hermit summit?"

"More like a hermit drive-by. Although Rudy is more outgoing than me."

Something in his voice made it sound like Davy didn't always like socializing with Rudy.

At Zoey's raised eyebrow, Davy said, "He's, you know, hearty. Used to being a big businessman. Always giving me unsolicited advice about how to succeed like him."

Very unwelcome advice, judging by Davy's frown.

"He's not really into animals either, so we don't have much in common. But it's fine, you know."

He picked up their trash and stowed it carefully. Then they went back upstairs.

"Should be coming up on the island soon." He seemed to take a deep breath and turned to her. "I'm serious, though, I want you to stay safe. I should give you a walkie-talkie, too."

"In addition to the phone?"

"I've mentioned that there are some animals."

"Right. Your big cat."

"You're sure you're okay with—"

The captain appeared at their shoulders. "Davy, we're going to be there in a few. We're set to help you unload but it looks like a storm is moving in, so we'll be getting out of there as quickly as possible afterward. You sure you want us to drop you there? We'd be happy to set you down in town so you can weather the storm."

"I'm well supplied for storms, but I don't want to speak for Ms. Fong."

Both men swung their eyes to Zoey.

Now was her chance. She could hitch a ride back easily and forget this pleasure cruise. Or she could stay here.

Davy said, "Zoey, we're well equipped, but this is one of the dangers I was talking about. If something happens to you, we might not be able to get off the island to get medical help. No one would blame you if you went to town."

"It's a nice town," the captain added.

Davy agreed. "Like I said, you can stay at my friend George's B&B on the mainland. It's in a little town called Narrow Falls. Tell her I sent you and she'll put you up for free. Really, I think this might be better."

"There are plenty of places to eat there," the captain said helpfully. "The Frasier serves an excellent salmon hash."

"I hear the blackberry pancakes are delicious."

Zoey held up her hand. "Gentlemen, it looks like you know the best ways of convincing me to stay in Narrow Falls. But I want to go to the island. I'm sure about this."

"Zoey, a storm on the coast is no joke—"

She looked straight up into Davy's eyes. "Bring it."

CHAPTER 5

A LITTLE LIGHT FLIRTING

Davy had a lot on his mind. He had many things to keep track of and, he had to admit, losing track was more of his specialty.

First of all, he was helping with the unloading. He had crates to direct, dollies to pull, his property over which to cast his eye, Zoey to watch, and the turbulent sky to brood over.

But at the same time, he was happy. The sea wind was fresh and cold. He was on his green and rocky patch, and he could hear the music of the waters. He was in a familiar place that he'd built for himself and for his convenience. And he was going to be able to show it all to the woman beside him. He had never had anyone stay with him before—his grandmother didn't even like venturing into Vancouver anymore, his sister and friends were wary of his big cat, Baby, which was entirely reasonable of them, he supposed. And his parents…well, that was a whole story unto itself.

So while he was worried, he kept that at the back of his mind like a hard stone. Zoey was there with her rosy cheeks, her round ass, and her dark cap of hair, her snap, and her smart, smart brain. And true to form, she'd taken to directing the crew as they played Tetris with his boxes in the small space in front of the house.

"If you put those too close together, we won't have room to open them or get them out the door," she was calling out, her beautiful clear voice a grace note against the sound of the wind.

He hadn't even considered that. He'd just been hauling and dumping crates in willy-nilly without a system, without thinking of how difficult it might be to get everything to different parts of the house and property. And grunting a lot.

The captain leaned in. "Seems like a keeper. Already arranging your life like she owns it."

Davy considered this as the crew made their final check and they hurried off to beat the storm.

"See you in a month or so," the captain called.

Zoey let out a small whimper.

Davy said, "I promise I'll take you to the mainland in a day or two depending on the weather. But this is your chance to get back now."

She looked a little green but shook her head.

Davy gave them a thumbs-up, and turned back to Zoey.

"Thank you for all your help. And welcome to…"

He paused. The island? *My* island? That seemed sort of annoying. "The place!"

Zoey was still holding her stomach. She seemed a little uneasy. "Does it have a name?"

"Oh, good point. The government had it down as Bell Island. The locals started calling it Davy's when I was building, but I feel like a land mass, even a tiny one, should have a more dignified name than *Davy*."

"But you shouldn't?"

"I'm used to it."

She opened her mouth as if to say something, then closed it again. She shook her head and gave a small smile. Then she put on what he was beginning to understand was her determined face. "Well, maybe while we're rooting through these crates, we can think of a name for your home. In the meantime, I'm guessing we're going to break these down to get them inside the house?"

"Yeah, it's not too bad. And some of these we can leave out here. But we have to do it one at a time. Sorry. This probably isn't what you were expecting."

"Well, I'm not exactly here for a vacation," she reminded him.

Right. That was true.

Not a holiday. She was here because she was doing important things in the world. Curing cancer! In kids! Trying to help her sister, even though her sister didn't need help anymore. Zoey wasn't here for the pleasure of his company, although he was afraid that he was already taking too much pleasure out of hers. Everything here was already better—not just the arranging that she'd done. But everything. The air seemed brighter and sweeter. The wind was making a happier sound. Maybe some birds would come down from the trees and start serenading them.

Hmmm. Where were the birds?

Right. A storm was coming.

"We unpack that crate of perishables in the house, maybe move a few more things, and batten down the hatches. The rest of the stuff will have to wait until the storm subsides."

"Which crates are the ones that need to get in first?"

"It's the blue ones, and also those light green ones over there. The blue gets sent straight from the store, so they should be pretty organized, and the green ones are where your slide should be."

She huffed. "Fine, let's get the dolly and move these a little closer to the door, then. It'll be easier to get everything else arranged so that we can find my specimen."

"You're a genius."

"No, I'm an organizer."

"That's its own kind of genius."

She pushed him gently toward the one she wanted moved. "Maybe it is. I'm not going to argue," she said, clearly arguing. "I can hear the wind whipping up. I hope the crew is safe."

It had started raining gently by the time they got every-thing they needed inside the glass-and-wood structure with its gentle sloping roof equipped with rainwater collectors on the side and solar panels on top. He loved the wide windows, the solid trees on the side that rustled musically on windy days like these. He hoped Zoey would like it, too.

Davy turned on all the lights. Not one flicker. That was a good sign.

Zoey was looking around the great room. It wasn't huge or beautifully decorated. Right now, it seemed cluttered with the unpacked crates left over from last time. But it had never needed to be a showplace. He said, hurriedly, "I turned the thermostat up if you're cold. Are you hungry? Would you like to clean up? I can show you to a guest room. It hasn't been used much—or ever, really. And, um, I can also find you some dry clothing in case you got wet."

He tried to keep his voice casual when he said *clothing—clothing!* It wasn't as if he'd said *zippers*, or *braaaaa*, or much less what they covered, and yet, here he was thinking of her *not* having clothing. He had done so at several points already during their acquain-tance, but right now he was presented with a picture of her legs, which he knew were made for stepping over idiots and kicking down doors, sturdy and practical. He wanted to run his fingers over the smooth, rounded muscle of her calf, or over her lush ass. He found himself wondering about her underwear, probably also practical, a plain covering for something extravagant and beautiful. And he let himself wonder, briefly, if she had dimples above that ass, two drops in cream, two spaces where he could lick her, press his thumbs in deep.

Whoa, okay. They were alone and he didn't want her to feel uncomfortable, especially not now, and the main—and only—person who could make her feel that way here was definitely him. He'd have to keep a tight rein on his mind lest it show in his face or demeanor.

He wanted her to like this place, although he couldn't say why.

Luckily, she didn't seem to notice that he'd gotten distracted. "Any dry clothing you could find would be fine. Well, maybe not one of your flashy jackets."

"Don't worry. I have some T-shirts and hoodies. Maybe we can cut a pair of sweatpants down to size—"

"You don't have to—"

"It's all right. It'll be better. Are you hungry?"

That amused her and his heart burst with sudden warmth to see her smile. "You're always asking me if I'm hungry."

"It's how we Taiwanese are. We lead with the stomach. We don't greet you by asking you if you're well. We don't say, *How are you?* We ask if you've eaten yet."

Between catching the boat and getting up to speed, Zoey hadn't had time to think, let alone plan. She was here to find her slide, but she wasn't averse to flirting with Davy, although her courage was failing her there. Davy was Handsome and right in front of her. It'd clearly never work out long term because he was a rich-boy island hermit, and because she was a serious researcher who was depleting all of her emotional energy to continue—no *finish*—her program. Plus, she was leaving as soon as she could. Perfect fling conditions.

But oh, it was pretty here. She already wished she could stay a little longer. The woods around were green, as far as she could tell, and she could smell the sea air even in the house. Davy's house was made up of a single low building, smaller than she'd expected, furnished sparsely, wide-planked floors. There were so many unsteady piles of books. And boxes. And boxes with books in them apparently. Somehow the clutter made it look like it could turn into a home eventually. If it had been sunny, maybe there would be lots of light, but right now, the rooms seemed dim and intimate. It had potential.

She showered and decided against the T-shirt she'd brought and dressed in the hoodie and sweatpants he'd left for her. She could hear him dropping boxes down in the great room and by the time she arrived, there was a stack of things for her to go through.

"Hey, you're under no obligation to start right now, but after I put the perishables away, I figured I'd try to bring a few more things in, get settled. Besides, this might give us something to do when it starts getting really dark."

She shivered. She should be looking for her slide! Priority one! For The Plan! But somehow it was hard to remember urgency and determination. It was as if when she'd told Davy about her sister, she'd let something go. Zoey's slide could very well be in this first box from this first crate, and then she could suggest other things they might do if it got really dark.

At the same time, though, she had to be practical.

There was also the fact that she was chicken.

Davy was moving around, shifting crates to one side of the great room. Zoey decided to station herself near the couch. It was near enough to the place he was working so she wouldn't have to shout, and it was far enough that he wouldn't get an eyeful of her butt every time she bent over. Although if she was thinking of having a fling, maybe that wouldn't be a terrible idea.

She sat herself down.

"You don't mind me going through your personal items?" she said, pulling open the nearest crate.

"Nothing too exciting. Mostly manga and fantasy paperbacks. I read a lot out here."

"Maybe you can tell me about how you started living here all alone, and about this house while we're sorting through it."

"My dad bought the land maybe twenty years ago, when he first moved us out here. He and my mom are *tai kong ren*—astronauts, they call them—because they spend more time in the air flying between family in Vancouver and business in Taiwan—and China—than they do on the ground."

"*Those* people," she said lightly.

He smiled ruefully. "Yeah, we're *those* people. Anyway, I don't know what he planned to do with the land, or even if he planned to do anything at all. He does that. Buys something because he thinks it's cheap, forgets about it. Next thing you know, someone wants it, and he sells it back to them and makes a profit. Business, you know."

"He makes it sound easy."

"Well, it's easy when you have money to buy land and let it sit unattended to begin with. Anyway, I guess he was thinking of selling it. My neighbor, the guy I mentioned, Rudy," Davy said, grimacing, "I think he made an offer and my dad mentioned it to me. I came out to take a look. It turned out I really loved it. It was wild and brambly. I was at a point in my life where I wanted to go far away from…everything, so I told him I'd buy it and come and live here."

From the hurried way he spoke, she could tell he didn't want to talk about that part. Too bad it made her curious. She inspected the contents of another box and set it aside.

Davy gave her a quick glance, strangely vulnerable, then cleared his throat. "He sort of laughed at me and said from the sound of it, it would take too much work and, well, it *was* a lot of work. I had a lot of ideals. I talked to architects and builders. I tried to use sustainable materials and solar panels. Repurposed the fallen timber we had on the land. But it was... an experience. We had to build shelters for the materials and clear staging sites and bring generators and heavy machinery. We had to dig so much of this place up. It looked really ugly for a long time. I've tried to shrink the amount of space I occupy. We're as close to the shore as we can safely be. I planted native shrubs and trees and let as much of it return to the wild as I could, but it's going to take years. I guess in the process I pretty much figured out that no matter how good I tried to be, I was destroying a lot. My residing here alone is not the most responsible way to live, ecologically speaking."

Zoey was sorting automatically through a box of electronics and papers. She knew it was definitely not the box with her slide. She should give up and start on the next. But instead, she watched him as he bent over a box, eyed the curve of his spine, the muscles flexing under his Henley. If only his shirt would ride up and reveal some of the skin underneath. But it didn't matter how hard she stared, the material stretched but stayed put.

Why would someone this beautiful want to live so completely alone? A love affair gone wrong? A horrible disfigurement requiring him to hide under the mask and in the shadows? What a shitty myth that was, as if there were a normal out there in the real world that people needed to adhere to.

Besides, Davy honestly seemed too well-adjusted for that to be true. All of the usual scenarios, the usual fictional scenarios that is, didn't seem to apply. Maybe he masked well.

Zoey found herself grudgingly rearranging her notions about

him. She had been judging him, his charming smile, his easy money, the fact that he had an island—okay, she held that against him a little bit even if the reality wasn't an entire house painted in gold leaf.

Even if she was enjoying herself just a little bit.

Moreover, she hadn't expected him to talk about…infrastructure? He'd put a lot of his own work into this place. And he also clearly was willing to look at it critically.

More critically than she. Because even though she hated admitting it to herself, even though she was technically working, emptying this crate, putting some things away, she felt like she could breathe for the first time in a long time, and it wasn't just the ocean air.

She tamped all of that down. "Is that why you're talking with Dr. Hisanaga about a wildlife sanctuary?"

"Trying to. Trying to find the right place to start instead of ending up halfway through the project and discovering that I've done it all wrong. Although it may be too late for that."

Before he could say much, a sheet of steady rain came pelting down on the roof.

"Oh, sounds like the storm's really hitting now."

He jumped up.

"Is there anything I can do?"

"I've got backup generators. All the windows are still locked so unless you opened them all up, we should be fine. But maybe I should double-check to make sure everything's in good shape."

The sky had gotten very dark.

She jumped up to follow him. She was a rational woman, and it was very rational of her not to want to be left alone in a strange place.

He didn't bother with the lights for the other rooms, just went to each window, running his fingers around them, inspecting the seals, she supposed. Making sure there weren't any leaks.

She watched. He was simply doing a routine check, trying to be careful. But even as he'd been admitting his faults, clearly feeling bad about this island project he'd undertaken, she had to admit, he seemed so—so *responsible*, so strong and sure. Even in the semidarkness of the kitchen, she could see the sensitive, methodical way his fingers ran across the tops and sides of each window.

Zoey followed him to the dining area with its casual, cushion-strewn chairs, to the kitchen, down the hall to the bedroom he'd given her, then without thinking, into his.

Davy finished with the last window and paused, and she barely even noticed that. She was so intent on the slow descent of his arms, the straightening of his spine, that she didn't notice that the air had become charged, that he'd been watching her reflection in the window.

He turned very slowly—excruciatingly slowly—and finally, she let her gaze rise to his face.

It took Davy a long time to get all the way to where he wanted to be. Because until coming to face Zoey, he'd be able to sustain the illusion that she was looking at him like she wanted him.

Then he was right in front of her, and surprisingly, the ghost of what he'd seen in her reflection seemed warmer. Hotter. Real. She was leaning toward him, her eyes dreamy in the darkness. She was close, so close. In another era, he would've grabbed her arms and pulled her toward him in a kiss.

But this wasn't that time. He didn't want to be a person who did that, and he couldn't manage to ask if he could kiss her. He closed his own eyes, and when he reopened them, the moment was gone.

"Everything good?" she asked, taking a step back, then another, then another.

"Yes. We're safe from leaks. Water damage isn't great for a place like this."

And…now he was babbling about water damage. What next? Was he going to talk about mildew and the dangers of heavy-duty bleach, and how to get stains out of the walls in an environmentally responsible way?

The silence stretched out. Was it uncomfortable because she was uncomfortable, or was it anticipatory? And if it was the latter, what was the right thing to say next? While they stood there. In his bedroom.

"How are they going to deliver the baby grand?" Zoey asked.

"Oh. Right. I decided not to bring the piano."

She blinked. "Just like that, you decided against it?"

"Yes."

"But you were so set on it."

"But I was going against expert opinion."

"So you just…listened and agreed?"

Her face was a puzzle. She'd looked aghast, even though he was sure that she'd never liked the idea of him transporting the piano to begin with. But then she seemed envious.

"Aren't you sad about it?"

He shrugged carelessly.

That was more along the lines of what she expected from him—an easy-come-easy-go attitude.

After a while, she said, "So no serenades for me?"

If she was going to attempt to be light, he would, too. "I have a pretty good electric keyboard with weighted keys. It's not the same, of course, but, well, you saw how worried Mr. Shu was about getting the baby grand ready for a trip. And again, I realized I hadn't given it enough thought. It's better to leave it with Mr. Shu for now and then figure out where I can store it."

"Your grandma won't take it?"

"She doesn't like instruments because then people want to play them."

"So, you're saying she doesn't like music?"

"I think she likes some Western classical pieces when they're in the background and mostly pretty quiet. But she gets annoyed when people who don't play well sit down at pianos. Which is kind of funny because it's not like there are a lot of chances for that now that she doesn't really get that many visitors."

He was in his bedroom, in the dark, with a girl he liked, and he was talking about his grandma. He really had no game. He wanted to hustle her out to end the slow punishment of not touching her, but at the same time, a part of him was enjoying this too much. Davy liked her here. He lived alone in this house for most of the year, with only quick visits to the mainland to check in on George at the B&B and to see his grandmother. But he liked how her questions filled the room. He was pretty sure no one aside from himself had been in here since the place had been built three years ago, and tonight, when he fell asleep, he'd have the echo of her voice on the walls.

"What kind of music do you play?" Zoey asked. "Are you a professional musician? Mr. Shu said something about that, didn't he?"

"I don't really play anymore. I write music for commercials and incidental music for TV programs in Asia. Not so much here."

She thought about this for a while. "I wasn't sure if you did anything—for work," she admitted.

Yes, well, for a while, he hadn't done anything. "I've been in the music industry for a long time" was all he said.

Zoey took a step closer—and oh, this was going to kill him, the way the distance between them widened and shrunk with every word he spoke. Of course, he could move himself closer. He could eliminate the divide between them, and he thought probably that she wouldn't object.

But all this talk about his music career made him unsure again. He wanted her to close the gaps. He didn't want to end up throwing his body into a space only to realize that he hadn't started it right, that he hadn't chosen the right path at all. So she had to decide, she had to bring herself close, and take herself far. She had to reach out for him.

That meant that he'd already made his choice, of course: he wanted her.

But when neither of them moved, he heaved a deep breath. "Let's go back downstairs. Are you hungry now?"

She smiled. "I could be."

It turned out Davy had bought some artichoke hearts, which turned up in the crate he'd started to unpack. He ended up incorporating them into the pasta he made. No, it was as if he'd expected to cook this dish. He had all the ingredients; he pulled up the recipe on his phone like he'd saved it. It was almost as if he'd listened to Zoey, thought of her while planning meals, thought of making it for her. But that was ridiculous. He hadn't known she would be speaking to him, much less following him onto the boat and onto the island.

But his attention couldn't be doubted as he watched her taste it, his eyes focused on her as she took the first bite, as if he were anxious to see her reaction.

"Thank you. It's good," she said. "I love it."

He beamed and that smile stopped her again. How he managed to look so uncomplicatedly happy when his life seemed less simple than she'd expected was beyond her.

She had to get a hold of herself. "The question is, do you like your artichoke experiment?" Zoey asked.

It was Davy's turn to chew thoughtfully. All she could hear was the rain pelting down hard on the roof, the clink of cutlery. They drank water from large plastic tumblers, and Davy had roasted up a platter of root vegetables that he'd found in the refrigerator.

"I think I like it, too. Although now that you've introduced me to the world of jarred artichokes, I feel like I should try all the different kinds of recipes with it as an ingredient. Do you cook a lot?"

"My roommate, Li-leng, does. She's supposed to be working on her dissertation, so instead she bakes."

"Sounds great for you."

"I do enjoy the desserts. But I wouldn't mind having more space to myself. You probably don't have to deal with someone who—"

Sees you a little too well.

"Uh, sets off the smoke alarm every hour. Though it's not that she burns everything. It's more that our detector is incredibly sensitive. It's as if the slightest whiff of anything good sets it off. It's like a critical parent."

"Or grandparent."

"But we don't want to take the batteries out completely because every now and then, Li-leng does get distracted, even from baking."

"What do you do when your roommate is busy avoiding her work and using the oven?"

"Aside from the lab? I was just thinking about that this weekend. Before all this happened. Li-leng says I need a hobby."

"I'm not taking you away from your Sunday night knitting circle, or a very important water polo tournament?"

"Just the lab."

"Right. The lab. Is it going to be okay if you aren't there tomorrow? Because aside from the fact that we haven't found the slide yet, this storm might last a while, or the waters might be too choppy for me to take you back right away."

"I asked one of my lab mates to babysit my experiments. It's fine."

Fine was definitely not the word. But her supervisor wasn't in this week at least, and she was feeling reckless. Maybe a little dangerous. This was a new Zoey. One who took risks, who deviated slightly from The Plan—part of it, at least. Davy seemed to bring it out in her. Just as she'd done among the beeves, and at the pho place, she forgot herself. She said with a breeziness she didn't quite feel, "I'm due a few days off."

She wasn't really. She took a big gulp of water and tried not to hyperventilate.

"No one at work is going to miss you?"

Whyyyy did he have to keep asking questions? She remembered what Li-leng had said about how much Zoey hated work. She thought of Alec and his passive-aggressive notes. She hadn't left anything there that he could snoop through. He stole her Post-its even when she was there, though. He would definitely tattle to her adviser. She could claim a family emergency. The slide was a sister substitute—practically family. She swallowed her doubts. "It'll be okay."

"What about your folks? Do they live in Vancouver?"

"Oh, no. My parents are in Ontario. Mississauga."

"It's far away. Do you miss them?"

"Yes, and no. I'm used to them not being around very much because they were always working."

"Same," Davy said with an expression that gave Zoey the feeling it wasn't the same at all.

"We have a good relationship now, though. When I was younger, they depended on me a lot, like I was a little grown-up.

But they've gotten more confident over the years, and I'm close to my sister. And she's how I ended up on the path I'm on now."

She wished for a minute that she had a glass of wine.

"How long have you been at this?"

Zoey counted it up in her head even though she already knew. "Oh, about four years. Still quite a few more to go."

It was going to go to waste if she didn't get better at it soon. More to herself she said, "I don't feel like I should be allowed to stop because then I might not want to keep going."

"You're the most energetic person I know," Davy said with a laugh.

"I'm not tired around you."

Maybe she did deserve a small break. She was looking at years and years more of dealing with slides and passive-aggressive lab mates and failed experiments. She couldn't *quit* no matter how much she wanted to.

Wait, what?

She stopped. She didn't want to quit. It was the slide. It was because the slide was still missing that made her think this way.

Davy hadn't noticed her small panic. He seemed lost in his own thoughts. "I never got good grades in school." He looked down at his plate. "Too busy fiddling with music or mooning around with my head in the clouds. I admired the people who did, though. My sister, Nina, was always the smartest person in the room. Although you'd probably give her a run for her money."

She was quiet for a moment. He'd talked about his schooling—or his lack—like it was something to be ashamed of. She didn't think he was stupid—maybe clueless or a little dreamy and distracted. But so were many people she knew. Then there was the fact that he'd actually listened to her and gone out and tried making some goddamn artichokes.

Jesus, she had to calm down about this. It was just pasta.

She took a sip of water. "I'd love to hear some of your music after dinner."

"Oh, well, the things I write are usually for shows or for the background. But it might be fun to play if you'll join in."

Now she was caught. "I don't really play. I had some lessons, but they were strictly of the classical, *learn this piece and then learn that one* variety—"

"A sing-along?"

"I don't know any songs!"

"You don't know one song off by heart? Not one pop song you used to play over and over when you were a teen?"

"I'm not doing a Fiona Apple *Extraordinary Machine* sing-along. Not for any amount of money."

His eyes gleamed. "Not any amount of money? Come on. I bet I could afford it."

Davy probably could, too, Zoey thought sourly as they stood up and gathered their plates. Well, once he heard her singing—he was a professional music person!—he'd probably pay her to stop. Scratch any chance of her ever being able to seduce him.

Still, as they washed up, she started to think maybe some singing would be kind of fun.

Davy said, "So your set list tonight—"

"*My* set list! I don't think so."

"Our set list: Fiona Apple, some Christmas carols—"

He was smiling again, that ridiculous man. But maybe she was, too. Still, she'd probably end up punching him soon.

"It's April!"

"C'mon, everyone knows carols. Unless you have a religious objection. I know, movie musicals—"

"Ooh! No, we can't."

"I heard the longing in your voice. What's your poison: straight-up Broadway, old-school MGM? Oh wait, *Disney* movie musicals."

She was in trouble now, and judging by the look in Davy's eye, he knew it.

Still, she wasn't a quitter. She tried to feign nonchalance, as if he hadn't seen into her secret soul. "How do you figure?"

"You're pink-cheeked, like a doll. Like a princess who can sing with the birds."

She kind of did like those songs, but mostly she'd watched a ton of them with Mimi when she was in the hospital. They'd been an escape.

"That's it, isn't it? I'm going to start playing and you won't be able to stop yourself. Don't know about you, but I can feel the love tonight."

She threw a dish towel at him.

CHAPTER 6

SOME ATTEMPTS AT SEDUCTION

Davy settled them onto the piano bench and thought of how nice it was to have contact with another person again, especially when that person was Zoey, so alive and snappish and vibrant and—

"I'm not joining in on a song I don't know," Zoey said snappishly and vibrantly.

"Even your warm-ups sound better than anything liable to come out of my mouth," she added.

She was nervous. Davy could understand that feeling. Meanwhile, he noodled on the keyboard, feeling more comfortable already. Would have been better with a real piano, but he was trying to do more with less.

"Let's try something everyone knows, then," he said genially.

He started playing "Chopsticks." She watched him. "You're right, I know how to do that," she said, joining in, an octave higher. They played through together one more time, then he started playing the bottom oom-pah-pah accompaniment.

"*Do-you-think/there-are-words/to-Chop-sticks/Do-you-think/there-are-ly/rics-to-this/song-Chopsticks/I-mean…*"

Miracles of miracles, she started singing, *"Don't-you-get/tired-of-kids/playing-Chop/sticks-Don't-you/get-tired-of/this-song-playing?/I-don't-know-how-to-go-on—"*

She had a nice voice, bright and clear and straightforward, a little higher than her speaking voice, but still so *her*. And when she smiled, the whole room warmed. He started doing variations and she held on to the rhythm of her playing without a hitch.

She was giggling. Her round cheeks were pink. They were sitting very close together, thigh to warm thigh, their elbows and arms bumping occasionally as they played. Zoey didn't move away from his touches, he didn't move away from hers. Davy wanted to kiss her.

They ended with a flourish. By now her enthusiasm was fired, and she leaned toward the piano. "Okay, let's play some real music," she said.

He clutched his heart. "What do you mean? That was a real song!"

"It was only 'Chopsticks.' Even I know it well enough."

"I don't know where you come from but 'Chopsticks' is a very important bonding song between you and the keyboard, between you and other kids who teach it to you or play it with you."

"Between the people who find it annoying."

"You sound like my grandma."

"Maybe I agree with her on this."

She pursed her lips primly. She was talking about his grandma, and he was turned on.

"But it's fun to play it. It's something easy enough to master as long as you can count to six. You can feel competent over 'Chopsticks.' Two fingers and suddenly you're making something that feels like something, that sounds like something. Plus, it's a waltz."

"Hardly elegant."

But her cheek curved as she smiled.

"What, you can't imagine being swept up in a long gown to the strains of 'Chopsticks'?"

"It's such a strange Orientalist name for a waltz."

He hummed. He hadn't thought of it that way. "We took it back tonight. Maybe we can do the same with 'Heart and Soul.'"

Her laugh was rich and beautiful. It was a good thing his fingers were occupied, otherwise he'd probably do something foolish.

"What are you playing now?"

He frowned down at his hands. They'd slowed down and were moving automatically through quiet chord changes into the song he'd been trying to work on. "Nothing worth mentioning. I was just thinking of you."

"Like you were writing a song about me? Oh, probably not. That's just silly."

But despite the quick backtracking, she had seemed excited by the prospect. Maybe he was, too. "We could try."

"Oh, no. You're just saying that. You weren't really writing a song about me. Were you?"

"I was playing some chords. I was thinking about you. That's another way that things start for me."

"Do you write lyrics?"

"My words to 'Chopsticks' didn't convince you that I do?"

Zoey rolled her eyes and scooched closer. "I should get a co-writing credit."

"I'll make sure you get a royalty check. I do sometimes put lyrics to the songs. They don't always get used."

He smiled down at the keyboard and modulated into a different key. The music that had been eluding him seemed to come easier with her nearby.

Zoey was quiet for a moment. When she spoke again, her voice was hushed. "Wow, this is…no one has ever written a song about me."

"I'm inspired."

She snorted. But there was something in her face that he understood—she wanted to believe his words. "Right. What would a song about me even say?"

"Something about how you're really smart."

"Ugh."

"You don't like being smart?"

"I love the fact that I learn quickly, but if I were going to be immortalized maybe I'd want to be known for—" She screwed up her nose adorably. "This is surprisingly hard. What do people even write songs about?"

"People with cruel, cruel hearts. But wouldn't you want your song to be different? A song about graduate school?"

"*No.* Not the lab."

They both seemed a little surprised at her vehemence.

"Not that I don't absolutely love everything I'm doing," she said, nodding as if to reassure herself. "But there's more to me than that. Isn't there?"

"I'd like to learn more."

"We could arrange that."

He stopped playing. They stared at each other for a minute.

"I'm glad you're here," he said quietly.

She ducked her head. "I'm sure you'd get more work done if I weren't."

"I don't have to work all the time. Besides, I wouldn't have anyone to share artichokes or play 'Chopsticks' with."

"You wouldn't have artichokes to begin with."

"And now I do, and I don't have to play one-handed 'Chopsticks.'"

"That sounds dirty."

Wait, was she flirting with him?

"Wait, are you flirting with me?"

She looked alarmed. But then she tried to seem casual. "A little."

It had been the wrong question to ask her, because despite her bravado she'd scooted away from him and was in danger of edging off the bench. How had she managed to get so red? He wanted to touch her cheeks, see if they were as warm and soft as they looked, like a sun-kissed peach. But a comment like that from him would probably send her onto the floor.

"If you have to ask, then I guess I wasn't doing it very well," she was saying.

"No, it was great! I enjoyed it. We could do it some more," he added hopefully.

"Oh, but now that you've said it out loud, I won't be able to. Why did you go and do that?"

"I'm not as bright as you. I need things to be clear."

She rolled her eyes. "Please, the way you look and the way you connect with people, you know exactly what's going on all the time with other people. You've got the gift."

"So, you like how I look," he said, focusing on the most important thing—to him.

"See, there you go again! Why couldn't we just flirt the way I'm used to?"

"Which is…"

"Ignore the other person until they go away."

"Hard to do in this situation, seeing as we're stuck here."

He gestured to the piano bench, their island on an island.

"I'm not like you," she said.

"And that's why I'm enjoying this."

She looked down again, but she put her hand on his knee. For an imaginative man without companionship, it was heady stuff. But even as her fingers traced his kneecap lightly, she whispered, "I'm a coward."

He swallowed. "You don't seem scared to me."

That came out a little rough, a little low. Her hand was bolder than anything she'd said, but her words didn't match the look she gave him. "Well, I'm terrified."

He touched her back, and when she didn't recoil, he put his arm around her and pulled her closer against him. He told himself it was to help support her—keep her spine up. But really he wanted more places on his body against more places on hers. If he bent down, he could whisper right in the whorl of her ear that she was brave and beautiful. But he was a coward, too, so he just said, "I don't think there are rules when it comes to flirting. Between you and me, at least. You can't really do anything wrong here."

"Of course I can!"

She looked right at him and sat up straight immediately. His support was working, so he didn't move his arm. Besides, he was too busy enjoying all of her movement, all of her *life* and energy and feeling.

She said, "There are plenty of things people can do wrong. You don't go up to someone and say, 'You have a nice butt.' In most contexts, it's creepy."

"Objectively speaking, you have one of the most beautiful asses I've ever seen. But I can see your point."

"Wait, I do? You do?"

Her face was a study of outrage and intrigue and…more blushing. He could kiss each apple of her cheeks and work his way to her mouth.

"But you're not even looking at it right now."

"It's true. I'm gazing deep into your eyes, and I'm thinking of your hand on my knee and my arm around your waist."

She took in two big breaths and then looked away. "Oh

God, this is hard. I thought I could be different for a minute, you know."

"What do you mean?"

"I thought I could be a person who flirts."

"You're doing great."

Maybe a little too well. His body was…turned on. Then again, it probably had been to various degrees ever since he'd met her.

"A person who's seductive."

"Honestly, it wouldn't take much with me."

Boy, that was that the truth.

"Who's cool when people write songs for them."

"No songwriter wants the person they're writing about to be blasé."

She threw up her hands, knocking him slightly aside. "I'm trying to be someone I'm not. You probably don't know what that's like. You're like a rock star. Swooping into labs and meat lockers and piano restorers, dazzling everyone."

He drew in a deep, dizzy breath.

Davy knew exactly what she was talking about, but he wasn't quite listening anymore anyway. His stomach twisted. He wasn't a star. He didn't want to act like one. That wasn't the point. Zoey was laying her fears bare, but he was trying to keep his under wraps. She thought he was a harmless, easygoing fool.

It was suddenly very quiet, and that's how he knew the anxiety was coming back.

Why now?

Why? Probably because he cared what she thought of him.

He hated this most of all, the rushing emptiness of his head before swirling worry took over. He didn't know what to do with his hands anymore. They didn't know what to play. Zoey was just trying to tell him something about herself. That was it. But he couldn't hear it.

"I'm talking too much. Spoiling the moment," Zoey was saying. It sounded far away.

"You aren't," he choked out.

He tried to control his breathing. He was Davy in the present. All of that was behind him. Except when the past walloped him the way it was hitting him now. This was why he couldn't live with other people around. Because an innocent remark could trigger all those dark thoughts that led to an anxiety attack. Davy hadn't had one for at least five years. He started rubbing his chest.

Still far away, Zoey was talking. "My point is, I've always been this person who thinks that there's a right way of being and doing things and is afraid of straying from the path, The Plan, no matter how complicated it was. And I don't know why I'm doing this—whatever this is. Losing the slide to begin with. Coming here and trying to talk to you like a normal person who's invited herself to your island and making a fool of myself. I just, every morning I wake up and for a few minutes, it's fine. And then all the feelings rush back, all the memories of all the things I did wrong, all the horrible things that started happening to my family when I was younger. I guess I missed out on that feeling of being a kid. And I just want to be able to take a break from it. To not have that sitting there. And to be able to just...be a person who flirts. You know?"

Zoey sounded so wistful. In the small, tight corner of his mind in which he could still think, he saw the child she must have been, trying to keep it together when her sister was sick. Trying to be an adult. "Maybe you can do that here, with me," he said.

But he'd been so wound up about even the mere mention of rock stars that his offer came out stilted, his voice tight.

Zoey's face fell a little. She was disappointed in his response. He stood up abruptly. "There are toothbrushes and toothpaste in the bathroom drawers, and all kinds of stuff like that."

"I'm sorry, Davy."

"You don't have to be. You don't even know what it's for. I'm feeling a little off."

"Is it your stomach?"

"No."

"Was it the artichokes?"

"No, I—"

"I did it. I spoiled the moment, didn't I?"

He almost laughed. But that would have choked him.

"It wasn't you. Believe me. I need to take a walk. There's a lot of food in the kitchen. I'll be fine, don't wait up."

He fled.

Zoey really knew how to seduce a man, yes, she did.

Start blabbering about a depressing time in her life, about her parents, her childhood during what had been a lighthearted moment, then watch Davy run as soon as she turned earnest. She'd told herself he wasn't serious, and that wasn't why she liked him.

She brushed her teeth with one of his toothbrushes and washed her face with his soap and water.

She texted Li-leng. Are you there?

Nothing. She really did have to be alone with her thoughts.

How's the hand? I'm fine obviously, she added. Safe. He's not a bad guy.

Oh, that was an understatement.

But she didn't want to admit to Li-leng how silly she'd been. How...hopeful she'd been. Because he had been attracted to her. To her! For a minute. She wasn't always the most skilled with interpersonal relations, but this time she could actually tell when someone wanted to kiss her. Or *had* wanted to, since at this particular moment he couldn't even be in the same house as her.

His lips had looked soft in the light. Every time they'd opened to sing or laugh, her eyes would touch them as if they were made of velvet, as soft and rich as the voice that came out of them. She couldn't imagine anyone walking by without wanting to brush up against them.

She could have had those lips on her. Instead, it was like she couldn't stop herself from telling him how scared she always was, despite her tough face.

This was what happened when she started making plans on the fly. Especially ones that involved other people and their feelings. She was only good when she stuck to the script absolutely. As soon as she deviated or tried to improvise, bad things tended to happen. It was like watching a Rube Goldberg machine, except the marble would drop through the funnel and hit her on the shoulder, causing her to put the pie in her own face over and over again.

Zoey reminded herself of The Plan. Find the slide. Get it back to the lab. Finish the degrees, help find better therapies for bone cancer.

She sighed as she got into bed.

It was still pretty early, just a little past nine, but as she gazed out the window, the darkness seemed complete. The rain had gotten heavier, and she could barely see out the window. Occasionally the wind seemed to howl—no, yowl, like a cat. She couldn't imagine Davy out there, but he'd said he needed to go for a walk, and who really went for a walk inside their own house, vast as it was?

So he was walking in the rain, in the slippery, rocky terrain, in that wind. Even if he wore a rubber suit, he'd be completely wet in minutes.

She had to admit that she did spend a minute picturing him in skintight pants, molded to the lean, muscled thighs that had pressed against her own earlier tonight. She imagined the water coursing over his bare chest. Why he'd be standing outside in a rainstorm with no shirt she couldn't say. But, of course, even as the picture flashed, lit up like a lightning flash in her brain, she started to worry.

What if something happened to him out there? What if he slipped and fell or was swept out by a huge wave? Well, she still had the satellite phone. She supposed she could call emergency services, and they could send a boat out. But that wouldn't help him if he'd struck his head or was bleeding to death.

It might be on her.

She crept down the stairs, because although she didn't want him to die, neither did she want to encounter him and embarrass herself *again* in case he really was taking a walk around the house. It was bad enough that she'd put her foot in her mouth, but for him to find her skulking in the dark, wearing his T-shirt and boxers and socks, would be embarrassing and suspicious.

It was odd tiptoeing around alone. He wasn't in the great room still crowded with crates. The bathroom also seemed to be empty. She went through the swinging half doors into the kitchen and almost screamed when she saw a movement opposite her. But it was just her reflection moving across all the gleaming surfaces.

She rubbed her finger along the counter as if trying to find a spot of grease, but no.

He cleaned up after himself.

She'd helped him with the dishes, but he'd put everything away. Even though it was not what she was supposed to be doing, she opened the cabinets. Cans ranged neatly in one cupboard with gaps where his new supplies would go. Pasta and cereal in glass containers. A spare smattering of bowls and plates and cups.

This was supposed to reveal something about his personality, but he didn't keep much here.

The rain had eased a little now, and she wandered over to the door to the laundry room. She hadn't paid attention before, but there was a door there, leading out to a deck of sorts. Part of it was protected by a long overhang, which was probably shady and cool on sunny days, but which tonight seemed scant protection against the blowing rain.

There was one single chair sitting right in the middle, like it had been planted there. Maybe darkness made it look heavier, more solid. It wasn't until it moved, and she almost yelped again, that she realized it was occupied. By Davy.

He was sitting alone in the dark.

So that's what he was doing. Watching the storm.

Maybe she should call him in. But maybe he was outside now because he didn't want to be in the same house as her.

The kinder, braver thing to do would be to go out there and try to get him to come back inside.

The thought had barely formed in her mind before he started to get up.

He stretched taller and taller and she couldn't look away. But in a minute he turned, and although he wouldn't have been able to see her face—she certainly couldn't see his—she leaped back from the window.

He was coming inside. He was going to catch sight of her and know that she was spying on him.

Half crawling, half stumbling, she fled, banging doors behind her, wincing at the noise, but eager to get away from him, and from herself.

★ ★ ★

Zoey woke up the next morning from restless dreams. For a minute, she didn't know where she was. This bed was a lot bigger than her twin and the covers were silkier. She spent a minute with her eyes closed, running her hands and legs over the sheets, admiring the cool, smooth feel of what was approximately one gajillion-thread combed cotton.

She liked this not knowing where she was or what she was.

Then, of course, because she was Zoey Fong, her eyes snapped open, and she scrambled up to sitting position.

The whole evening came flooding back to her. The pasta and artichokes, the piano, singing, laughing, and then her careless statement, her mad dash through the house at night, the pounding of her heart as she'd scooted under the covers, imagining strange yowling coming from outside.

The caterwauling had even penetrated her dreams. She'd imagined that she was chained to a cliff face and that a giant tabby cat was coming to butt its enormous head against her, and that she wouldn't survive its love. But luckily, just as that was about to happen, Davy had come along wearing a sparkly jacket and no shirt, his well-defined chest bared for her to stare at, and he'd chucked the tabby under the chin and the enormous beast had settled down for scritches.

She had no idea what it meant. She shook her head, feeling stupid.

Zoey slid out of bed and peeked out the window. The rain had stopped and a little sunlight was coming through the clouds. Birds were chirping madly, eager to share news of last night's storm.

Today her goals were modest: she was going to go through the rest of the boxes, and she was going to find her slide, and then she'd hitch a ride back to civilization on a passing yacht or ferry or ocean liner—or maybe swim if she got really desperate—and return to her work, her lab, and her narrow, slightly uncomfortable twin bed. And she would do all this without being in the same room as Davy, or meeting his eyes, or hopefully talking much to him.

As soon as she got coffee.

She climbed out of the bed and patted it mournfully. It was a really good bed, and she was going to miss it. After changing into a new T-shirt and another pair of oversize shorts and examining the mysterious bruises she'd gotten, most likely from her mad dash through the house last night, she made her way slowly down the hall.

There was coffee waiting in a French press for her, and a note:

Good morning! Help yourself to anything in the fridge or pantry. Sorry I don't have dairy, but there's oat milk in the fridge, and sugar and agave on the counter if you want it. The grounds go in the compost under the sink.

No sign-off, no signature. No XOs. Although, given the fact that no one else lived on this island, it was pretty obvious who would've left the note, and it wasn't as if they were on hugs-and-kissing terms. Maybe that might have happened last night, but now he was writing to her about compost.

As if she didn't know how to do that.

She made herself some toast with peanut butter and drank the coffee. It was delicious, damn him.

She made another cup and took her mug to the great room where the containers were waiting for her, one after another. Lined up neatly so that she could go through them easily and methodically, as was her way. No one around to bother her. Plenty of air and light. She could even switch on some music if she wanted to. Ideal conditions for her to conduct her work, secure her slide, and be off on a boat by tomorrow.

Instead, she turned on her heel and headed back into the kitchen.

CHAPTER 7

WILD GOOSE CHASED

When Davy got back from doing chores and inspecting for damage from last night's wind and rain, he found Zoey in the kitchen standing amid what appeared to be a flour explosion.

There were also cookies.

"I baked."

"I see."

"There weren't any eggs. Or butter. But there was coconut oil and tapioca starch. I found a recipe. Hope you like vegan cookies. I'm also making bread."

"This is incredible. You didn't have to. I didn't know you were a baker."

"Oh, well, Li-leng, my roommate, she does it more than I do. But, you know."

She wasn't quite meeting his eyes. And her voice was a bit too perky.

Zoey wasn't the only one who felt uncomfortable. Davy hadn't had a full-blown attack last night. But he didn't feel relieved. He could still feel the faint ache of it in his chest. He should probably explain to Zoey what had happened, but the words seemed stuck near that buzzing hornet's nest close to his heart, and he didn't want to poke it.

Still. He looked at her little face, her mouth still slightly downturned, and he had to say something.

"I get anxiety, and last night that started to happen. What I mean is, I started getting anxious."

"You?"

"Yes, me."

"About what?"

He almost laughed. Zoey *would* ask so baldly. "Let's say it's a kind of performance anxiety."

"Oh." A pause. "Oo-oh." Then another. *"Oh?"*

He didn't know what all the ohs meant. Or maybe he did and didn't want to get his hopes up.

"Is that performance anxiety a euphemism, too?" she asked.

"Too? How many euphemisms have we had between us?"

Zoey threw up her hands. "I don't know! It seems there might be a bumper crop on this island."

He felt his chest ease subtly. She was teasing him. She didn't seem horrified by his condition. She didn't offer advice.

"Let's just say I'm working some things out."

She was curious, though. He could tell. But Curious Zoey was normal, and better than Sad Zoey—for now at least. He had to distract her. "What's in these cookies over here? They smell amazing."

"There's a lot I don't know about you," she said pointedly. "I've noticed you're maybe vegan?"

"I'm vegetarian and mostly try to keep vegan, but I'm not strict about it."

She nodded. "Well, you can eat them if you want. I mean, they're your ingredients and it's your kitchen so obviously you can. But they don't have any animal products, is what I mean."

He wanted the cookies. They looked good. The bread smelled better.

He should probably wash his hands and his whole body, though. He was grimy from hauling things and walking around.

She saw his hesitation.

"They also freeze well," she said hurriedly. "I mean, I won't be here that long to help you eat them."

Despite the awkwardness, he wished she were. "Maybe you could become my personal chef."

Her laugh sounded a little wild. "Don't tempt me. I'd probably like it more than my graduate program—not that I don't love it, of course. Sort of. It's really, uh, fulfilling."

"Sounds like it."

"Plus, this island could use a henchman. Someone to unpack your crates, and pull levers that lead to huge electrical boxes, and laugh maniacally, and say, *Yessss, Davy*, in a creepy voice."

"Don't think I haven't thought of that."

Was everything okay? He peered at her from under his hair, but she was tidying and frowning. Although he was quickly learning that maybe her expression had nothing to do with him.

"My friend Li-leng would probably be better for you. She's a better cook. Although more likely to set fire to things. Not on purpose, of course. But she should really just finish her dissertation, get it over with."

"Even though she seems to not want to do it?"

"But she's so close to finishing her plan!"

Davy shrugged. He didn't know the woman, but he did know what it was like to put a lot of work into something only to feel like it was ruined for you at the end.

Too well.

"I'd prefer you anyway."

What did it matter if he flirted? Davy needed to be alone, and she had a world to save. Keeping Zoey here because he liked her and liked talking to her, and he liked her black, shiny hair, and the way her soft face looked with a smear of flour across her cheeks was selfish and he'd been selfish enough in this life.

As if she knew the direction of his thoughts, she tried to clean herself up with the apron. "I should really, really look through the crates," she sighed.

He could understand why she was reluctant. It seemed daunting to sort through them. Even to him. Which reminded him, he had some goals of his own to take care of. "I need to go check around, see if anything else was damaged while I was gone. But you can always call me if you need help prying off the lids and things like that."

"No, it's fine. You don't have to help me. I can do it on my own."

"You don't have to do everything on your own."

"People say that to me a lot."

She crinkled her nose, and he resisted the desire to pinch it gently. Where were these affectionate gestures coming from? It wasn't like they were together. "Do you ever listen?"

"No."

But she was smiling a little bit now. And she stepped closer to him, and for the first time that morning looked him in the eyes. "I'm sorry that something we talked about triggered your anxiety. I hope you feel comfortable telling me about it one day. Or someone. Because you shouldn't have to go it alone, either."

He leaned closer and said in his best imitation of Zoey's voice, "People say that to me a lot."

Zoey giggled and snorted, then clapped her hands over her mouth. He couldn't help the smile that crept over him, too, and they stood looking fondly and foolishly at each other. It wasn't so bad, this…getting to know people a little better thing. He'd forgotten how much he liked their quirks, the funny things they told themselves, their crooked smiles, their pretty shoulders emerging from a slightly too-big T-shirt.

Wait, that was just Zoey's shoulders he liked.

He enjoyed having her around, even when she made him feel off-kilter. What was that about? She was right. He did actually get along with people, and he could be good with them. The anxiety hadn't changed that. Oh, being a hermit devoted to music was fine in theory. But it was like that beard he'd tried to grow in order to take on the role: it was just a little odd, maybe not so much a discomfort so much as it made him self-conscious, which was a terrible thing to feel when he spent so much time alone. He saw it when his eyes flicked down and even when he'd had it for a few months, it startled him. He'd dropped his guitar pick into the sound hole of his acoustic and spent a few minutes trying to shake it out. In the end, he'd shaved off the beard and cut himself doing it, but at least no one was around to witness his embarrassment.

He wished someone like Zoey would have been around to tease him about it.

"Would you like a tour?"

"What?"

He'd been a bit abrupt. "I know you're busy and have to find your slide. But it stopped raining, and I wanted to know if you wanted a tour. Of the island."

He was being inane. It wasn't as if he had a carousel and pony rides to offer or something.

She dropped the cloth she'd been using to scrub the flecks out of the granite. "I'd love one!"

"You would? Oh—great! I'm so glad."

He was probably beaming like a fool. He hadn't realized

how much he wanted her to spend a little more time here, to get to know the place. Or him.

"Well, okay. Do you want to borrow a pair of hiking shoes, maybe? And let me get some gear together. You'll have to grab the satellite phone."

"Can't I just use my regular phone? I'm not planning on making any calls."

"It's still better to take precautions. Your phone won't work out there, but in case something happens to you, or me, I'd rather that you have it handy so that you can call for help. The number of the nearest RCMP station is programmed in."

"Wait, what exactly are we expecting here? Elephant stampede? Tigers?"

"There are a few animals on this island. They're as harmless as wildlife can be, but it's still important. Or, you know, I could fall into a deep pit and need rescuing."

"What kind of wildlife?"

"Rabbits, birds. And there's the cougar."

"The what?"

A wooden spoon clattered to the floor.

"I mean, she was raised in a zoo and she's elderly, and at some point, someone took out her claws."

"That's really cruel."

"Yes."

"But a cougar!"

"Yeah."

"This is the big cat you were talking about! Fuck! A cougar! I thought you were talking about, like, a Maine coon, or maybe just some tabby that you'd overfed."

"With big haunches of beef?"

"I thought those were for you! Except you don't even eat meat. God. A cougar!"

"Her name is Baby."

"A cougar named Baby!"

"I didn't come up with that. But she answers to it."

Sort of. As much as a not-domesticated-because-you-can't-domesticate-a-cougar could respond to having her name called. She was probably more interested in the meat than in his endearment.

"I paid for her vet care. And I wanted to try to, I don't know, re-home her. But it's surprising how few people want to take in a cougar."

Zoey choked out a laugh. He wasn't sure if the sound meant she was freaked out by him or if she found it funny. Maybe both?

"She couldn't survive in the wild without her claws. There was nothing I else I could do for her."

"You can't just keep a cougar on a remote island."

Ah. He was going with freaked out.

"Better than a populated one."

She gave him a look.

"I was trying to arrange for a place for her to stay last year, but it fell through. I was never trying to run a wildlife sanctuary for a big cat—maybe some bird rehab at most. I was minding my own business. Trying to do my work. So that's why I've been trying to get expert help, like from Dr. Hisanaga. But I really don't know what I'm doing yet. Although if it makes you feel any better, at least I'm not as irresponsible as the guy who gave Baby to me—who abandoned her."

"You're not irresponsible," she said.

Zoey seemed to have recovered from her shock if she was snapping at him about being too hard on himself.

"That was what the yowling was about," she mused.

"I think that was just the storm."

"I can't believe there's been a cougar here all this time."

"Like I said, I was trying to get her into a proper sanctuary.

But in the meantime, there aren't a lot of people who want to foster a cougar."

"She's unwanted."

He clapped his hands over his ears. "Hush, don't ixsay that in front of the ougarcay."

"Don't…six that in front of the cougar? She's not even here. Or is she?"

She looked wildly around the kitchen.

"Well, no, that's not what I meant to say, but don't do that, either. She has good hearing."

"So the yowling was because we were talking behind her back?" Zoey started to giggle. "Most people don't usually want little cats. Even the cutest kittens. But no, you took over this island, built a house, and started living here so you could take care of a former zoo animal."

"I didn't plan it this way. But that's what ended up happening. I don't know, people give you mugs, and they give me elderly animals. I don't know why."

"Because you're a soft touch."

He couldn't deny that. Dammit.

She was still giggling. She may have snorted. He wished he could keep that sound somehow, put it in a hot water bottle and hold it to his chest every time the nights got too cold. "So there were other animals? Please don't tell me you have an incontinent liger."

"No, just a couple of injured hawks for a while. But I eventually re-homed them at real wildlife sanctuaries."

He wasn't sure what to make of the laughter. Especially because she was repeating, "A cougar named Baby," between snorts and giggles.

Davy stood a little helplessly while Zoey worked it out of her system. Yet, that angry drone of anxiety had loosened with her every laugh until he couldn't feel it anymore. He could breathe easily again. He could hear how beautiful the world was.

He handed her a tissue. When she'd finally wiped her eyes and stopped hiccupping, she said, "Okay. Sure. A cougar named Baby. Why the hell not? Bring on the tour."

It felt like a date, even though Davy was rather grimly packing a tranquilizer gun.

The tranquilizers alone probably made it better than most dates she'd ever had.

Zoey felt absently for the reassuring weight of the satellite phone. She'd borrowed some boots, thick white socks, and a flannel shirt, which she'd tied and retied in an effort to make it look flattering.

She supposed she should be concerned that she was going out with a strange man who had a firearm (Tranqarm? Medarm?) and a large clawless cougar. Except that Davy didn't seem like a killer, and he was being responsible. Maybe too responsible if he was running this show for an elderly cat.

He was genuinely worried about Baby.

But for some reason, *she* wasn't anxious about anything right now. How…unusual for her. She glanced again at Davy's equipment and asked, "Do you know how to use that?"

"I'd rather not, but yes, I do. I took classes."

What was it about a man who admitted to getting proper training that made her swoon?

Better yet, judging by the serious way he'd briefed her about what to do if they came in contact with Baby, if he had to choose between her and the cougar, he'd choose her. That was a warming thought. Especially since he'd done all *this* for the cougar: created a sanctuary, went to the mainland to buy her large meat treats.

Why was that exactly?

Davy didn't lock the doors, but he did run a final check to make sure things had been put away—no burners left on, no food left out, no windows open. His face was serious and careful, and she had to admit she liked it, liked the firm set of his jaw, the patient and slow movement of his hands as he ran his fingers around sills.

It was the kind of thing she might do if she were acting like herself.

He closed the heavy door, took a deep breath, and looked around him, as if preparing to meet heavy traffic, and they stepped right out from the narrow porch around his house, the thin perimeter of clearing, and into the woods.

Zoey wasn't sure what she expected. The house disappeared behind the thick veil of branches not long after they left—or maybe it was because she was a city person who needed signs and streets, and Google Maps to tell where she was going. Even in spring, with many of the leaves just beginning to bud, she could hardly see the solid structure. She wondered if they'd be able to see it in winter, with all the leaves completely gone. It must have been quite a job to clear.

But it was beautiful, with all the delicate greens of spring a bright mist even while the sky remained gloomy. And the air. She sniffed in a deep breath and smelled rain and wood deep in her lungs.

"Careful of the brambles over there. Am I going too fast?"

"I'm fine."

Zoey was more than fine. She could see why Davy spent all his time here. For the first time, she felt the heaviness banding her chest loosen. She could breathe.

"Do you have enough water?"

"We set out less than ten minutes ago."

"I just want to make sure you're okay."

"I'm great!"

"I'm not used to being responsible."

That made her stop. "Of course you're responsible. You're in charge of all this."

She waved her hands around at the greenery around them. He had a whole minor land mass.

Of course, it was hard to indicate scope when her arms hit branches as soon as she tried to open them wide, but Davy got the idea.

"It really mostly takes care of itself."

"The cougar feeds herself?"

"I probably don't track her eating as well as I ought, but she hunts smaller wildlife on this island, too."

"You're not her parent. You're not a vet or a biologist. You aren't obligated to track her feeding. You don't have to go and buy meat for her, or try to think of safe, ecological ways of maintaining this island. You kept most of it untouched and keep her safe. You chose that, and that's maybe the most responsible thing of all."

Davy had turned to listen to her, and as he swung around to the path again, she could tell he was thinking about what she'd said. She meant it, too. He put a lot of work into it, and money, obviously. Was this part of his anxiety, too? What could have caused such a thing?

It was a sobering thought, especially because of what Zoey had thought of him just two days ago.

She couldn't even keep track of a slide.

She cleared her throat. "Are there other animals out here? Aside from, you know, the big cat, and rabbits?"

"There are raccoons, of course. There's a beaver dam up near the stream—we'll go see that. I've seen a white-tailed deer some years—no idea how they got here. We also get all sorts of ducks, and sometimes even some loons."

"So mostly harmless animals."

"White-tailed deer are deadly. You could get Lyme disease from the ticks. That reminds me, you should do a check when we get back."

"Will you relax? I'll be fine-*ulp*!"

She'd tripped across a branch that wasn't on the path, because she'd wandered slightly off the narrow track he'd cleared on his walks, because she'd been trying to prove a point to him.

He was at her elbow in an instant.

"Can you stand? Did you twist your ankle?"

For a giddy moment, she thought he was going to hoist her into his arms and sweep her back to the house. She was going to let him. But then Zoey realized she would rather make him feel like he was doing a good job shepherding her through the woods—because he was—than be carried.

She shook her ankle out. "I'm good. I was just startled."

"May I?" Davy asked.

He knelt to carefully unlace her boot, to peel down her white sock, the ones he'd insisted she wear, and examine her limb for himself. His hand was warm on her skin. "Lean on me a little so I can see if you can rotate this."

She almost wanted to laugh. Because now that the initial surprise was over, there was hardly a twinge. But she put her hand on his firm shoulder and thought about how steady it would be even if she rocked against him. She closed her eyes briefly at the idea, then lifted her leg and let his fingers move her one way, then the other. "Did you learn how to get a lady to strip her boots during first aid training?"

He looked impassive, probably because she was trying to flirt again. That had gone so well last night.

"I went in to get certified when we first started digging this place up. There was so much heavy machinery and the nearest hospital seemed so far away. Then I kept it up because for a while I thought I'd have people come and visit."

Davy's fingertips ghosted a little higher, up her calf.

She could hear the wind in the leaves, the call of birds in the distance. She could even smell the peaty smell of woods and water, and the underlying cool spring scent, the sign that better times were coming. And she could feel. Every nerve in her body thrilled to the touch of his hand slipping softly back down her skin to cup the curve of her heel. He squeezed gently, as if it were some precious thing that didn't bear the impact of her foot strikes all day, every day. She didn't feel delicate. She wasn't. But she felt precious.

When he tested, trying to see if she was sound, she felt it like a bell tolling deep in her. She was never sure of much, despite her bravado. But in that moment, she knew she could depend on him and on herself.

Somehow her hand had moved up, into the softness of his hair, the warmth of it, the solid architecture of his head, the sudden stillness of him as she stroked once, twice.

She opened her eyes and he was looking up at her, his eyes searching her face. She could see everything open to her, the dark brown eyes, the handsome cheekbones stretched out, the strength of his neck. He was the one vulnerable right now. She could press his face right to her thighs, right between them, and he would never put up a fight. That thought made her hand tighten in his hair.

"Can you put your weight on it?" he asked her softly.

She wasn't sure she could stand because her knees felt strangely weak. But of course she did. Of course she was fine. She'd always been fine. That didn't stop her from wanting more all the time. From wanting him.

She was thinking of kissing him again.

Zoey's big brown eyes had softened and her mouth curved gently. Everything about her was ripe for kissing. He could just reach up, meet her halfway, like he'd been wanting to this whole time, pull her body to his and fall down onto the earth and revel in the way that she tugged at his hair.

Oh, Davy wanted it. But it had to be good. It had been a long time for him. He didn't just go around talking to anyone, let alone kissing people anymore.

God, he was supposed to be taking care of her in these woods. Not thinking about how her foot had felt so strong and alive in his hand, how slowly and carefully he'd traced her ankle and calf because he hadn't wanted to let go.

This was the very worst first aid he'd ever rendered.

He looked down again at the sturdy leg and pulled the sock gently over her again, put her foot in the boot and laced it up.

All in complete silence—well, as much silence as one ever achieved in the woods. The birds seemed especially chatty today.

When he looked up again, her face seemed to have closed off.

Good. Right? He'd self-destructed trying to please other people at one point in his life. He liked other people, but they worsened his anxiety, especially if he cared about them, and the cycle would start again. It was better for everyone if he stayed alone.

Sometimes those seemed like good reasons.

He stood up and brushed off his knees, and his disappointment.

"You're okay."

"Of course I'm okay."

She really seemed to be. She was a little flushed, of course. She had a lot of layers on, and they'd been walking.

After a few more minutes of pushing through branches, they turned down the path that led to the small duck pond.

Or should he say goose pond? Because as he approached, he

noticed that the vegetation around the water seemed stripped down. There was no sign of the smaller waterfowl that had nested there earlier in spring.

It had been pretty and cheerful just a few weeks ago. The wind had ruffled the tree branches, and all around the pond the ducks had quacked merrily. Maybe a little too merrily. But now there was no cheerful flapping. Instead of a teasing breeze, the air felt stiff and cold. The grass around the pond was completely stripped.

Plus there was the goose slime.

"That's a lot of big birds."

He crinkled his brow.

"There were mallard and wood ducks, and I wanted to show you them. It's usually much prettier here with the cattails and water lilies. Sometimes there are frogs, too. Really tiny ones."

Did geese eat frogs?

"Well, maybe it's early in the season," Zoey was saying diplomatically.

But he didn't want her to have to be tactful. He wanted her to like it. It was absurd and childish, like trying to show someone a toy and hoping that they'd play with it and love it, too. Except that it wasn't a toy and what he wanted her to do was to want to stay a little longer, just to get to know the place. And him. Even though she shouldn't.

"Davy, look out!"

He leaped backward to avoid one large specimen of hissing waterfowl that was coming toward him, and almost slipped on the muddy earth.

A few more geese were definitely glaring at them and flapping their wings menacingly. God, he'd been so concerned about protecting Zoey from a big cat, but it turned out that the native birds were the danger all along.

Could *nothing* go right today?

"Maybe let's back away slowly," he suggested. "They seem to be feeling a little aggressive."

"Did the hissing clue you in? Or was it the fact that they all started waddling toward us with their noses pointed down."

"Not all. Just, like, four of them."

One of them honked as if offended. "The four biggest ones."

"They just look bigger when they're beating their wings like that."

Zoey, by contrast, was hunching down as if to make herself smaller. Her face threatened to disappear into her hood. "Yeah, that's a great trick."

He glanced at her. "I'm trying to get us out alive."

She rolled her eyes at him and for some reason he found that comforting. For a minute. "I've never heard of a goose fatality."

The lead goose was aimed right at them like a frying pan-shaped bullet.

"Although I guess I don't want to be the first. Sheesh, where is that Canadian politeness we're all so famed for?"

Davy said tightly, "It's a facade. We're all just glowering, bullying waterfowl advancing on any invaders who try to come into our space. Maybe we should turn and run."

"No. You have to maintain eye contact."

"It doesn't perceive that as aggressive?"

"I have a lot of experience with campus geese." Zoey got a faraway expression in her eyes, like she'd been through a lot.

"These geese don't look like they've been to university."

They were running out of clear space in which to back up. Any minute they'd be in the sharp brambles.

"Get behind me," he muttered.

"But then I'd break eye contact."

"I'll keep it. They can focus on me."

"I have a better idea. Why don't we both turn and run?"

"That's what I said earlier. Then you were all like, *I'm the goose whisperer.*"

"I changed my mind. I'm not the goose whisperer. Although once we're out of their territory—"

"Everything is their territory. They're *Canada* geese. As far as goose names go, it's a pretty imperialist one."

Another goose seemed to take offense at their politics. Or it could have been that they were talking too much and not retreating enough. A few more steps and—

The goose put its head down, then up, then down and looked about ready to charge.

"Go first behind me," Davy said. "Really, I mean it."

"I'm only getting behind you because you have a larger wingspan and that seems like the kind of thing they respect."

"Nice goosey goose," Davy said, sounding like a cartoon villain who suddenly realized he was in over his head.

Davy grabbed Zoey's hand and they both turned just as the lead goose charged.

The narrowness of the path worked to their advantage and their disadvantage. It was difficult to run together, and Davy wasn't about to leave Zoey to the mercy of angry waterfowl, so he kept pulling her and hurrying her deeper into the bramble.

At the same time, it turned out to be difficult for a goose of a certain impressive wingspan to follow for long and as soon as Davy was sure he couldn't hear any more angry hissing, he slowed down.

"I'm all right—" she said even as he said, "Your ankle!"

She held up her hand to catch her breath. "My ankle is fine. It's always been okay. Will you quit asking about it? I took a small tumble and then I recovered. Story of my life."

"I should have been taking better care. I should have thought this through. Instead of a nice, scenic hike, I took you through a bunch of trees and bramble, exposed you to murderous wildlife—"

Her mouth twitched. "You told me about the big cat, but you failed to mention the attack geese."

"I didn't know they were there! I hope they didn't get rid of the ducks. What are they doing here anyway? Aren't they supposed to be flying north? Or south? It doesn't matter. As long as you're okay."

She'd really started laughing now. "I thought you were this laid-back surfer-skier dude when I met you, but you're not at all. You're as bad as me."

"Of course I am! It's a lot of responsibility. We were nearly maimed."

"I mean, the geese are scary, but at most it would've been a few bruises and maybe a nasty nip or two."

He stared at her.

She admitted, "Okay, you're right, it wouldn't have been pleasant. But we're fine. It was an adventure. It's funny in hindsight."

She was giggling again, and he didn't know what to do with that. On one hand, it was adorable. On the other, didn't she know she'd been in danger? Was she reckless? Why was she even here? With him? A total stranger who'd almost made goose feed out of her.

"Let's just go back."

"Can we explore a little more? I like it out here."

He couldn't help himself. He waved his arms around. "How can you like it? It's cold and blustery. The path is so narrow we have to walk single file and you can't see through the wood. We haven't spotted any animals except those attack geese, which apparently you see all the time on campus. And even if we do see wildlife, I guess we're going to have to pray it isn't the cougar I was gullible enough to rescue. It's a danger. I'm a danger to everyone I care about. I don't know what I'm doing!"

"Davy."

All trace of laughter had gone. Now her voice was only warm and concerned. He couldn't look at her.

He lowered his arms. Great. Just great. Now she was trapped in the woods with a cougar, some homicidal geese, and an anxious yelling man.

Why had he agreed to let her come here? Why had he thought it was a good idea? How could he have ever thought he was helping anyone at any time?

"Davy."

This time her voice was closer. Then she was standing in front of him, looking up at him, her eyes full of concern. She grasped his wrists, and he let her. "Take some deep breaths. Sit on this stump. Put your head down between your knees like that. Good. We're okay. No one was nipped or pummeled. Maybe you don't know what you're doing all the time, but who does? Your heart is in the right place."

He heaved in a breath. "That's useful."

She started stroking his back. "You're doing your best, and that is a lot, even though you may not think so now. From what I can tell, you've done a lot to help an island full of misfit animals."

"It's because I can. I can afford these things."

"No, it's something. Because you've decided to take on all this responsibility yourself. I really admire that. I don't know if I'd do it."

His breathing was calming. "Because it's misguided. *You* wouldn't screw up this badly."

She knelt in front of him. "Because I'm so smart that I misplaced a valuable slide, and forced you to take me to your sanctuary and spent most of my time not searching for the item I lost?"

Davy shook his head. But he bent into her embrace to bask in her warm breath on his skin. "You're too hard on yourself."

"I could say the same for you." Her palms slid higher up his back, up over his biceps to his shoulders, and then thrillingly to his chest. His own hands slid to her waist.

"Well, aren't we a pair?"

Had she leaned forward to whisper, or had he started doing it first? All he knew was that they'd created a quiet secure world together with their voices and their breath. Her nose was almost touching his, her lips were closer, closer, and then there she was, pressed to him, sweet and gentle.

She pulled him down more firmly against her, and he let himself go, let his arms circle her, his hands moving up her back, pulling the thick layers of fleece and flannel more tightly around her even as he wanted to lift them up, slide his fingers underneath and touch her with his cold hands until she shivered. All the while, her tongue stroked lushly into his mouth, and he felt every breath, every flutter of her lashes, every delicate movement of her against him.

He'd tried so hard to be good for such a long time. Maybe he could deserve just a little bit of her, a nip of her plump lip, a gentle stroke across the slope of her ass?

"Davy," she said, and her eyes were soft.

Of course he had to kiss her again to stop her from saying his name in a way that made him want more.

He would have gotten lost in her, if the rain hadn't started coming down, although the first few drops splattering down hadn't fazed either of them. But the next moment water poured from the skies. Still, he wouldn't have cared about anything except her lips. If he concentrated very hard on putting as much of her body on his, as much of his on hers, he wouldn't feel anything else at all.

But she was starting to shiver. He was being careless again. "Come on, we should get back."

His voice was hoarse. She lifted her eyes hazily. Or maybe it was the rain blurring her features. "Won't it stop?"

Maybe eventually. Maybe they didn't have to, and they could wait the rain out. Maybe they could make each other happy. But he had to think. He had to be the sensible one.

God, that was always such a bad idea.

"It might, but we should get to shelter. It will be better for us."

She shivered again. Right. If he were alone maybe he would crouch underneath the overhanging rocks a little south from where they were, but he wasn't going to take a risk with her. The house wasn't that far away. They'd go back the same way they came.

If they could see where they were going.

The rain got worse, almost blinding, despite the dense cover of the forest. By the time they struggled back to the door, back to the clearing where the water hit them full and hard, she looked numb, and he was cold through and through himself.

He shoved her as gently as he could through the door and leaned back against it, as if that could keep the weather out.

Zoey was gasping, still breathless from the rain and cold. So was he. They both slid down to the floor and helped each other with their wet boots and socks.

"Go change," he said. "Get out of those wet clothes. Have a hot shower."

She hesitated. But her practicality seemed to return to her, and she trudged out of the kitchen and toward her room.

He waited a few more minutes to catch his breath, then stripped off his own Henley and angrily started trying to get his jeans down. He dumped everything straight into the washing machine and slid to the floor.

It took a while for him to mop up and get himself into dry clothing again. He hadn't seen Zoey in a while so he knocked on her door. Nothing. Worried, he called her name, and heard only a muffled groan. He opened the door.

She was sleeping under the blankets. Her face blissful and smooth. It was tempting to crawl in there himself, but he reminded himself he hadn't exactly been invited.

His date was asleep. "Well, Davy," he told himself, "you sure know how to show a girl a good time."

CHAPTER 8

POP SECRETS

What time was *it?*

Zoey rolled over to check her phone. It was dark and she'd been asleep for hours?

She touched her lips. They still tingled. Her body felt relaxed, and apparently dozing off had been enough to make her lose track of the fact that she'd been cold and uncomfortable before, but not enough to make her ever forget that Davy—the Handsome—had kissed her like he hadn't wanted to stop.

She hadn't wanted it to end, either. Unless he moved his mouth down her neck, to her breasts. That would have been acceptable.

Right. Good word choice. She could almost picture him grinning up at her while she said, *Yes, oh yes, that is acceptable,* and nipping her gently.

God, she really needed to get some clothing on because sitting in bed naked and having these thoughts was doing things to her. It could almost make her forget that she was supposed to die of embarrassment.

Again.

She'd fallen asleep! She could have been down the hall doing it with him on the dryer while their clothes tumbled around inside! Multitasking!

Maybe he was even in the laundry room waiting for her. Maybe she, Zoey Fong, was making a man wait for *her* in sexual frustration. Davy only ended the kiss because it had started raining hard, and they'd both begun to feel the rain more than they felt each other. Very sensible of him to get them back inside where they could dry off.

But maybe she would have been willing to ignore her discomfort, and his recent panic to have sex in the rain?

Who was this impulsive person she was becoming?

She should definitely get dressed now and march up to Davy—no, marching wasn't sexy, and neither was getting dressed. She should shimmy or sway her hips or something. Anyway, she should let him know that she would like to continue what they'd started with the kiss.

If he was okay.

Zoey rubbed her eyes and looked at her phone again so she could avoid thinking about what she had to wear and how she planned to walk and how she intended to completely change her personality in order to seduce the man.

She had a message from her annoying lab mate, Alec, who she was planning to avoid forever, or at least until she'd found the slide again, and three from Li-leng.

Zoey frowned. She hoped Li-leng hadn't set fire to the apartment or dropped anything hot on her toes or stomach or any of the other places on her body that could easily be scalded. At least if she was injured she probably couldn't do much more damage to herself.

Or would she?

She scrolled through Li-leng's last message: How going with Davy X?!? RU alive? Doing fine eting sandwhic.

Good. Well, good as of several hours ago. Zoey thumbed a message into her phone. Don't try to cook anything while I'm not there.

Right away, her roommate sent her what was supposed to be an eye roll emoji.

Maybe Zoey could call Li-leng and talk to her about Davy. But nothing had really happened. Except a kiss. In the rain. Maybe she should tell Li-leng about the geese and the flirting, and the piano. But she felt weird talking about it without a definite course of action.

She was hungry. That was all. Plus she wanted to see what Davy was up to.

Then again, she wanted to hide in the bedroom until she had a better plan for...what? Seducing Davy? Pretending it never happened?

She wished *she* had a sandwich. She'd probably be able to think better.

Li-leng picked up right away. "Thank God you texted back. I started to get worried when you didn't reply."

"I sent a message the night before."

"*I'm safe. He's not a bad guy* is exactly the kind of text I'd send if I'd taken your phone and I were a bad guy and you weren't safe."

"I don't always get back to you right away."

"Not when you're in the lab. But I figured you'd need a break from looking for your slide. I'm kidding, though. I wasn't really worried. I guess you were also preoccupied with handsome Davy X."

Her tongue certainly had been preoccupied with his mouth. "Uh."

"Anyway, everything's fine here."

"The hand is okay?"

"Can't type at all," Li-leng said a little too cheerfully. "I don't know how I'll get any work done on my diss for weeks."

"There's plenty you could do. You could research."

"Eh."

"There's also dictation software. I heard it's improving."

Li-leng gave a familiar sigh. "I'm not asking for advice, Zoey."

"I know, I know. I'm just—"

"Trying to help. I know. If you actually practiced medicine, you could do this and be paid to tell people what to do."

"We're not talking about that."

"Fine, then we're not talking about my dissertation. Let's talk about Davy X instead. Is he fascinating and mysterious? Has he told you any war stories? What he's really like?"

"Why do you keep calling him Davy X, like it's some sort of title or something?"

A silence.

"Oh wow," her roommate said. "He hasn't told you."

"Hasn't told me what?"

"You made him send over a copy of his ID. And his grandma's address in Burnaby."

"Okay, so is Davy X like a nickname for someone?"

"Then I thought his driver's license photo looked familiar so I googled around a little."

It was annoying when Li-leng knew more about what was happening than she did. But wait, was Davy an internationally known animal kidnapper? Importer of killer geese?

"Zoey, Davy X was one of the original members of 5 Boy Thunder! You know, 5BT?"

"Of course I know 5BT!"

She didn't really—maybe a little. Li-leng was more interested in this kind of thing.

"They've been around for a surprisingly long time, since

back before Asian boy bands were big in North America. Plus they were more of a C-pop phenomenon, but they never quite made it here."

"So they're obscure."

"Not in China and Taiwan. They also had a lot of lineup changes. But oh my God, their music brings me back. Davy X was one of the first boys they recruited to be in it, but he was kicked out after the first year and a half, and no one knows why. It was a minor scandal at the time because they were just starting to take off. There were some wild rumors."

"He was in a boy band?"

"Keep up. He was in one that became famous in Asia. Tours, commercials. There was a lot of talk about them potentially being breakout stars in North America, but we weren't exactly into boy bands at the time, much less ones who sang in another language. Although why 5BT needed to get an audience here is a mystery to me. *Breakout* is another word for appealing to white people, I guess. *I'm* in Canada, and I knew about them."

"That's because you study pop culture," Zoey said stiffly.

Zoey was glad Li-leng wasn't here to see her face flaming. Davy had been in a boy band. She hadn't recognized him. He probably thought she was stupid, or one of those second-generation kids who didn't know anything about their own culture. Girls likely kissed him, and hid in his hotel rooms, and stowed away on his boats all the damn time. And she'd gone on about how he was like a rock star.

Li-leng was oblivious to Zoey's turmoil.

"But like I said, he left before the band got bigger. I went through some old footage. He used to wear this black jacket with a lightning strike down the back and no shirt underneath—it was pretty daring at the time. His hair was streaked white, too. Does he really look like his driver's license? I mean, people are never attractive in those, but he still managed to convey the hotness. Or is he one of those people who just photographs well?"

"No. He's very handsome."

"What did you say? You sound like you're trying to talk without opening your mouth."

Her stupid, kissing tactless mouth.

"Anyway, you should get a selfie with him. And get him to sign some part of you."

"What?"

"Chest, butt. It doesn't matter. Then take a selfie of that and post it on IG."

"What?"

"Instagram. Which you don't have. I'll post it on mine."

"Why would I get anything signed, let alone by someone who used to belong to a boy band that I've hardly even heard of?"

She had kind of heard of them, though. Maybe. Perhaps her little sister had liked them. Maybe they'd even listened to 5BT together in a hospital room.

"Think of what a great story it would make."

"To tell the grandchildren? *Hey, when Grams was your age, she made out with a member of a boy band and had him sign her boobs.*"

A silence.

Oh, shit.

The screech that could probably be heard across the entire greater Vancouver area filled Zoey's ear. "You made out with Davy X?"

"A little."

"Like, tongue and everything?"

"Are you fifteen?"

"So yes, tongue! Oh my God, what was it like? I can't believe it!"

Something like admiration was tempering Li-leng's squeals. "Wow, I didn't think you had it in you!"

"What is that supposed to mean?"

"You kissed Davy X! You're usually so self-contained. Like, not in a bad way, but look at you! You let go and mashed faces with him! Wait, are you going to *do it*?!"

Yes, please. "No."

"But then you could say—"

"To my future grandspawn—"

"To your grandkids that you spent a wild weekend with a pop star."

"So I should do it for the children."

"Yes, absolutely."

"I'm hanging up now, Li-leng."

"You're no fun."

"I've never been fun, remember? That's the whole fucking problem."

Zoey hadn't come out of her room all night.

Davy had texted her to let her know he'd made some soup. It was one of his better efforts. He covered her bowl and left it on the counter, then went to the great room to work, but she never replied. Later, much later, he went and put the food away.

He'd exhausted her. What had he been thinking, trying to take her outside when foul weather and, well, waterfowl threatened? But he hadn't been thinking, of course. Story of his life. The pills he'd accepted from his manager that led to messing up his career. The time he'd crashed the car in George's garage, which led to her having to leave her longtime home and move to Narrow Falls. At least when he was alone out here, the only person he could mess up was himself.

Zoey was waiting for him later, though, in the dark kitchen where the storm still raged on. Nevertheless, he was so relieved and happy to see her that he didn't notice how angry she was until he'd asked how she slept.

"I'm fine. Oh, I'm just fine."

"Well…great!"

"The thing is—" she began.

That's when it hit him that she was furious.

Of course, it was hard to tell. She was thumping some dough around on the cold floury counters. More bread? They'd eaten most of the loaf she'd made yesterday. Her face was red with exertion. Also something that looked like embarrassment. And anger.

With him? There wasn't really anyone else around, was there? Unless he counted the animals, but he doubted that the glowering looks she cast at her creation were directed at yesterday's geese, unless, of course, they'd decided to storm the building.

He'd opened his mouth to ask what was going on when she interrupted him. "You pretend to be this naive, transparent, earnest person! Like, you act all compassionate and understanding and all that, and like you wouldn't hurt anyone because you care about animals and people. But it turns out you're Davy X."

It was always a jolt when someone recognized him and associated him with the less-than-savory way his brief career had ended. It usually didn't happen in Canada, which was why he spent most of his time here. It definitely didn't happen when he was alone on an island with only a clawless cougar and a pantry bursting with canned goods to keep him company.

She thumped the bread dough again. "I found out yesterday from my roommate. After you and I, after we—never mind."

After they'd kissed.

The roommate had probably told Zoey all sorts of rumors about him. There was one where he'd been kicked out of the band because he'd gotten into a fistfight with one of the boys because he'd wanted to sing lead for their hit "You You, Me Me." In another, he was let go because he'd tried to steal another's girlfriend, or he'd quit in a fit of pique and heartbreak because she remained loyal. One of his favorites was that he'd been ejected after someone found out he was putting butter in his bandmates' food and causing them all to gain weight, and thus securing his position in the band as the svelte one who never had to wear a shirt. Even now when he made a smoothie, he sometimes imagined himself blending a whole stick of butter into it and rubbing his hands while laughing maniacally.

Of course, it was funnier now that he *was* allowed to eat more or less what he wanted. At the time, he and his bandmates would probably have killed for a butter smoothie.

He hoped they were better fed these days, too.

"I wasn't trying to hide it on purpose," he said, pulling up a stool and sitting.

"Management romanized my stage name as Davy *Xie* instead of *Hsieh*, but it's the same character. And I know you won't believe me, but being in the band for a year was the least interesting thing about me."

His voice was half-hearted. Davy *didn't* hide it, but he didn't volunteer the information. At first after he'd been kicked out, he hid from the press, from the fans, some of whom loved and defended him, some of whom hated him for various wrongs they imagined he'd wreaked on the band.

Davy took a deep breath. "I was let go because I had a drug problem. Prescription drugs. I'd started getting panic attacks, and I was a teenager and I didn't believe in taking care of my mental health, and neither did management."

Zoey blinked. "Davy. I'm sorry. I didn't know. I didn't know anything about the band until Li-leng told me. She recognized you."

He didn't want to look Zoey in the eye, but his hand crept across the counter and touched hers. She gave him a squeeze and didn't let go.

He tried to enjoy it. Maybe she wouldn't be so sympathetic when he continued.

"I wasn't doing well. I was pretty young, and far away from any family I knew. My Mandarin wasn't as good as everyone else's because I grew up here so that made it even harder to make friends with my bandmates. But I'd auditioned on a whim while I was visiting my dad, and it seemed like the best way to get to be an independent person. Earn my own money. Like I said, I was never a great student."

Zoey made a noise in her throat and made a motion with her other hand as if batting his words away.

"My parents resisted, then they decided it might be good for me. Or they were glad someone else was taking care of me. When I got in the band, it was like I'd finally done something right in their eyes. I'd shown a talent. I'd get structure. And money. So, of course, I couldn't quit. I was disciplined, for a while. There was training all the time, singing, dancing, appearances, recording. The pace was really frantic. As a recording artist here in North America, you can release an album a year and that's fine, but the cycle is faster there, so we were already up to four albums in a year and a half, most of which had done pretty well.

"My anxiety started up then. We didn't get days off. We weren't allowed to be sick. Luckily we were all teen boys with teen boy energy, although it would've been better if we'd been allowed to eat more. Maybe that would also have helped with my mood."

"Davy! They starved you?"

Her voice was soft. But he still didn't dare look up. He kept his eyes on their joined hands.

"They didn't want us to gain too much weight. The fans didn't like it. It didn't look good on camera.

"When the strain started showing, my manager suggested I take some pills to calm down. I took the drugs, then stopped, but it got harder to get up there, so I took more. But to tell you the truth, I kind of enjoyed it. That was something I could do something about. Take a pill, feel calmer. Take more pills. Feel a lot steadier. I mean, sorry, the real reason I took them is because they helped me be *better*. I was a better singer and dancer when I had my meds. I got along with people. I didn't get frustrated. But who knows what the pills really were. They'd stop working after a while, so I'd up the dose. And that becomes a habit, or an addiction. And pretty soon, you're taking them all the time. *I'm* taking them all the time." He shook his head. "*I* took them, I should say. I don't anymore. Now I just take… responsibility, I guess. And tea. I drink a lot of tea."

Zoey got up to cover the bread dough and washed her hands. For some reason, she hadn't been expecting this. Davy was so… pure. He seemed so enthusiastic and open and not like a person who had anxiety. But she hadn't looked for shadows, had she?

Davy was fiddling nervously with his mug right now, peering at her from under his flop of hair. She wanted to reach out and touch him again, still his fingers. Instead, she put the dough away in the fridge and took a moment to breathe.

But she was still angry, although now the feeling had changed targets. "Where were your parents in all this? Why weren't they informed? Who was in charge? I don't understand."

Why had they abandoned him?

Her nails dug into her palm now that she didn't have the bread to occupy them. Her sister had been sick, and yes, she'd translated on occasion, she'd been told to look after Mimi because she was the big sister. But her mother and father had at least always been at the hospital. They'd sat through the treatments. They'd *been there*.

Davy glanced quickly over at her as if for reassurance, then put his head down. "My parents have never been very hands-on. And I didn't tell them. How could I? It's not like they would've understood. My manager, Mr. Li, was the adult in charge. No girls, no late nights unless we were performing. He did all the things a parent should do—or so it seemed. You get used to the idea of being taken care of in that way, until you're not. Until it becomes clear you're a way for your management to make money. A lot of things seemed one way until they were another way. That's part of life."

Zoey wasn't sure about that. She preferred to think that some things were straightforward enough. Davy had seemed that way at first. Wouldn't it be easier if he were just another stupid, handsome man? Instead, today he was looking older somehow. The bones of his wrists seemed to stand out more than they had yesterday. She'd met him four days ago and already she knew his arms, his hands, how powerful they looked when he was hauling heavy boxes or pulling her to safety, how gentle they were when they skimmed her face. She wanted to grab them and run her thumbs along his skin, his arms, to soothe him. But what right had she? She'd hardly scratched the surface. She shouldn't know him well enough to understand that his eyes were tired and that she'd done this.

"The day we were scheduled to make one of our big appearances—" He laughed without humor. "What am I saying? They were all the biggest, most important ones. Every single one was vital, according to Mr. Li. But before this appearance, I took a handful of pills. I don't think I even counted them. I used to be careful. Just one more, one at a time. This time I just shoved them in my mouth, and I don't remember what happened next.

Apparently, I tried to go on the show—the one that was sup-posed to be our big break—without clothing. Which, in my defense, I was shirtless guy."

"What do you mean, you were shirtless guy?"

"You know how every band has the cute one and the deep, quiet one, and funny one? I wasn't any of those things, so I was the one who always wore a fancy jacket but no shirt."

"Wait, how were you not the cute one, or the deep one? Or the funny one? I don't remember shirtless as a category of boy band members. Weren't you all cute, really? Doesn't this mean you were the sexy one?"

His eyes flared briefly with amusement and maybe desire, then died down again. "We were all cute, but you know how it works. You establish your roles, and that's who you are. So I was the shirtless one. I thought I was so clever taking that title, because that's how a fifteen-year-old thinks—or this one, at least. Except I worried, of course. Plus, I was cold all the time. Cold and hungry and anxious. It's kind of funny when you think about it. But that's why I have all those fancy jackets in my closet. The linings always stuck to me when I danced. If I'd been allowed to stay in the band longer, maybe I would've gotten better linings made up. You know, if I had to do it over again."

He gave a short laugh, and maybe Zoey did, too. She wasn't sure what to do. She felt angry—she was often angry. But there was nowhere for this anger to go, and she didn't want it to hurt him. So she restrained herself. Sort of. But she sat down and took Davy's hand again. "You don't have to make jokes."

"Jokes are all we have sometimes. Anyway, I don't remem-ber much else about that day, but apparently before the show went live, I even took off my underwear backstage, which is sort of funny. But I guess I also told everyone it was my time to outshine my bandmates. I wasn't allowed to perform, not that I could have.

"So between my addiction and the pants thing, I got booted. Not that the last thing would have made a difference, but all of it was enough for the manager to say I was too unstable. I was, though. There were no second chances. So that was it. I was out. I know from the outside that seems like it's the worst thing that could've happened to me, but it's what I did afterward that pains me. That's why I don't want to talk about it."

"Oh, Davy."

"Don't Davy me until you've heard the rest."

"I promise not to interrupt. But they were starving and abusing you, and they gave you the drugs. You were a *kid*."

The whole thing seemed so removed from anything she knew or understood, and yet she knew it was so profoundly unfair. Worse, despite his friendliness, he was a private person and she'd forced the confession out of him.

Yet, there was Davy, leaning his elbows on the counter, drinking his tea like a normal human being. Davy shook his head. "The manager didn't tell me to keep taking the drugs. He didn't tell me to hide how bad it had gotten from him."

"He must have had an inkling if he was supplying you."

"You shouldn't promise not to interrupt, if you can't keep it," he said.

But there was such a sad fondness in his voice.

"Anyway, the band isn't the point. The fairness isn't, either. I don't really care about that anymore. What's worse is I was a jerk, Zoey. In addition to all that. I think you have to understand that. I was really angry for a long time. I wasted nearly half a decade asking people variations on *Do you know who I am?*, which is embarrassing to think of now because I was in a band for a little over a year."

"You were a kid, Davy."

He shook his head and stood up. He moved restlessly around the kitchen, opening cabinet doors and shutting them. "But now I'm an adult, and I hate to remember it. I don't like talking about it because I loathe how much I needed to cling to my status. I was in bad shape. I wasn't willing go back to a normal life—school, work, anything. When I tried to think of what I'd do next, I started getting the anxiety attacks again."

He darted a look at her from under his thick lashes, and Zoey took in a breath. That's what that had been about at the piano, and in the woods. It hadn't been about her at all.

Davy continued his aimless prowl. "My family finally ended up checking me into a hospital. Anonymously. Rich Taiwanese families don't want to admit they have children like me. Although I guess the drugs were more okay than the anxiety. Any sign of mental illness is still taboo with my parents. Especially with my dad."

She pulled his hand to her mouth and gave it a fierce kiss. And then finally he seemed able to look at her, to hold her eyes.

"The only person who stuck with me was my old babysitter, George."

"Your friend on the mainland, the one who runs the bed-and-breakfast on the Sunshine Coast?"

"Yes. She was still in Vancouver at the time. She took me in after I left the hospital, and I was still so angry. She made me finish high school. She fed me, and talked to me, and I repaid her by getting into an accident with her car, wrecking her garage one night when I tried to drive off to get away from her. I'd get so mad at her—this sounds terrible—I'd get so mad at her for being supportive and believing in me."

He stopped and sagged again, and Zoey didn't know what to say. Her chest ached from everything he'd already told her.

Davy smoothed down his shirt as if to make sure it was still there. "I was immature. I didn't think of how expensive it was to get it all fixed. It was like I magically expected someone to step in and take care of it. It wasn't until she sat down and explained to me she wouldn't be able to do any repairs because she wouldn't be able to afford the mortgage on her house…"

He paused for a moment. Zoey squeezed his hand.

"I could have asked my family to step in at any time. They would have yelled at me, but my dad would rather send me money than actually be in the same room with me working it out."

Zoey couldn't help snorting at that, and she was pleased to see him give a brief smile, a small flash of his old Handsome dazzle.

"But for George, I decided to try one thing first. I sent in a song, the song George told me she liked, the one that she'd *believed in*, to a studio musician the band worked with, a keyboardist I'd bonded with. I heard back right away. He sent it to some contacts of his. It was a simple little piece, and it ended up in a yogurt drink commercial. I turned over the money to George. Instead of repairing the house and garage, we decided to sell it on the Vancouver market, which was even wilder back then than it is now. It was snapped up almost right away and torn down the minute George handed over the deed."

"I'll bet."

"It's a McMansion now. George hates it and refuses to drive back to her old neighborhood. I think she still misses that house, no matter how drafty it was."

Zoey snorted again.

"With the money, George and I bought an inn on the coast. She'd always wanted to retire there. And after getting over myself, I'd started sending more songs out, and earning my own money that way."

"How old are you again?" she asked suddenly.

"I'm twenty-seven. Why?"

Good Lord, he was younger than her. He'd already had a lifetime of glamour and grief. How could anything she said to this person be anything more than empty platitudes? And yet, here he was looking at her like he wanted her to tell him something important, like her opinion was worth something to him. She was confused, and angry at *something*. Not at him, anymore, but at his family and the people around him, and at the unfairness of it all. Yesterday had already been dizzying enough. There'd been a cougar that didn't show up, geese who did, and his (famous!) chest dripping from the rain, each rivulet outlining the tendons of his shoulder, the dips and ridges of his abs. No wonder he'd spent so much time shirtless.

There'd been his kiss, which had reached down so deep into her that, apparently, she'd shut down like a reverse Sleeping Beauty.

She shook her head to try to clear it, even as she squeezed his hand again. "It's a lot to process."

He gave a rueful smile. "Considering I still seem to be doing that myself, I'm not surprised."

"So all this, your whole project with this island, and going in to talk to experts, and taking all of this on yourself, why are you doing this?"

"Aside from the fact that I'm a sucker for a sob story?"

"You and me both," Zoey said gruffly, trying to hide her true feelings.

"When I was staying with George on the mainland, I came across an injured bird. The wildlife officer told me it was a Cooper's hawk. Its wing had been broken and it was hopping around, and…it was angry."

"Hawks usually look pissed off."

"Well, this one was pretty terrible all the time."

"You seem to like a project."

Davy cast a fond glance at their joined hands. "I do. Anyway, the officer took it to a wildlife sanctuary inland, and I drove out to visit it a few times. It stayed with me, the idea of a sanctuary. That hawk. And when I decided to build on the island, I realized I really wanted to do this. I was still living with George in the B&B in Narrow Falls, but I wanted to carve out a place of my own, a sanctuary for me, too. For all those zoo animals who were old and tired of being looked at. For birds who couldn't fly anymore. Maybe it was selfishness."

She was learning that this was such a Davy thing to say. He was so frustrating sometimes she thought even as protective affection swam dizzily through her. "It's not selfish, Davy. You obviously do care about the animals. You're trying to help. You're—" she raised her chin at him "—you're trying so hard. I can't understand why you can't see that."

"But I've been going about it all wrong. Sometimes I think I should have left this island alone, instead of, like, building a septic system and—and importing a cougar."

He looked like he was going to start roaming again. "When you put it that way, of course it sounds ridiculous. But listen, it doesn't really matter if you do anything or not, if you make some sort of contribution. Like, we're all trying and we don't know how to figure out if what we do matters at all."

She waved her arms around. "I mean, I stare at bone slides all day. I'm told that someday, somewhere this might help do something for people, or animals, or something. But it's felt very different compared to what I was doing in medical school."

"Why didn't you just become a doctor?"

She sighed. Now she wanted to fidget. "I'd gotten into this prestigious MD/PhD program. Plus theoretically I thought I'd prefer working with less people. But it turns out I currently hate the few people I do work with. To tell you the truth, thinking about doing future good doesn't really get me through the day lately."

Her words slowed. "I don't know if I'm doing the right thing," she confessed. "Which is why I started carrying around the slide like it was some kind of talisman, even though that turned out to be a bad idea."

She stopped and Davy didn't say anything. She took a deep breath. Was she…unhappy with The Plan? Well, yes, obviously. But those were typical bumps, weren't they? If she simply re-thought some parts of it… But there was no wiggle room in it. She'd made it too perfect.

A perfect trap.

Zoey shook her head. "It's important work. It's meaning-ful to me, or it will be in the long term. Plus I've already put so many years into it. But that isn't the point. You're doing something important and worthwhile, here, okay? You being you is worth something,"

Davy was watching her carefully. "Are you all righ—"

She couldn't let him finish that sentence, because she was pretty sure she wasn't actually fine. "No, listen to me, Davy. I can tell by the look on your face you don't want to believe me. Adults let you down, and maybe you made a couple of mis-takes when you were a kid. But what matters is now, and you are *trying*. God, you try so hard, and yes, it isn't perfect, but honestly, what is? I don't think I try with my whole heart as hard as you do. Not that you need to. Not that anyone has to all the time. Sometimes just getting through things is enough."

She wasn't making sense to herself, but she *felt* it, and she hoped he could feel how much she meant every word.

Well, when it came to him, at least.

She sprang up from her seat, unable to sit still anymore. Her own restlessness paced like a big cat under her breastbone. Be-cause if she was standing here trying to console a former pop star and making bread instead of searching for her goddamn slide, the one that she'd deemed so important that she'd taken a car to Burnaby, stowed away on a ship, and now she was actively doing everything in the world to avoid looking for that slide, then that told her something, didn't it?

Zoey had spent so much time, so much money, so much energy and guilt already. Years of her life following The Plan.

Fuck it.

She dusted off her hands, grabbed Davy's head, and yanked him toward her.

"I hope this is okay with you," she muttered as she pulled him in and brought his lips to hers.

CHAPTER 9

START ALL OVER AGAIN

Davy hadn't realized how tense he was until Zoey was kissing him again.

She'd towed his head down with a surprising strength and urgency, and screwed her eyes up tight before her lips met his, as if she were afraid of what might happen. But as soon as their breaths mingled and their skin touched, he felt her body go pliant with recognition. His own eyelids drifted closed as he let himself uncoil under the warmth of her tongue, the plumpness of her flesh under his gentle teeth, the taste of her, until his head was liquid, until he was swimming, drowning in her.

She sighed deeply and drew away, and he thought for a minute he'd done something wrong. He must have if she wasn't kissing him anymore. His hands had traveled up inside her shirt to the smooth skin within. As his knuckles touched the undersides of her breasts, he noticed she hadn't been wearing a bra. But now, as he let her lean back and slide off the stool, his hands were cold again.

Until she stripped off the tee.

The hem of her shirt caught the tip of his nose as she pulled it off, but that wasn't what startled him.

He blinked. If he'd bothered to think about it he wouldn't have known where to affix his greedy gaze first, but his eyes zoomed immediately to her breasts. Still, the whole of her, all that maddening glorious skin, made it difficult for him to linger long in one place. It had been a very long time since he'd seen a naked woman in front of him. And this was *Zoey*. He never could have imagined how the light and shadows played across Zoey's chest, her ribs, how they made the slight curve of her belly look velvety and soft.

But she was real, and this was happening. He could press his thumb at the side, right there, and move his hand up her ribs until he felt the silkiness of the undersides of her breasts. With every breath she took, every small movement, everything changed. She was a living, breathing person, close enough that he could feel the heat radiating off of her. He could reach out and touch her. He should, because he'd been quiet and watching so long that she was starting to look worried—more worried than usual, that is. Then she shivered.

Someone so full of life should never be cold.

So Davy took a deep breath and stood, the stool screeching as he drew her to him. He was touching her bare waist, his palm sliding along the smooth curve as if it were a path made for him, and into the gentle groove of her spine and around to those indentations above her ass. He'd lick them later.

His fingers continued down beneath the waistband of her underwear, the pressure of the fabric keeping his hands tight against her plush skin.

Slow down, slow down. But she was moving her hips and he could feel her breasts, the swell of her stomach moving against his cock. His pulse was anything but slow, and the rest of his body was already pulling hard at him, pulling his hips toward everything lavish and welcoming about her. He tried to take his time, starting with the tender skin of her earlobe, until she murmured and pressed closer. He was never going to be able to balance his hunger against his desire to hold out for her.

Davy gritted his teeth. "I need a minute."

His voice was a strangled whisper.

"It's been a long time for me. I..." His tongue stumbled over the words so instead, he took a breath, stepped back, and did what he did best and took off his own shirt.

The small space between them seemed charged. Zoey's eyes were huge, almost amazed. She reached her hand out tentatively—so slow. Her fingers pressed flat on his chest, trailed down toward his erection, then up, then down.

God.

It was too much.

She pulled his sweatpants down, carefully stretching the elastic away from his cock and down underneath.

"Let's go and—"

"I want to touch you," she said.

He groaned, because he really wanted that, too. "I won't last very long if you do. I'm already very close."

"I don't care."

He licked his lips, trying to form a reply. Her tone was reckless, and it made him feel the same.

The feeling of her hand, the sight of her breasts, was too much. It was maybe inevitable. "I really am—Zoey."

He couldn't quite bring himself to tell her to stop because the pleasure was too intense. Her hand, wet with him, her breath on his chest. He was pushing himself into her hand. And, of course, she squeezed and kept going. "Zoey, we need to stop or I won't be able to—"

But she kept going, and it was too late. Everything in him

pulsed rapidly, drawing energy from every corner, every hollow in his body. And it all came into her hand.

They were both quiet. He slumped forward on her, not quite letting her support him, not quite able to stay upright himself. For one moment, his body felt pleased, relaxed. In the next, he realized that he'd come before she'd even had a chance.

She let go of him gently. Still looking down between them. Her expression was a mixture. A little pleased? A little rueful?

He knew the feeling.

Another deep breath. He could recover from this. It wasn't even a setback. He didn't have those anymore.

He led her to the sink and washed her hands, cleaned her up. "Thank you," he said.

She was staring at the water. "You're welcome."

He took a breath, shut off the tap, and stood up straighter. "It's your turn now."

"What do you mean? Oh! You really don't have to."

He shook his head. "Oh, but I want to."

"But after that, how—?"

"Wanting doesn't stop there. And I want to be a part of whatever you do, everything you enjoy."

Well, Davy X had completely lost it, hadn't he?

She, Zoey Fong, had done that. She'd never made anyone come with just her hand—well, aside from herself.

Another new experience on top of all the experiences she was having.

Except, she was left with this ache, and all this nakedness, hers and his. It was startling.

He'd pulled off her underwear and the rest of his clothing and was nudging her toward the great room, where it was dark, despite it being morning. Rain beat against the windows.

"Sit," he said, propelling her down into the deep couch.

Then he put one of the pillows on the floor in front of her and knelt. "Oh, I—"

Zoey was not quite ready for this. She scooted back in the couch and ended up sinking deeper.

"Only if you want this. But you should know that I want to."

Davy wasn't lying. He was barely holding himself back—again. She had never met a man so eager. And all of this anticipation was for her. His hands clasped her knees gently, but his wrists, his forearms were tense. And he was licking his lips. Even in the gloom, they glistened. She ran her hands up and down his arms.

It was her turn to groan. "Yes," she said. "Okay."

"Yes?"

"Yes, please."

He smoothed his hands along her thighs until they felt almost liquid under his touch. His hands found the groove of muscle at the side of her legs that she was so secretly proud of, the strength she'd worked on all year bicycling everywhere. He lingered there, his face turning up to watch her. Then he moved, pulling her legs apart, letting himself fall into the sensitive skin between her thighs.

She may have gasped.

Something about that sound made him move more quickly. Abruptly, he slid his arms up and around her again and hauled her ass forward until she was near the edge of the couch, until she could feel his stubble on the sensitive insides of her thighs. The anticipation made her hips squirm in his grip, and the spot between her legs throb.

Zoey tossed her head restlessly. She didn't want to watch him as he looked at her, as one of his hands, wet from touching her, stole up to give her nipples a quick stroke, but she couldn't help herself.

Davy's grip with his other hand was as sure as ever against

the small pulses of her hips. He looked up at her again, to check if she was all right, to smile, to reassure her. He cupped his palm right there, his thumb moving through the dark thatch of hair, sliding down through the crease of her. Then he closed his eyes and put his mouth on her.

She let out another groan.

Zoey was excited, yes, and his mouth and hand were firm enough, gentle enough. But a little niggle of worry slipped over her. It usually took her a long time to come, even this way. Maybe she should help him along. Her own hands slid down over her breasts, flicking her own nipples, down to his hair, the top of his ears, which she almost wanted to grip, as if that were a way she could bring him closer, deeper.

He made a hungry sound deep in his throat and pushed his fingers deeper.

Oh.

He was enjoying this. Somehow, even though he'd told her he wanted to do this, she hadn't expected how into it he was. It was strange to be so intimate with someone she hardly knew. But that wasn't true, was it? She knew the truth about who he was—not the facts that old fans might want, but the expression he made before he took a sip of tea, and the serious look in his eyes when he felt like he had to protect her. Now she could see the strain of his arm, the muscles in his back working as if he were throwing his whole being into trying to give her pleasure. His other hand was below, unseen but felt, circling her, spreading the moisture from her and from him as he worked his lips and tongue up to her clit. She panted, hearing the wet clicks of his tongue and lips, her own quiet grunts.

And the rain, always the rain.

There was no one else on this island.

No one to hear her enjoying this.

"Yes," she said quietly when his tongue slid over a particularly good spot. "That's good."

He raised his head as if to ask what she'd said, still teasing her—so close to where he'd been before. The frustration rose again. "Right there, right where you were," she said more clearly.

His hand tightened on her thigh, and she could swear she saw a glimmer of a smile.

"No smiling, more sucking," she said thickly.

This time he really did laugh. She could feel the happy vibration against her even as he bent his eyes and head down, back to task.

She was wide open, more open than she'd ever been before, her legs stretched out, her toes straining, her arms making snow angels on the soft nap of the cushions, her chest and breasts pushing up and out. She could feel the contrast between the heat between her legs and her cooler, uncovered body, gleaming with light in the dark room. And she wanted to be open. She could be, for the first time in her life. It was as if she could receive the abundance of his body, of hers, if she opened herself wide enough, if she opened herself up enough.

"Davy," she said low. Then louder. "God, Davy, keep doing that. Go deep. Please, deeper."

He heard her, his mouth and fingers making sloppy smacking sounds as he moved through her. She groaned loudly. And his free hand, the one that had been gripping her thigh, moved up to caress her waist, her chest, to warm her. She wanted to be louder. She wanted so much right now. "Please, please. Give me this," she half screamed.

Hearing herself ask, hearing her own need, her demand, her desire, hearing how close she was, pushed her over. Her body stiffened and then the waves radiated out of her. She could feel his fingers pumping frantically, his tongue still moving, his eyes on her watching her come apart. She took it all. She took everything he had and wanted to give her.

It was still raining hard after they both fell asleep. Davy had stayed on the floor for a while as Zoey gathered herself up reluctantly and went to the bathroom to clean up. She was quiet when she returned, but she wordlessly dragged him up onto the couch with her and they wrapped themselves with blankets and dozed.

When he woke another couple of hours later, sweaty, and tangled in Zoey's limbs, he wanted her again. One of her smooth shoulders, soft and gently rounded, was tucked into his chest, her head lolled back. In the dim light, he could see the curve of her cheek, the tufts of her hair sticking up. Under the blankets, her chest, so round and inviting, rose and fell against him. She was still apparently exhausted, so he quieted himself and slid carefully out of the blankets and padded off to take a shower. He pulled on some pants and a T-shirt. He cleaned up the kitchen. Put all the clothes they'd discarded into the washing machine. When he got back to the room, she was sitting up, the blanket engulfing her once again.

But she was smiling, if a little tentatively. Her face poked out adorably. He really liked that face so he bent down and kissed her nose and tried not to wonder if she might want to have sex again soon because apparently even the glimpse of her cheeks and eyes, of a few of her strong fingers holding the blanket together, was compelling.

The fingers relaxed even more at his kiss.

"It's a little chilly."

"I can help you with that if you let me in."

A laugh. "You showered," she said, her voice slightly muffled.

He sat down gingerly beside her and ran his hands through his hair. "I did."

WILD LIFE | 149

A pause. "I really need to brush my teeth."

"Zoey."

"I feel weird! Ordinarily I make sure to wake up before the other person or never fall asleep. Then I gather my stuff and run away. But you've put on clothing! Well, not much, thank goodness. And—" she moved that nose closer "—you smell like soap. And I can't run because this is an island and there's a flock of deadly geese and maybe a big cat out there. And... and... I don't want to."

Her nose was close to his. He wanted to kiss it again, kiss her.

Instead he looked down and touched the edge of the blanket. "It's odd for me, too."

But not for the same reasons. It was strange because he was happy to have her here. But he didn't want to scare her by telling her that. "I'm glad you're here and haven't run away. How about I make us something to eat?"

She sniffled. "Okay."

Okay.

He could handle sandwiches. So he got out some bread and hummus—might as well use them up before they went bad. He peeled carrots and found some vegan cheese.

Now he was nervous.

He hadn't had a morning-after in a long time. Being a hermit tended to help with that. When he was more in the habit of it—well, he probably hadn't thought much about other people and how he affected them.

He glanced anxiously over at the kitchen door, as if expecting Zoey to storm in and demand he somehow be better.

But that wasn't her. That was about him. She came in a little shyly, but soon she was eating her sandwich and bumping elbows companionably with him, maybe on purpose.

"This isn't bad," she said slowly.

"What, the sandwich, or the company?"

"Both."

"Why do you run away?"

"I don't know. Why would anyone stick around after? It's not like we're going to fall in love and live happily ever after."

He said mildly, "Well, of course that's not going to happen if you aren't there. I don't think happily ever after means what you think it means."

She paused. "I don't think about it that much, I suppose. I have some vague idea about animated blonde princesses in castles, which clearly isn't The Plan."

She seemed to say it with capital letters. *The Plan.* Or maybe he'd misheard. He shook his head. "It depends on where you end the story, doesn't it? If you end the story with Baby abandoned and with her claws taken out, then it's a terrible tragedy. Or with me being kicked out of the band, then I guess it is a story about one man's downfall, a cautionary tale about a kid done in by fame and drugs. But here I am, still alive. And right now I'm happy. I've had many false starts and new beginnings. I'm still here."

She shook her head. "One of my profs told me it doesn't matter how smart you are, or how talented you are. In the end, it's about hanging in."

"That sounds sad."

"Maybe it isn't. At least I enjoyed med school. It wasn't until the research program that I realized one of the great things about being a physician was the fact that I'd always get different patients bringing me challenges. Now I'm stuck with one professor to please and some other students who don't like me much. And now I've half convinced myself to quit The Plan just because it's a little difficult."

There it was again. The capital letters.

"Tell me again about your whole Pla—" he wanted to avoid

the P-word "—path to curing cancer again? Why not just go to medical school? Isn't that what most people do?"

"I did think that was what I'd do at first. But I heard about the program, and it was amazing I got in. It's really difficult to get one of these spots, so giving it up—"

As if realizing what she'd said, she added, "But the main thing is I'll help so many more people this way. In the long run."

He didn't try to do the math. He'd always been bad at it. "So you'll be a doctor with a doctorate. Doctor doctor."

"Yes, yes."

She sounded morose.

"But you don't like the current part."

"It turns out I didn't like it then or now. I *should* enjoy it. That's been the hardest thing to understand. I've always liked school. Maybe if I keep at it longer it'll get better. Plus I've already been at it for so long."

The lights flickered, and Davy frowned as much from that as from her statement. "It's not like you could call yourself a quitter at this point. You were working late on a Friday night when I met you." Had it only been three or four days ago? "Futures can change. *The Plan* can change."

"People in my program would call me a quitter. There's always whispering and betting about who'll drop out. And really, I don't know what to do without The Plan."

He could understand investing a lot of time in something and not having it work out, but that wasn't helpful. He wasn't sure what was, so he pulled his chair closer to her and put his nose in her hair.

Zoey said, "When I was young, I used to think that was the worst insult in the world, telling someone they were a quitter. Maybe I still think that even though I want to stop. Oh God, I said that out loud."

"Quitting one thing isn't the end of the world. It can be the start of something else."

He kissed her as he said it, and maybe she understood because she pulled herself into his lap. The wind had started howling louder, and the lights flickered once more, but sitting with her in that kitchen chair, their bodies tucked together, he felt like he could withstand anything.

"What the hell is wrong with me?" she said into his chest. "Just a while ago I feel like I made a decision to stay with it. Then I admitted I wanted to quit, and now I'm panicking. I'm quitting being a quitter!"

"Maybe this isn't the most productive path to go down."

"And if I decide I don't like that, I'll quit being a quitter who quit quitting!"

"Stop," he said, all the affection bleeding into his voice as he held her tight.

"Davy."

She sighed into his neck. The lights blinked again as an especially high gust of wind almost seemed to shake the house.

"I like being here with you too much," she muttered into his hair.

That was good, wasn't it? After everything that had happened over the last few days.

He was about to pick her up and take her to bed to solidify his case, but before he could move, the lights went out.

CHAPTER 10

GOING DARK

"The backup generators will come on at any minute," Davy said.

Zoey felt confused as they stood, not scared by the sudden darkness and silence. She felt him take her hand without any hesitation, his fingers closing around her palm, as if he always knew exactly where it would be. She leaned on him, and he put his other arm around her. She realized she'd been holding her breath, worried that if he saw how screwed up she really was it would change things between them.

Davy made her feel safe. That was the worst and the best thing about him. An overdeveloped sense of responsibility had kept her afloat all these years, but it was so tiring. She hadn't realized how much she needed to let go. While it wasn't necessary, it probably helped to take refuge in a pair of strong arms around her.

So here she was holding him like he was a life raft, like she hadn't been *managing*.

She buried her face in his neck, and almost missed the fact that the lights came back on dimmer than before.

"There," he said, his voice so deep and satisfied that it made her toes curl. "We should try to make sure all nonessential electronics are turned off—lights, the Wi-Fi, things like that. We don't want to tax the backups, and when the real power gets fixed, we won't have a surge. I have some high-beamed flashlights, though, if that helps."

He was still talking, still holding her, his voice full of responsibility and backup plans. No wonder she felt so good with him. Her hand traveled up his back, up the solid line of his spine to his shoulders, hard and strong. They were used to bearing weight. They could take hers.

His breath had hitched, even though she knew her fingers were light. His voice stilled. She was kissing him softly now, her lips finding the underside of his chin, still bristly, the hollow of his neck.

"Zoey," he sighed, "Zoey, Zoey," and she loved the way he said her name, like he was finding music in it. *Zoey,* he murmured, the soft buzz of an instrument on his lips, against her skin, in her ear.

"Storm day," she murmured. "We shouldn't have to work."

He hoisted her up and they stumbled through the rooms, kissing and turning off lights, unplugging appliances. Every room was going to have a memory now. A nip of her neck stolen while he made sure all the great room lights were switched off. A tumble followed by making out as they bent to unplug his keyboard in his office.

They were thorough.

By the time they got to her bedroom, the blankets they'd been wearing were gone, and while the rain lashed at the windows, they were warm together under the covers.

Zoey wanted to laugh and keep laughing. She felt giddy and ridiculous. She didn't have to think. She couldn't go poking through the crates right now for some slide she didn't really want to think about after all. It was a relief, such a relief that she was absolved from being mindful about the future for now. That she could simply enjoy Davy's hand on her thigh, pulling her open, as her own hand closed firmly around his cock.

She knew exactly how careful to be with his body now. When he groaned, she let him go, opened her legs wider to his hand, let him cup her, slide his fingers through her slickness. Every flick against her clit made her thrash and hiss. Then it was no longer easy, and she was desperate for him to be inside her.

"Condoms in my backpack," she said. "First zipped compartment."

He hurriedly dumped everything out, and she hardly thought about the mess she'd have to deal with later. He turned around again, and she pushed him down on the bed, her hands lingering on his shoulders, on the warmth of his chest. When she slid her body over him, he groaned until she kissed him quiet. The wet click of his lips and the inhale of his breath made the desire throb so hard through her that she had to pump her hips against him. She could feel her own wetness overwhelm her, the warm tide of moisture tracing the folds between her legs, onto her thighs, onto him.

She straddled him again and raised her hands to cup her breasts. She'd never felt like this before, so sexy—no, so full of sex, so overflowing with sex and heat and energy and a kind of relentless rhythm. This was her! Every part of her body felt full, bursting, every pore and nerve and limb so heavy with want and power that she could hardly move, so heavy that if she didn't move she would die.

His hands covered hers. Together, they ran their fingers over the smooth skin of her chest, over the nipples puckered and alert. "Oh, Zoey," he whispered, his own hips pumping, "please fuck me. God, I need you to fuck me."

She raised herself, and grasped him, teasing his cock over her entrance, glided him inside until she felt full of him. And oh God, even though she felt the hot ache of him in her, even though he was finally there, this wasn't enough, somehow she was still restless. His hands moved onto her hips now, pulling her up as he began to pump into her. And somehow she found the desire to move up and down, to rub herself hard against him, to dig her fingers deep into his biceps and crouch over him and let her nipples bump up and down and tease his chest, tease her with the friction as he moved in her.

He was watching her avidly as they found their rhythm, his mouth open in concentration. She lowered herself to bite his chin, and he grasped her head as if desperate and drowning, and she was the one giving him the breath of life.

Her muscles were burning from riding him, her thighs were sticky, one leg was tangled so badly in the blankets and she couldn't move her toes, and she was panting as he grasped her hips and pulled her up and down faster and harder, but she didn't want to shift, she didn't want to move, because she was so close, so close, and it was curling out of her reach. She wanted everything to be exactly as it was at this moment, except she wanted to reach the next moment so badly.

He gasped and paused.

"What do you think you're doing?" she whispered fiercely. "Don't stop."

He grinned at her frustration. Then he'd braced his hands under her and was rolling her over onto her back, then to her side. Her foot, stuck in the blankets, twisted and he pulled her out with a laugh. "That didn't go as smoothly as I'd planned," he said as he resettled himself behind her.

His breath tickled her ear.

She was on her side, one of her arms trapped under her. She could still feel him firm against her, hard and slippery against the crease in her ass. She couldn't help moving against him even now. In a moment he was nudging her open, and she twisted to help him inside her again. He'd put one arm under her to pull her against him and used the other to stroke her between her legs.

It was like feeling him all around her, his breaths and murmurs right behind her, the luxurious lick of his tongue against her ear, the way his hands moved slowly down, pressing into her back, then around to grasp her stomach, her breasts. If she could think she'd probably be angry at him for being so perfect. His hips thrust. She felt that right up into her chest. She gripped his forearm, gilded with sweat, her hand sliding through light hair and along tense muscle. It wasn't fair of him to be this generous, this handsome and talented. Each tendon moved under his fingers, his head bent studiously over her shoulder as he worked on her clit. She pressed his hand down hard. She wanted him to keep doing that, *There. Right there.* Even as she wanted him to stop because it was so much.

But every part of this overwhelmed her. Every part of this scared and thrilled her and made her want more and more. And she knew at least here, she could open herself and he would be good to her.

She lifted her free leg higher, trembling from effort, and pushed herself harder back against him, twisting her head back to try to see him, to try to hold on to anything of him. She bit his shoulder, the nearest part of him, and cried out as he braced one leg deep in the mattress and slammed into her, harder and desperate now. She squeezed against him, wanting to hold him there, to hold him to her. If she could just keep the pressure and pleasure there between her legs, they'd never have to leave. But already she was open, as wide open as her mouth and her chest and every part of her pouring out.

"Zoey," Davy whispered.

They'd spent most of the day in bed while the storm raged outside.

Sometime early in the morning, she'd fallen so completely asleep that the sentence she'd begun murmuring petered out, and he was left waiting and laughing at her.

He, on the other hand, was wide awake. He had a lot to think about. Mostly sex. Because sex was very good and with Zoey, it was very, very good, and because Zoey was small, soft, and glowing like a juicy apricot beside him under the warm covers, and because he was still naked, which made him very aware of her nakedness.

He was pretty sure he wanted to take a big bite out of her.

She probably wouldn't object if he woke her up right now to have more of the very good sex he was thinking about constantly, but he got the feeling that Zoey never had enough sleep. She was almost always wound up and worried, and seeing her curled up like this in his presence made him sure he should let her brow stay smooth in sleep, let the tension around her mouth slacken as she fell deeper, let her breathe. It felt like a duty, but one that was a pleasure.

One thought kept distracting him from how much he was enjoying all of this right now: How could he make this moment last? He'd screwed up so many of the most important things in his life: his music, his health for a while, his relationship with his siblings and parents and George, the preservation of this island probably.

Zoey stirred, as if disturbed by his spiraling thoughts.

He should leave her. He should go and stew somewhere

else where his negative energy—his negative self—wouldn't muddy her dreams.

Maybe he'd head to the great room and try to get some work done.

He sighed and started to ease himself out of bed. "Where are you going?" Zoey mumbled.

In an instant, she was awake and anxious again.

He knew, even by the way her breath sounded. He knew.

"I was just going to let you sleep," he whispered, kissing her hair.

It must have been the right thing to say—the right thing to do, because immediately, she relaxed. She *let go* again, and it was such an honor, a gift. He'd never understood the English phrase "She let herself go," as if it were a bad thing for someone to do.

"I don't want you to worry," he said out loud.

It was true. He wished she wouldn't, but at the very least *he* didn't want to be the one who worried her. He was weary of being the one who made people anxious.

She surprised him by laughing. "Well, good luck with that."

She stretched her compact body out, quick and long, and he was so distracted by her legs peeking out from under the covers, by the long line of muscle that ran down her calf, down to her perfect pointed toes, that he didn't pay enough attention to what she'd said. He wanted to bite her big toe and lick the divot on the inside of her ankle. When she let go of the stretch and her body softened again, her eyes were glinting. He'd caught her foot, and he was about to suggest he help stretch her legs a little more when she stiffened. Startled.

"Do you hear that?" she asked.

He slid out of bed and crossed to the bedroom door. He could hear a muffled pounding.

Zoey had followed him.

"Someone's at the door," he marveled.

"Who? Who could be at your door?"

"I have no idea. This has never happened before."

"What do you mean?"

"I mean, no one has ever knocked on this door."

"How— What?"

"I mean, it's an island with no one else on it. The workers didn't have to knock. They came right in. And the animals, well, there's a fence, but they don't bother with etiquette when they want something."

Then, realizing what this meant, he said, "You should stay back. Let me get dressed and I'll go see who it is."

"If they're someone who wants to rob you, they wouldn't be making any noise," she said, looking reasonable and delectably naked.

"Yes, but let's still be cautious."

He'd pulled on a pair of red track pants he found in the closet. They had a stripe of sequins going up the side. Very athletic. That's probably why he'd kept them. No matter.

More pounding.

He looked around the room for a weapon that didn't look like a weapon.

"Get the sat phone, just in case," he told Zoey.

"Mmm-hmm."

She was unpanicked, paging curiously through the other outfits in his closet. People probably knocked on *her* door all the time. He had, after all. That's how they'd met.

She held up the matching red jacket with the same sporty stripe sequin, and he winced, leaving before she could suggest he go answer. He wasn't sure why he'd thought he could salvage some of these costumes. He'd had vague ideas of figuring out how to recycle textiles at some point, but it was pretty clear now that he wasn't equipped for it.

Davy forced himself to be alert. It was probably some poor fisherman who'd gotten blown off course, he told himself as he headed down the stairs. On second thought, he casually hefted a small lamp. It wasn't a weapon per se. *Oh, this? I was just planning on sitting down with a good book all by myself in this dark house when I heard your knock.*

Unease skittered along his spine. No one had installed a peephole in this door? He hadn't even gotten a doorbell. Why bother? It wasn't as if he had neighbors who would pop over to borrow a cup of sugar.

Now he wished he'd thought to install something, though.

"Who is it?" he yelled, trying to sound authoritative.

No answer.

He tried it again, this time, growling and clenching his fists. "Who's at the door?"

"You look like a guard dog," Zoey said behind him.

He jumped. "Zoey, I thought I told you to stay back, just in case."

"I have the phone."

She was also wearing the matching jacket to his pants. She'd zipped it up, thank goodness, but with their paired glitter stripes, she and he probably looked like a down-at-their-heels ice dance team.

"Why don't you hide a little out of the way in case it's someone with bad intentions."

"They've probably already heard me. It sounds like the wind and rain have died down."

"True."

But he motioned Zoey behind him anyway, then cautiously cracked open the door.

There was no one.

Of course, they could be waiting in the—well, there weren't

a lot of places nearby to hide unless they were down around the dock. He opened the door a little wider.

"Did they leave already?"

"Zoey."

"I mean, we took a while to select some clothing, and you had to get your, uh, lamp."

He gripped the lamp tighter.

Someone had come to the island, knocked on the door but not tried the knob, which, admittedly, hadn't been locked because no one ever landed here, and then had just gone off?

"Maybe I should go to the water and see if there's any sign of them."

"Maybe they left tracks."

"Thank you for believing I'd be able to spot those."

A bang came from outside. He threw the door closed and got Zoey well behind him.

After a few moments of silence, Zoey whispered, "Maybe it was the wind?"

"You said the wind died down."

"We should go and secure the back door, too," he said, turning.

"Yes, sir. Batten down the hatches."

She saluted smartly. The jacket rose up her thighs. She wasn't wearing underwear.

He harumphed to cover the ache of renewed desire. "You worry about other things, but you're not worried about this?"

"I figure if they had bad intent, they would've already come in."

"Yes, but I'm responsible for this. We can't just have people come here willy-nilly."

"I doubt it was a casual decision that sent someone to a remote island in the Georgia Strait to knock on a door in the middle of a storm."

Zoey was right. Being here on this island mostly alone was making him selfish and suspicious. Any outsider, except her, seemed like an intruder.

But before he could answer, they both heard something, like the screech of metal, like the high whine of a drill, but also like animal anger and teeth and blood all together in one.

"Was—was *that* the wind?" she asked.

"Oh, no. It's Baby."

CHAPTER 11

THE SOUND AND THE FURY

"That sounded close. Really close."

Zoey couldn't help the way her voice rose, with alarm.

She'd been brave outside, when the cougar was unseen, theoretical even. But the growl had made her skin scream in fear.

"It's okay. Besides, don't you study animals?"

"Human animals! Maybe mice sometimes. Both things that can be killed by cats with huge teeth! I don't know anything about cougars, or the kinds of sounds they make when they're incredibly pissed off and nothing will satisfy them except tearing open the flesh of delicious, delicious people!"

Davy gave her the stubborn look he'd been giving her all morning. She couldn't help noticing his chest, his famous bare chest, which was actually pretty perfect, and which she hadn't had an opportunity to admire properly, not that now was that opportunity and not that her admiration was proper. "If it comes to that, I'll protect you from the wild animals."

"How?"

He thought about that. "Well, we have this big house."

"But the cougar sounded like it came from inside."

"I don't think she's inside. She's close—closer than usual, but it would be unreasonable for her to be in the house."

"It didn't sound like she wanted to be reasoned with."

"She can't open a door."

"Maybe she knocked first and did it anyway."

"It wasn't Baby. It was someone else."

"But who else is there?"

"Let's just go to the mudroom and get the tranq gun."

"What if she's in the room with the tranq gun?"

"Like I said, I really doubt she's inside. But let's go get it to make sure."

"Did you lock the back door?"

"I don't think she can open doors, Zoey."

"Right, so that's why she knocked."

"If it's a person who's intruding—which I still think it is—maybe we'll need it."

She followed Davy so closely that she almost tripped on his heels.

"You keep using logic to try to protect us."

"I also have my muscles."

She narrowed her eyes. She had been admiring those muscles, but she was still practical. "So do I. But big cat teeth beats muscle. It's like some prehistoric version of rock, paper, scissors."

He got the tranquilizer gun and checked it carefully, as always unhurried. But oddly enough Zoey found this comforting. She should have been quivering with impatience.

"Baby usually doesn't come this near this house," he said. "Something must have disturbed her."

"Something or someone?"

They bolted the back door shut. It seemed flimsy, relying on a couple of pieces of metal and some screws to keep whatever was out there from coming in here.

"I'm just going to check out the kitchen window," he said.

"You should get some clothes on first," Zoey blurted. She bit her lip. "You'd look less vulnerable with your chest covered. I don't know. It's weird. I know it's not like a piece of cloth will stop anything from happening to you. But I still want you to be safe."

His face softened.

"We should both put on some of our clothes."

He picked up the shirt she'd discarded in the kitchen. "Here."

They went through the house, gathering all the clothing they'd thrown off in lust and excitement, and by the time they got back to the kitchen with slightly more expanded wardrobes, Zoey felt more whole again. As Davy pulled on his things, he never stopped looking strong and handsome, but somehow she felt better having him cover his heart.

The house was buzzing with electricity again. But even with the wind now settled—not dead—she heard everything better, she heard *him* better, the way he blew out a soft breath before pursing his lips and checking on her, the light murmur of satisfaction he gave. Even his smile had its own small sound, a note in his throat, as if the happiness started as a song, before the corners of his mouth twitched up.

"For the record, I preferred being naked with you," he said, that small melody letting her know he was about to say something cheeky.

"There's a time and a place," she reminded him, although she couldn't help her own answering hum and smile. Now that she heard it, she couldn't help calling back to him, it seemed. It was as if she wanted to be on his frequency. Oh God, she was a dork.

"Several times and several places, I hope."

She would like that.

But every time she thought of the future, that slow, horrible fear started to crush her.

She breathed sharply.

"What is it? Did you hear something?"

"Nothing. I—I thought of something scary."

Davy buttoned his last button and strode to the window with the tranq gun.

He lifted a corner of the blind and took a look outside.

How could she have thought he was lightweight and self-involved?

His eyes were serious, trying, as if by will, to take in every inch of this terrain that he'd tried to protect and cherish. Then he turned that thorough glance to her, and she felt it. She could feel it on her face, over her body. It made her tingle down to her toes.

Another small sound escaped her. He was by her side.

"I won't let anything happen to you."

A choked laugh escaped her. *He* was the thing happening to her.

"What is it? Are you sick? Are you hurt? Are you coming down with something?"

"I'm all right."

He set down the gun carefully and she let him touch her forehead, because God help her, he soothed her, or lulled her. She wasn't sure which, and she couldn't tell them apart. Maybe there was no difference. She'd been scared for her life. She'd been scared about her work. Now the only thing that scared her was that this was all going to end too soon.

Zoey was anxious again, and Davy wanted to fix it.

He squared his jaw and pretended he was fine. "I don't think there's anyone out there. So let's try not to worry—" he winced "—and just try to be prepared."

Zoey laughed a high-pitched laugh. "I'm usually always prepared. But I guess my life before this hasn't really let me experience a lot of large felines, or private islands, or really anything worth more than two thousand dollars, except my degrees, but that's more of an intangible, isn't it?"

"Zoey?"

She waved her hands at his home. "I know, we could make some sort of extra weapon so I can be armed, too."

"Who do you want to attack, Zoey? That wouldn't be good for us, or for the animals. I don't want to harm Baby. She's just being herself."

"Well, you should've let them be animals on their own turf."

He should have. He should've left Zoey alone, too. But he'd seen her, and he'd wanted some of that vitality for himself. He'd agreed so readily to spending time with her not just because he wanted to help her, but because he wanted to help himself.

That always ended badly.

"Why is it that we're always told we shouldn't make sudden moves around animals, but they make sudden moves on us all the time?"

"Because they're protecting themselves. Zoey. I think the real problem isn't Baby."

"It's the geese, isn't it? They learned how to knock."

"It's a person who was knocking at the door."

She sprang up and started pacing.

"I don't know why I don't want it to be a person. I guess I was so happy for a while. Alone with you. And now that real life is intruding I'm losing all reason. I haven't made sense in days, but being in this bubble with you made its own kind of sense."

She stopped.

"It's probably nothing," he said, far too late. "We can sit

tight for a while. We have a backup generator and it's working. By tomorrow we'll have forgotten about it. It'll be fine."

But it wasn't. Zoey was right—well, about the last thing. Somehow the outside world had managed to invade their sanctuary.

No man was an island, he'd once heard someone say. And no two people were a sex bubble.

"I'm sorry. You're right. I don't know what I was thinking."

"Hey, hey." He put his arm around her shoulders because he could do that now. He'd seen her shoulders bare not that long ago. Her skin was soft there, although the rounded muscle under that skin wasn't. Such a study in contrast. "It's just one person outside who seems to have gone away, and one big cat who is frankly pretty shy—"

"Plus some terrifying attack geese."

He pulled her closer. "Yes, the geese are vicious."

"I feel stupid for being afraid of people. And waterfowl. I hate feeling stupid. It's worse than fear—but I've got a good case of that, too."

"But fear isn't stupid. Sometimes fear is a sign that you've learned something."

They'd moved into the great room now, onto the couch. She buried her head in his shoulder. It felt good. Her voice was muffled. "Easy for you to say when you aren't afraid all the time. I know I sound like I'm sure of myself—I like to boss people around—but most of the time I'm terrified. That's why I have The Plan. Had it. It stopped me from being terrified of all the things that could happen to me and the people I loved. Eventually I'd be able to solve it all if I stuck to The Plan."

His hand crept under her shirt where it was warm. He was stroking her gently, but it was more for his own comfort than for her.

"But, of course," she continued, "it's stopped me from doing

170 | OPAL WEI

things. Kept me from saying what I really wanted to say to people, from doing the things I really want to do."

He kissed her head. He wanted to tell her the only reason he wasn't scared all the time was because he lived mostly away from where he could harm others. That people were the most terrifying and fragile things he knew. But that wouldn't help either of them.

"I really am okay now," she said after a moment. "You didn't see anything out there?"

His hands curled around her waist and up around the ridge of one rib. "Nothing that I can tell. I mean, the wind and rain did something, and I'm going to have to go out and inspect it. But I don't see anything out here out of the ordinary. Too bad they didn't leave a sign."

"Geese can't write, *Give me your entire lawn or we'll get you.*"

"Maybe they did. In any case, I'll have to go out later to check the generators. And I'll radio the guy on the nearby island. I haven't in a while, and he's probably worried. Although with the storm, maybe he's lost track of time, too. I hope he's okay."

Rudy, his neighbor, was probably somewhat better off. His island was like a fortress against a coming disaster. He had foods, gadgets, cleaning products, stockpiles of gasoline and fuel, a couple of boats. The man was equipped like a Bond villain. Davy suspected he might be one, to be honest.

Rudy would definitely survive. That kind always did.

Still, Davy was thinking he should probably ask Rudy to escort Zoey to the mainland. She was scared, and Davy wasn't helping. With the knocking he'd heard, and how close the cat had come to the house, he wanted her to be as safe as possible—to *feel* safe. And despite how much he wished to wake up and see the sun shining in her hair, how much he wished he could kiss her, and feed her, and keep her rounded body against his, the softness of her cheek against his chest. But when Zoey started feeling cornered, she started thinking she should go back to the way things were, and Davy didn't want her to worry that either of those things had to happen. Davy was anxious enough as it was. He didn't wish that on her. No. He didn't want her to regret this time with him any more than she already did. It would break his heart.

He had to cut this short.

Davy gave her skin one last stroke and pulled his arm back. "Come on," he said. "We're safe now. There's nothing else we can do. It's time to look for your slide."

He stood.

Zoey looked up at him, confused. "My slide?"

"Yeah, the one that's in the boxes."

"Oh yeah. The slide."

"That's why you're here isn't it? There aren't that many left to search through. We'll use the flashlights if you need stronger light. Later, I'll go out and check the generators. Then we'll talk about getting you back to the mainland."

She dropped his hand.

"Zoey." He scrubbed his hand through his hair. "You've gone through a bunch of big decisions, a lot of changes lately, and even though you've maybe changed your mind about your…future—" he was not going to say Plan in capital letters "—I know it's not always easy to let go of things you've held for so long."

"This is because I panicked a little."

"It's not panicking, it's processing."

"Oh, spare me the shrink talk."

"I know you, Zoey. You're going to need some time to think."

"You know me? It's been four days!"

"Four days where we haven't thought much. Maybe you

need some space. We both need to clear our heads. I had a plan, too, and I feel like maybe I'm about to change it."

Because I met you.

"We're getting attached and I just don't want you to do something you'll regret. So maybe you should get your slide. We go back to where you feel more comfortable. And then we can talk things through."

He knew her? She was getting too attached? She needed some space? Oh, Zoey had changed her mind all right: How could she have ever thought Davy was brilliant? The man was a bonehead. And she knew a lot about bones.

Zoey glared at Davy's back as he left to check over the generators, but somehow she failed to singe holes in his shirt. She stomped over to the crates. She wasn't in touch with all of her feelings. In fact, maybe she tended to ignore most of them. But she was familiar with anger. *And* she was very sure that she was unhappy with her program—or was it her experiments? Or her supervisor? All three. This time with handsome (but annoying) Davy had helped with that.

Zoey did not need to clear her head. She was probably sniffling from allergies. Funny how the crates were newly moved here and already they were so dusty.

She wiped her eyes on her sleeve and harumphed and dug into another crate.

Still a little voice whispered, what was she going to do if she didn't have her future mapped out for her? Could she return to a different school, another program or supervisor? Could she finish her clerkship and residency and practice medicine instead of continuing the research track? But no, she couldn't start all over again. She wasn't getting any younger or any richer, and she'd already wasted so much time and money.

Then there was the fact that she still did care a lot about helping kids like Mimi.

But sometime in the last few days, she'd quit *thinking*. That was the problem. For some reason, she hadn't thought beyond hanging out on the island with Davy. But that wasn't realistic. He hadn't offered to let her stay here forever eating SpaghettiOs. And even if she could stay here, what would she *do*?

Maybe Davy was right, dammit.

Even if he had hurt her just now.

She had to admit the growing pit in her stomach was not just because she was worried about her future. It was because in a few words he'd distanced himself from her. Put her off the island. That was all it took.

Zoey put her hand on her hips. At some point, the new unopened crates had mixed in with the old unopened ones. She moved through the stacks automatically, sorting them into more coherent categories, labeling some of them, not because she wanted to help the big, dumb jerk, but because it bothered her when people were so disorganized. Like she had been over the last few days.

So disorganized that Zoey hadn't noticed that maybe he didn't feel the same way about her that she was beginning to feel about him. But no, Davy was being realistic. Even she couldn't map out a plan in which she ended up with him, not unless he left the island, became less of a hermit. Not unless he felt the same way, or she changed the way she was built.

Zoey was rooting through a box of clothing, turning the pockets out automatically. She found scraps of paper with little scribbled notes and drawings, which she smoothed out and sometimes looked at. A bird, a bear. They weren't very good, she supposed, but she could tell what they were. Sometimes, there was probably some musical notation she couldn't read, or a note in English or Chinese.

His Chinese characters were messy. She should take satisfaction in that. He was right, but she had one thing over him—Zoey had great handwriting.

She should also note the number of coins in his pockets. Her mother, who'd always scrimped and saved, would have been horrified by all that free-floating change. Those coins could be turned into dollars, which could be an entire meal. But it was obvious that Davy hadn't gone through his pockets in years. There were pennies. Pennies hadn't been in circulation in Canada for years, although Zoey's mother had some old ones that she hoarded in hopes they'd be worth something someday.

What they were worth now was almost nothing.

No. Their value lay in reminding Zoey that she was the daughter of a person who kept track of pennies and nickels, and Davy X was the kind of person who had so many pockets in so many outfits in so many houses that he didn't have to worry about small change. If he even considered letting her just stay with him she'd be at the mercy of his whims.

No, that wasn't true. Davy took responsibility—maybe too much. Just like he took care of the animals and people in his life.

She had to be her own person, no matter how seductive the idea of letting go was. Three days ago, she'd known who that was, where her responsibilities lay. Today she had no idea.

She thought of Mimi, who was probably studying for her exams right now, finishing up her first year of university. Mimi had never asked Zoey about why she was in the field she was in, but her sister had to know. Didn't she? And if she quit, she'd also know that Zoey was failing her.

Zoey pulled out her phone and texted Mimi a quick **Missing you** message and a GIF of a giraffe with its head popping out of the trees that she'd saved to her phone. The icon whirled around, taking its time sending. The connection had probably been disrupted by the storm.

But Mimi didn't reply. It was probably a sign—not that Zoey believed in those. She dumped all the change into an empty shoebox. She folded another sweater and set it aside and pulled out a windbreaker.

No coins in this one. No telltale jangle. In fact, there didn't seem to be much except a thick piece of paper tucked under more items of clothing.

She smoothed it automatically and was about to put it in the pile, when she recognized the envelope.

Holy shit.

She pulled her arm back so suddenly that her elbow knocked the flashlight off the chair, and while her elbow tingled, her eyes smarted, and the light went flying, she almost—almost—dropped the envelope again.

But no, it was in front of her. She shook her other arm out and breathed in quickly, blinking away the sudden tears. Then she picked up the flashlight, placed it carefully back on the ottoman, and sat down with the envelope.

She unfolded it carefully, and with steady fingers pulled a glass rectangle out.

Her goddamn, no-good, stupid aggravating slide.

The light winked off its transparent surface.

Maybe it was a sign.

Zoey hadn't even gotten the chance to label it, although the words came back to her disconnected from meaning: *cytological specimen from an osteoblastic osteosarcoma.*

She shook her head, trying to clear it. She'd have to check it when she got back to the lab to make sure it hadn't sustained any damage.

Back to the lab.

Even if she'd faced some of the truths she'd been avoiding,

real life was still waiting for her. Consequences. Zoey didn't think about how much she wanted Davy to ask her to stay. She stuffed that envelope into her bra. She put all the clothing she'd folded back in the bin, took the notes and placed them on the ottoman. Then she looked at the shoebox full of pennies and change, got up to wash her hands, because she'd always been taught to wash her hands after handling money, and steeled herself to find Davy.

CHAPTER 12

IN WHICH ALL SORTS OF THINGS TURN UP

"I found it," Zoey said.

"Found what?"

"The slide."

She held out a box to him.

Davy had managed to get the main power back online. The lights were humming in their familiar registers again. The house was suddenly and subtly louder.

Oppressive.

Before, when he'd been alone out here, he never felt like the sound of the house was closing in on him, but now, with the old-new noise of electricity, the little beeps and boops of the various machines that he'd plugged back in, he felt trapped.

Or maybe it was the accusation in Zoey's eyes that had him feeling that way. Her hurt was the plunging bass note to all of this.

He'd expected finding the slide would at least mellow the sound, but the box clinked and *rattled*.

Was it broken? Had it shattered into a million jingling pieces?

She thrust the box at him once more, and he wiped his

178 | OPAL WEI

hands carefully on his jeans before glancing inside. "These are…coins?"

"I found them folded with your clothing."

"Uh, thanks."

"Aren't you going to take them?"

Zoey held it and shook it again.

Davy had no choice but to accept the box.

She said, "There must be at least five dollars in there."

"And some pennies."

"Yeah."

He cleared his throat. "I haven't seen a penny in a long time."

"You would if you ever checked your pockets. If you want to do some good in the world, you have to be organized and thorough. Not just come up with ideas."

She still sounded mad at him. Sad, lovelorn man that he was, that made him want to pull her into his arms. "Zoey, it's not like I want you to leave. You're welcome to stay here as long as you need. It's just… I don't think you'd be happy. Longer term."

"So you're doing this for my own good. I get the intent. I might even agree with you. But I don't have to be happy about how you decided it for me."

He'd hurt her.

He wanted to say it was part of his plan. Make her think he was a huge jerk. But he wasn't really one for strategizing about people's feelings, and it killed him a little inside that he'd made her think less of him. He just knew she wouldn't thrive here, and if she didn't leave sooner, it would hurt him more.

"I want to want to stick to The Plan. I want to like my work. I hate the idea that I'm giving up this responsibility. How am I going to stop feeling guilty? I texted my sister just now because I felt like I had to tell her. Except I never really told her about The Plan in the first place."

"Surely she's never expected you to make her illness your career."

"It sounds bad when you say it that way. I don't know. Kids these days with their avocado toast and their wanting their siblings to cure cancer."

She sobered. "But it's hard to just…let go of that way of thinking, you know? I've had this in my mind focused for so long, I don't know what to do with myself when I'm supposed to let go. Except when I'm here. With you."

Then stay, he almost said. But he'd already told her to go because she would never be the kind of person who would be content with that—with just him. She had too much crackling energy. Too much curiosity, and anger, and vitality. It wasn't like they really knew each other.

Except, he wished he could know more about her, more than the way her hair stuck straight up in the mornings, more than the texture of her skin, the pink along her cheeks and shoulders and breasts when she was excited, more than the sound of her voice when she said his name in exasperation, and laughter, and passion.

He cleared his throat. "Well, I'm glad you found the slide. I'm going to try radioing Rudy again. But if that doesn't work, I'll be able to take you out on the water myself, as long as it clears up a bit more."

"Why offer up someone else?"

Because he didn't want her to go.

But he said, "Rudy's a better boater. He's more experienced in these waters. You'd be safer with him than with me."

She stared at him. "I should be happy that I figured this out. I should be relieved that I have this chance to make a new plan, start afresh, but I'm not."

"I'm sorry."

"No. Davy, stop. You don't have to make it up to me. Stop acting like you're the only one whose fault it can be, like you have to spend your entire life making up for mistakes you made when you were a teenager. Everything that has happened here, between us has been as much my responsibility as it was yours. Maybe even more so, because I certainly was the one who handed you the thing to begin with, I was the one who got on that boat, and I was the one who wanted you."

Oh, he was not strong enough for this.

"Zoey, I want—"

A pounding sounded at the door.

Fuck. Fuck. Fuck. He went years without hearing a knock at that door, and now it was twice in one day?

Before Davy could move, Zoey strode over to the door and flung it wide open, and he threw himself in front of her.

But it was only Rudy. And an RCMP officer.

Davy was confused. He'd just been talking about Rudy with Zoey, and the man was already here? Worse, the part of Davy that wasn't sunk in misery flashed in warning looking at the older man's face. Rudy hadn't brought an officer in for a friendly post-storm check-in.

There was something about the greedy way Rudy's eye was taking everything in that made Davy pull Zoey back behind him.

How could Davy have considered sending Zoey off with this man? Then again, that small alert part of him whispered, how could he consider sending Zoey off at all?

"Oh, Davy," the weedy, older white man quavered. "It's so good to see you're all right, son."

Zoey could feel Davy stiffen next to her. "Thanks, Rudy," he said, his voice oddly flat.

The policeman, a tall South Asian man, consulted his phone. In a deep, rumbling voice, he said, "Mr. Hsieh? I'm Constable Dutta of the Royal Canadian Mounted Police. I'd like to talk to you about—"

Rudy interrupted. "Why don't we go inside and have a seat. Maybe get some coffee and talk about this?"

He eyed Zoey as he said the word *coffee*, and Zoey instantly loathed him.

They hadn't even been introduced and she'd already been relegated to bringing him and all the other men things in *mugs*.

"This is Zoey Fong," Davy said, ushering them into the great room. "My friend."

That felt both inadequate and too much to describe their relationship. He'd painted this Rudy character as a sort of friend, too, and she didn't want to be on the same level as Rudy. Then again, Rudy didn't get the sparkle of Davy's full smile.

She did note that Rudy had his arm in a sling over his yellow golf shirt. He wouldn't be taking her to the mainland anytime soon. Davy would have to see to his own chores.

Zoey grasped that flash of anger she had for Davy. It helped cover the unease she was starting to feel with the arrival of the constable and Rudy.

"I'll get that coffee," Davy added.

"Why don't you just get your girl to fetch it," Rudy said. "We have some sensitive things we'd like to discuss with you."

"It's Ms. Fong to you."

She couldn't help baring her teeth at Rudy in satisfaction at his startled look that she'd talked back to him.

At the same time, Davy was shaking his head. Still in that same, flat voice, he said, "You can discuss anything in front of Zoey. There isn't anything she doesn't already know."

The officer finally interjected. "Then let's get down to it.

Mr. Hsieh, Mr. Durrell here alleges he was attacked earlier by an illegal animal you're harboring here on your property."

What the hell? She glanced at Davy to see his reaction, but his face was hard to read. It made her shiver.

"Now, son," Rudy began saying even before Officer Dutta had finished. "I didn't want for this to happen. But I did warn you that something like this was bound to occur sooner or later.

"We've discussed those wild animals before," he explained to the officer, who looked bored. "When I came down to see if you were all right after that storm, I didn't know you were entertaining. I guess you were too preoccupied to answer the door."

He winked at Zoey and something about the way his face shifted from fake concern to suggestiveness made her want to bathe in disinfectant.

"I went round to check on everything. And—" Rudy was back to pathos. His throat worked. "That's when it happened."

He paused and stared into the distance.

"What happened?" Zoey asked baldly.

Rudy glared at her for a moment before seeming to remember that he was supposed to be acting paternal and heartbroken.

"Are you sure we should be having this discussion in front of a lady?" Rudy asked.

Except when he said *lady*, Zoey felt her skin crawl.

Davy, who'd been quiet until now, said, "Rudy, what were you doing walking around the property? I've told you, you shouldn't be wandering around on it."

His voice still seemed flat. Zoey couldn't help checking. She wasn't sure if he was exhibiting signs of an incipient panic attack. Despite the fact she had no right, she reached for his hand. His skin felt cold. But after a minute, he squeezed back.

Then he pulled away.

That hurt.

"Davy," Rudy was saying, "I was worried about you. We're friends, my boy. That's what makes it painful to be here like this."

He turned to Zoey. "It was bound to happen sooner or later. Doesn't have a head for business, my Davy. Doesn't think of consequences."

Oh *no*. He did not go there.

She couldn't explain it. Yes, she *was* angry at Davy for wanting to send her away, even if she was probably going to have to leave eventually, for wanting to send her away with this jerk. But she was damned if she was going to let Rudy make Davy doubt himself or his goals.

"You take responsibility and consider consequences just fine," she told Davy before whirling on Rudy. "I think the person who didn't think of consequences here is you. You trespassed on private property despite being warned not to do so. And this injury that you say you sustained—" She pointed her chin at his sling. "What was it? A sprain? A bite? We have only your word for it. And we do know you're well enough that you got it this morning and you're already out and about attempting to intimidate Davy by dragging an officer into it."

"Ms. Fong—"

"Just say you don't want a wildlife sanctuary here instead of wasting everyone's time and telling Davy it's his fault that *you* are choosing to involve the law," Zoey burst out.

"Wildlife sanctuary!" Rudy sneered. "I'm not wasting anyone's time. His animals are a real threat!"

"To whom? It's an island! There are no neighbors! Unless you're trespassing, you're not in danger."

Rudy rolled his eyes, but his voice had become shrill. "What is she, a lawyer among other things?"

It was clear from the way Rudy said *among other things* that he didn't have much respect for anything she might do.

"Mr. Durrell," Constable Dutta said.

But Davy stood up. *No, Davy. Please don't have an anxiety attack now*, Zoey wanted to beg.

Instead, he said very quietly, "Ms. Fong has medical training, and you owe her an apology."

His voice wasn't flat anymore. Zoey heard the fury under the soft syllables. He was mad, Zoey realized. She didn't think she'd seen him angry before, but he was slowly, slowly working himself up to furious. On her behalf. Maybe he cared about her a little?

"To her?" Rudy asked.

A rumble started in Davy's throat.

Was he *growling*?

Did she like it?

"Davy, my boy, I didn't mean anything by it."

"Apologize. And don't call me *my boy* or *son*," Davy said.

Rudy held his hand up. "I don't mean anything by it—" *It* meaning her? "Sorry. It's just I know your father, Davy. When I talked to him about buying this piece of land—"

Davy snarled. "Well, I own it now, so don't bring my father into this."

It seemed Rudy had hit a sore spot. Zoey tried to think of any times Davy had mentioned his parents. All she could think of was how they'd abandoned him when he needed them.

Zoey reached up and put her hand on his arm as if to tell him she was here with him. She knew she was getting a glimpse of a younger, angrier Davy. A more dangerous one. But she didn't feel scared. She was almost glad to see him. At least that Davy fought. The mood in the room had definitely shifted. Constable Dutta, no longer sleepy, watched them. Rudy seemed to be realizing for the first time that his sob story wasn't entirely convincing, Davy stood furious beside Zoey's chair, and Zoey... She was still furious, but the rage was a wonderful change from feeling hurt and apprehensive. She squeezed Davy's arm and went with it.

"Let's start from the beginning," Constable Dutta said after a moment. "Mr. Durrell, you said you came to Mr. Hsieh's property and knocked on his door."

"A few times. I was worried, because we'd had a big storm. Knocked over a few trees on my property. I was lucky, I—"

"Mr. Durrell."

"Right, so I hadn't gotten Davy's usual communication, and he hadn't responded to mine. Although this isn't the first time. The boy's a little absent-minded."

"I told you I might not be around a couple of weeks ago. I went to Vancouver to resupply."

Rudy ignored him. "When the waters seemed calm again, I thought I'd swing by, check and see if everything was all right. Come up to the property, you know. So I docked and came up to the door. The electricity didn't seem to be on. The house looked abandoned. So I thought I'd walk around the property a bit. Davy's father picked it up a while ago for a song. It's a nice piece."

"So you came to scout it out?" Zoey asked.

"No harm in it."

Davy said, "Except I've told you before that there are some injured animals here. I don't want them disturbed."

"Davy," Rudy said a little pompously. "We've spent time together in good-natured intellectual debates about what we should do with the land in this area, conservation, all that. We agreed to disagree that maybe this wasn't the best place for those animals."

Zoey snorted. He made it sound like Davy and Rudy had sat in front of a roaring fireplace wearing silk robes and ascots swirling snifters of port while deciding the future of the coastline.

But she knew he'd never even been in this house before.

"Ms. Fong."

This, sternly, from Constable Dutta.

"Yes, please let me continue," Rudy said. "As I was saying, I only wanted to take a little stroll about the young man's property."

"Why didn't you come in the door? You know it isn't locked," Davy asked.

"I did *not* know. That seems awfully trusting."

"You're such good friends and spend time in intellectual debate, and you don't know the door's always open?" Zoey countered.

Davy's arm shifted, but Zoey kept her grip.

Ruby ignored her. "I took a little walk around to see what you'd done with it, and then from out of nowhere, one of your animals came at me!"

"You were warned," Davy said.

Rudy pointed a trembling finger at Davy. "Listen to that, Constable. *You were warned.* He's uttering threats to me, even as I describe the—the assault I received at the hands of his attack animals."

"There was more than one animal attacking you?" Zoey snapped.

Rudy passed his good hand in front of his face as if to try and erase the memories. "I can't say. It all happened too fast. May I also add that these animals hardly seemed to be ailing, if they could come at me with such swiftness and fierceness."

"So multiple animals attacked you and you injured your arm?" Zoey asked.

"I also bruised my ribs, and my coccyx."

"Were you assessed by a medical professional?"

"It's an old injury."

"Then how are you sitting?" Zoey asked.

"I'm enduring great pain."

She was enduring great bullshit. She leaned forward.

"Are you experiencing numbness?" she asked.

"Yes."

"Swelling?"

He shifted uncomfortably. "A little."

"Leg weakness?"

"Some."

She was enjoying using her medical training at least. "Bladder control problems?"

"No!"

Constable Dutta very discreetly inched away from Rudy.

Zoey said, "If I may examine—"

"She's hardly objective if she's been dallying with Davy, here."

A growl from Davy. Zoey shivered. They said pets and owners sometimes sounded alike. Maybe Davy was starting to sound a little like Baby. Except, of course, Baby's growl didn't make Zoey tingle or make her knees weak.

Maybe *she* had the bruised coccyx.

She shook her head.

"So you fell down, sustained some bruises. But the animals didn't devour you. Unless, of course, you're painfully sitting there with half your organs gone."

"She's making fun of me, Constable. Isn't that against the Hippocratic Oath?"

Constable Dutta looked tired. "No, and you can't bring someone up on charges for that, either."

He turned to Davy. "Mr. Durrell seems to think you have some illegal wildlife out here that poses a danger to people."

Davy's voice still held that growl. "It wouldn't have posed a danger to anyone if he hadn't started wandering around. I'm the only one who lives here."

Constable Dutta looked at Zoey.

"She's only visiting," Davy added harshly.

Only visiting. But Zoey stayed quiet. For now.

She didn't withdraw her hand.

Davy continued, "The wildlife isn't illegal. I'm not keeping Baby as a pet."

"You've named her Baby," Rudy piped up.

Davy turned to Constable Dutta and said with barely concealed impatience, "Baby, the cougar, is a former zoo animal who was mistreated. I applied for and was granted permission to have her here to rehabilitate her, but her injuries are enough that she can't be released just anywhere into the wild. She'd never survive."

"Do you have those papers?"

Davy's mouth firmed.

Oh no. The papers were somewhere in the crates.

She knew it. She could read it in his disorganized, handsome face.

Davy said after a pause, "I can look for them."

"I'll help," she offered.

He turned to her and looked down at her grip on his arm. "This is my mess."

"That doesn't mean you have to clean it all alone. Just because you feel responsible doesn't mean you have to take everything on yourself!"

That was what finally made her let go of the stubborn jerk. She threw up her hands. But before she could yell more at the Handsome, Constable Dutta stood. "Maybe we should meet this cat."

CHAPTER 13

A SERIES OF PERSONAL ATTACKS

"That is not a great idea."

Davy was trying to stay calm. This would not be a good time for his anxiety to come back. But maybe this wasn't anxiety he was feeling. It was the once-familiar burn of reckless anger. The desire to burn it all down.

He breathed in deeply, thinking relaxing thoughts. He hadn't had time to tour the whole property again. He wasn't sure how safe it was. There would be branches ready to come down, slippery paths.

And, of course, Baby was out there somewhere. She would probably hide away from a group of people tromping through the underbrush. But there was the fact that they'd heard that grumpy growl from her.

He wasn't sure how she'd react.

"What have you got to hide?" Rudy Durrell demanded.

Davy stiffened. He tried to tell himself at least it was good to know that Rudy, whom he was ashamed for disliking, was truly a shitweasel. Rudy had tried his best to seem neighborly, and invited Davy over to "talk business" several times, and Davy had always declined because he suspected Rudy just wanted to try to convince Davy to sell. He'd tried to feel grateful for Rudy's unsolicited advice, especially in the first year when Davy truly didn't know what he was doing. But he'd always felt a little uncomfortable about the whole thing, and he'd never been able to put his finger on why.

"I'm not trying to hide anything. Zoey, you should stay inside."

"Aha!" Rudy said as if he'd caught Davy admitting a great secret. "Because your animals are dangerous!"

He was, Davy realized, trying to pull a Zoey. But Rudy was no Zoey. Zoey had been sharp in her questioning. Davy had been attracted to her intelligence and vitality from the start, but to feel all of it turned toward a defense of him made him wish he could have more of her. It made him more selfish. He couldn't afford that.

"All animals are dangerous, Rudy. We don't want to frighten the cougar."

Zoey looked mutinous. "I'm coming."

"Well, I'm not," Rudy Durrell announced.

"I'd like you along to point out where you were attacked," Constable Dutta said mildly.

"I've already been traumatized enough."

Zoey said, "You shouldn't let him stay here on his own, Davy. Who knows what he'll do to your house."

"I resent that implication."

"I wasn't implying anything. I'm saying he'll definitely do something."

God, he was so stupid for associating with Rudy. And Zoey, beautiful, smart Zoey, was stuck in the middle of this.

Before Rudy could object, Constable Dutta snapped, "Everybody's coming."

Davy's heart dropped to his stomach. He'd hoped he could

get the constable to ask Zoey to stay back with Rudy, but he also didn't like to leave the two of them alone together. This was like that brain teaser that he would know the answer to if he'd been a better student, except instead of trying to bring a fox, a duck, and a bag of grain to the other side of the river, they also had a snake. *(That was Rudy. Sorry, snakes.)* So instead they were all going to pile in and hope the canoe didn't sink.

It was a good thing he wasn't in charge of solving big problems.

"I'll need to bring a tranquilizer gun," he said quietly, realizing how damning that sounded. "It's for our safety."

Mostly it was for Zoey's and Baby's. He didn't give a shit about anyone else at this point.

Rudy looked like he was about to speak again, but Constable Dutta cut him off. "You can give it to me."

Davy didn't argue with that.

He could feel it slipping away, everything he'd barely begun to build, the sanctuary project, his ideas for bringing a bird rehabilitation program to the island. This was how Zoey felt, he realized. Her plans had collapsed softly as she watched. It didn't matter if it wasn't fully formed yet. It had been his, and he didn't want to let go of his idea.

He got the tranquilizer gun to Constable Dutta, who checked it and nodded at him. "I'm assuming this is licensed."

Davy gave a tight nod back.

Even Rudy had quieted down, although he still grumbled as he waited for Zoey and Davy to put on sturdier clothing.

Davy edged toward Zoey. "You don't have to come," he said quietly.

Her expression was hard to read. "You don't want me there."

"I want you to be safe."

"That again. *Leave the island, Zoey, for your own good. Don't come, keep your eye on Rudy, for your own good. You* aren't going to be safe! Do you ever think of that? Not with *him* there."

She jerked her chin toward Rudy, who was making an exaggerated pain face as he pulled on his boots. Her voice was low but fierce, and he frowned. She thought she was protecting him. From what, he wasn't sure. It wasn't like Rudy would conk Davy over the head with Constable Dutta there to witness it. Would he?

It didn't matter. The main thing was he didn't want to flush Baby out of her solitude. Because if the elderly mountain lion got spooked and sprang at them, then he wouldn't be able to save both Zoey and Baby. At least Constable Dutta looked relatively calm and sleepy again.

Davy took a deep breath as he zipped up his jacket. He was all right, he realized. He knew what he had to do: he had to keep between Zoey and the cougar at all times. As long as he stayed close, he'd be able to manage it. For the rest, he'd have to trust Constable Dutta.

Their boots squelched in the mud as they stepped out onto the property.

Davy stayed close behind Zoey, close enough that he felt warmed by her nearness. Close enough that he could see the deep breath she took outside in the cool air, the way she glanced around—at him.

Wait, was she trying to make sure he was around her?

It had been a terrible day, but for some reason a tendril of warmth bloomed in him. She kept looking out for him.

Something about having this small fierce woman on his side made him feel stronger. She didn't need to defend him. In fact, he wouldn't blame her if she kicked him in the shins and ran screaming away forever. But instead she was outside on his island in a bulky jacket—one of his—that somehow made her look both slight and adorable. Her hair was getting mussed in the wind, and her cheeks were pink. If Rudy and Constable

Dutta weren't here, and if he didn't have to be on the alert for a disgruntled cougar, and he wasn't furious and sad, he would have pulled her to the still-wet ground and rolled around with her until mud stuck in their hair and all over their naked bodies.

Good to know his fantasies were all still impractical.

"Why don't you tell us where this happened," Constable Dutta told Rudy.

Rudy glanced around contemptuously. "I don't know. It all looks the same out here. Too many trees."

"Not everyone wants their own personal golf course," Davy snapped.

He was rewarded by Zoey's snicker. God, she was rubbing off on him.

Constable Dutta sighed. "I need more of an idea of what happened, Mr. Durrell. We've been walking for a while and so far we haven't encountered any animals at all, and we haven't seen any evidence of where any of this could have happened. From what I can tell, there's very few clearings or locations that indicate any damage from the attack you described."

"I'm disoriented. I suffered a lot of emotional distress."

Zoey's snort set off another round of squabbling. Constable Dutta was probably going to shoot them both with the tranquilizer gun. But Davy turned his head. There was a rustling sound.

"Zoey, get behind me!"

Out from the bushes it came, huge and angry.

Rudy screamed. "Not again!"

The older man fell down face forward as a toweringly angry goose, hissing and flapping its enormous wings, aimed itself right at them all.

Constable Dutta yelled something—probably telling them all to run.

But Davy had already grabbed Zoey's hand, and they were sprinting away.

★ ★ ★

"Don't you dare leave me here."

"I'm going back to help Constable Dutta and Rudy."

"Dutta has firearms and Rudy has bluster. They'll be fine. And what if Baby shows up here while I'm alone?"

Davy was about to reply when Rudy Durrell burst out of the bushes. Given his speed, it did not look like he'd reinjured his coccyx.

"This is your fault!" he screamed as he hurtled past them.

Constable Dutta strode into sight, looking unruffled, but not sleepy anymore. A cloud of feathers flew around him. His mouth was a grim line and he exuded menace. If she weren't already half in love with Davy—

Wait.

Already in love?

She glanced at the object of her inappropriate and ill-timed affections and blushed guiltily. Too bad he was too busy glaring at the officer to notice. He'd been trying to rid himself of her, after all, because he knew this would happen. There was no reason for her to try to protect him from the Rudy Durrells of the world. She could leave him and his chest and his overdeveloped sense of responsibility to this island, take her slide, and make her merry way to the mainland with Constable Dutta.

Davy stepped up to the policeman. "What happened?"

"I took care of it."

They looked like they were staring each other down.

Dutta said tightly, "I didn't have to fire or anything. The flock dispersed."

He crossed his arms over his chest.

Davy did the same.

Were they going to jut their chins out and strut around each other all day? Was she going to have to get herself a deck chair and some knitting while they sorted it out?

But Rudy Durrell had limped back now that he found the coast was clear. "See, what did I tell you, Officer! This—this man is harboring deadly animals on this island. I demand you arrest him."

It didn't quite have the same ring to it.

"They're geese," Davy said. "I'm not harboring them. They do what they want, and they go where they want."

"Were these the animals who attacked you?" Constable Dutta said.

Rudy looked cagey. "It was all a blur."

"So it might not have been the cat as you implied."

Dutta was breathing heavily and it looked like he was having a hard time containing his temper.

"An exam of Mr. Durrell's injuries might help," Zoey offered.

"I will not be violated this way."

Davy said, "Even if it was the cougar, you still shouldn't have been on private property, Rudy. I don't know what you want to do here. You want me hauled off so that you can turn this into a golf course, too? Is that what it is?"

Apparently Davy's anger, once roused, was difficult to quell. Not that she wanted to. She was plenty pissed off herself, but a corresponding fury rose in her once again as she thought more about it.

If they had Baby destroyed just because Rudy, the stupid, malicious man, wanted Davy to abandon his project—

Then, as if her anger manifested itself, a gnashing razor screech tore the air apart.

Baby.

"What was that?" Rudy cried.

He was about to run into the house and doubtless lock himself inside while leaving the rest of them out.

"You ought to know what that is," Davy said. "If anything you said before was true."

Baby shrieked again.

Zoey felt herself stiffen. She wanted to run and panic. She stayed still and watched Davy and Constable Dutta exchange a look. The officer quietly and carefully drew out the tranquilizer gun.

But between the gun and Baby's next unearthly cry, Rudy lost any composure he might have left and threw himself on Constable Dutta.

"Get off me!"

"Give me the gun!"

Davy went in to help.

"No, Davy. Be careful!"

But it was too late. The gun went off.

Rudy looked down at himself in horror and started backing away. "You shot me! I'm suing the RCMP for wrongful death. I'm suing you all."

"If you hadn't lunged for the gun, this wouldn't have happened," Zoey yelled.

She was so done with all of them. She pointed at him. "You're not even hurt. You're fine."

"So what happened? Where did the dart go?" Davy asked, looking around wildly.

Constable Dutta opened his mouth, but the words that came out of his mouth were strangely slow and garbled. "All of you," he said, limping forward, favoring the foot with the dart stuck in the toe of the boot. "All of you...under arrest."

CHAPTER 14

BACK TO THE MAINLAND

Zoey was too busy tending to a woozy Constable Dutta to pay much attention to Davy, but somehow he managed to wrangle Rudy and radio for a helicopter to transport Dutta to the mainland. Even though the officer was still conscious, he could develop an allergic reaction. And Zoey wasn't sure about his foot, either. Despite the thickness of the constable's boots, the rifle had gone off at close range.

It was bound to be painful.

Rudy insisted his injuries were also serious enough that he needed to be flown out, too. Which meant that Zoey couldn't travel back on the helicopter because there was only room for Constable Dutta—who had eventually passed out—and one other.

But because a constable had been hurt, and because Davy insisted on coming clean and telling the authorities that Constable Dutta had wanted them all hauled in, a detachment of more RCMP officers came to escort Davy and her off the island pending investigation. They weren't under arrest exactly. They were going to be "questioned."

Zoey had never been questioned before in her life. She should be worried. She worried about every goddamn thing.

But instead, she felt energized. If the authorities had questions, then she certainly had answers for them, including a few choice words for how Rudy Durrell had endangered them all. She was ready to defend herself, defend Davy, defend the entire pack of injured animals if she needed to. She'd even had a chance to use her skills on Constable Dutta, who from all appearances would probably be fine once the drugs wore off.

She had a Plan for the next day at least.

Her mind was humming. She hadn't felt this way in years.

"You're really eager to get back to the mainland, aren't you?" Davy asked.

"You can bet on it."

For some reason, his face fell.

Maybe Davy was worried, if she could judge by the way he was fussing to reassure her as they sat inside the stuffy police boat, cruising their way back across the strait. At least his anxiety hadn't manifested. He said, "The bed-and-breakfast George and I own? We can stay in town if we need to. It has plenty of room. You can have privacy. You may have to stick around until Constable Dutta recovers."

Zoey didn't want to say out loud how relieved she was that she could put off getting back to the lab for another day. She could avoid serious conversations and questions she couldn't answer about her future and stay in a hotel. She could stay with Davy.

Zoey grabbed her backpack and some extra clothing—well, a selection of Davy's extra clothing—with her. The slide was still safely tucked in her cleavage. Very safe, considering Davy was probably not going to be looking there for the time being.

"Plenty of rooms, huh? I should still pay my fair share for staying with you," she said. "I can, it's not a big deal."

She'd just…get a job. That was all. Pay him back in install-
ments for a stay at his Sunshine Coast B&B.

"Zoey, let me do this for you. Let's not argue."

He seemed sad.

She didn't want to be difficult, but she couldn't help herself
most of the time. She opened her mouth to protest despite the
fact he'd just asked her not to, but he cut her off.

"I'm sorry for all this," he said.

"No. Stop. I don't want you to continue with that, and I
don't to hear whatever it is you want to say if you have that
expression on your face."

"What expression?"

"Like you're sorry for me."

"I'm never sorry for you. You're the least pathetic person I
know. But I do regret dragging you into this."

She was furious with him. "Stop that!"

An officer looked over at them curiously. "Stop that," she
shout-whispered, which ended up being louder than her original cry.

She took a deep breath and tempered her voice. "I'm getting really tired of this. Is blaming yourself the way you keep
people from getting close to you? Who needs an island when
you've got that thick wall of self-regard masquerading as self-
blame keeping people out?"

His lips thinned. "You're not exactly one for letting people in."

"Well, at least I'm open about it. I tell people I'm prickly.
You're all like, *I'm so easygoing and handsome and floppy haired.*
Not that your handsomeness or your hair has anything to do
with it, but it helps with the image. But me, I don't hide the
fact that I'm this way all the way through."

"What does that even mean? That doesn't make sense. How
are you better because you're madder about it?"

"I'm not saying I'm better because I get angry. I'm saying I let people know it's hard to love me by being the way I am. But you, you don't warn people that it's hopeless to let people love you."

And…her voice broke.

It was not one of her finer moments. This was why she stuck to goals and ran away from relationships. Because she was mortifyingly, brimmingly full with feelings. She let the anger out, but everything else she kept tightly shut down, afraid she'd form another difficult and improbable Plan around them. But now, the one time she'd actually run toward someone full tilt and thrown herself on his boat, his island, and into his life, he wanted her to leave.

She bit down on her tongue and turned her face away, but his hand had already caught her cheek so gently that it hurt.

"Zoey," he said in that way he had, except this time the song in his voice was like heartbreak.

The officer said, "Sorry to interrupt, but we're going to have to take you into the station."

"I'm not sorry," Zoey muttered.

She wasn't sure if Davy heard her.

Davy wondered if he'd understood correctly. Was Zoey in love with him?

Despite the fact that she'd also said something about being angry with him, he grabbed her hand, wanting to hear about that love over and over. He wanted to write songs about it. He wanted to get up and dance even though the RCMP would definitely arrest him if he made any sudden moves. He wanted to confess every single feeling he'd been having. But the constable, a big white guy this time, hustled Davy and Zoey off the boat and toward a beat-up old cruiser. Reality, in the form of a car that smelled like fries and baked leather, sank in.

"Do we have to sit in the back seat?" Zoey asked.

Like criminals.

He could hear her thoughts so loudly. The officer shook his head. Davy winced and squeezed her hand before letting go. It was a good reminder that they were in a bit of a mess.

He'd sit in the back.

He opened the door for Zoey and spent the brief ride staring out the window.

The station was less three minutes away from the dock. They probably could have walked. At least then he'd have had more time breathing the same air as Zoey, because as soon as they arrived at the station, they were immediately separated.

"Wait. Where are you taking her?"

The constable was leading her off down the hallway while a new person blocked Davy's path. "Please come with me, sir," the blocking woman said in her polite Canadian way.

"But I can't leave Zoey, not now," Davy protested.

Zoey turned around, looked at him distantly, and allowed herself to be led into a room.

The door shut.

"I'm Sergeant Major Green," said the woman. "Would you like some coffee? Water?"

He was led into a small room of his own. There were two chairs and a table. "Am I being arrested?"

"We have to ask some questions. An RCMP officer was injured in the line of duty."

Sergeant Green watched him calmly, her face impassive. She was in her forties, maybe, although her brown skin was unlined. It was something about the way she held herself. Authoritative, unhurried.

"The report says that Constable Dutta was asked to investigate dangerous animals being harbored on your property."

"Yes, that's why he was there, and he did end up getting

attacked," Davy said. Maybe that was the wrong way to put it. "By geese. They didn't belong to me. Or anyone. The geese were fully self-possessed."

"I see."

Davy wasn't sure how she could. He hardly could himself.

"Why don't you tell me in your own words how this led to Constable Dutta being shot in the foot."

"Well, we were in a clearing near my house after we'd fled the geese—we being Zoey, that is Ms. Fong, Rudy Durrell, and Constable Dutta. We heard a…a growl."

"From a goose?"

"No, it was from a large cat. A cougar."

"A wild cougar on your property."

"She's not *undomesticated*. Although technically it's not really possible to domesticate a large cat like this one. But she's elderly, she doesn't have claws, has been around humans for most of her life, and she has some health issues."

"Was this the animal that Mr. Durrell claimed injured him?"

"That's what he says, but Rudy shouldn't have been wandering around my property."

Sergeant Green looked at a tablet. "He told us he had a standing invitation."

"Radioing in with the neighbors is not the same as giving leave to walk around another people's property. Especially because I know…"

"Especially because you know what?"

"Because I know Rudy better now. Anyway, I don't usually invite people to the island."

"And yet Ms. Fong was with you."

"That was a special circumstance. We didn't venture far from the house, and when we did, I tried to take safety precautions."

"Like having a tranquilizer gun."

"Yes."

"How was my officer shot with your gun, Mr. Hsieh?"

She pronounced his name correctly. Like she'd been studying.

The worst thing he could do was act guilty when he was not. "When we heard that the cougar was possibly nearby, Constable Dutta drew the tranquilizer gun—"

"Your gun."

"Yes. As you noted. I gave it to him willingly. He drew it and Rudy Durrell threw himself on it, and in the struggle, Constable Dutta got shot in the foot."

"Mr. Durrell says it was because you intervened in the struggle that Constable Dutta was shot."

"Rudy was threatening to take a gun from your officer!"

Davy's fists clenched.

"Maybe Constable Dutta would have been able to protect himself," Sergeant Green said coolly.

"That thing could've gone off in any direction. It could've hit Zoey," Davy said, gritting his teeth. "I was trying to help."

A long pause as Sergeant Green tapped on her tablet. Finally she said, "You're free to go, but assaulting an officer is a serious charge. We're talking to Ms. Fong now, but I'd advise you both not to leave town until Constable Dutta wakes up, and we get to the bottom of this."

Davy wanted to say that Zoey could back him up. But he didn't want to bring her into this any further than he already had.

He said out loud, "I shouldn't have let Zoey—I mean Ms. Fong—come to the island with me. She wasn't involved in this. She's an innocent bystander."

He was going to say it was all his fault again, but Zoey would hate that. Besides, Sergeant Green would probably see that as a confession, and while he did tend to blame himself for a lot,

204 | OPAL WEI

he felt safe in saying that Rudy had been the one to jump on Constable Dutta in a panic.

Zoey was right about that. She was right about everything. Maybe he shouldn't have been so quick to try to send Zoey away. Maybe he could let her into his life. But how could that ever work out?

She was smart, though. Maybe she could figure it out with him. If he let her.

Davy stood slowly, Sergeant Green close behind him.

He'd wanted to linger, to see if Zoey was there, but the hallway she'd disappeared down was a blank of closed doors and quiet.

Instead, he walked slowly outside into the sunshine and texted Zoey to see if she was out. No answer.

He shouldn't worry. She was a grown woman. He should just…trust her to take care of herself.

He texted her the address of his mainland property and called George to let her know he'd be there in a few minutes, and he walked down the road toward the house.

Zoey was settled into a booth and enjoying a truly enormous cup of coffee and eating a pile of pancakes with blackberries that apparently came from the bushes outside of town. Her phone wasn't charged, she'd realized belatedly, and although she was worried that she hadn't seen Davy come out, surely everything would be all right for him. The solicitous police officer she'd talked to had decided that she wasn't really at fault for any of this, and yes, she may have flirted with him a little bit out of spite, and because she realized she could. His aunt owned a diner on the main strip of Narrow Falls, and he'd told her to mention his name. She felt relieved, and oddly sure that it was all going to be fine.

How strange. She seemed to have become an optimist over

this weekend. The extremely massive cup of coffee was probably helping.

Besides, Zoey could see the station from here. When Davy walked out, she'd be able to wave over at him and make him sit down and eat with her.

Except that would mean talking to him. Embarrassment twisted through her, making her push her plate away. Why was it so easy to tell him everything? As much as she wanted to be sure he was all right, she also didn't want to talk to him right now. Let him see what it was like without her.

"Visiting here?" the waitress, a young East Asian woman, asked, refilling her coffee.

Zoey swallowed. *Try to answer like a normal person.* "Yes, I'm staying at a bed-and-breakfast somewhere in town. I should find out where that is."

"Oh, what's the name of the B&B?"

"I think it's called the Innlet. Get it?"

Oh no, now she was repeating Davy's jokes.

The woman frowned. "The Innlet?"

"It's supposed to be around here somewhere," Zoey said, feeling stupid.

"I thought I knew all the places in town," the waitress said. "Unless you mean George's place."

She made a face.

That didn't bode well.

But the diner was empty, and the waitress was happy to chat for a few minutes. Zoey found herself oddly willing to talk to a stranger. Davy must be rubbing off on her more than she thought.

Interestingly, the waitress had a different, but telling expression when Zoey carefully mentioned Rudy Durrell.

Zoey ate and found herself wishing she could speculate with Davy about Rudy Durrell's ambitions for this chunk of territory—no, that wasn't true. She wished she could tell Davy to follow his instincts about trusting people like Rudy Durrell.

After she finally scraped the last bit of pancake from her plate, she peered out the window. It was a pretty town, near the water. Trees lined the sidewalks. She could see what looked like a small drugstore and a real estate agent's office with signs for vacation rentals in the window. That was nice, wasn't it?

She wasn't an expert on these things, though. She didn't know anything about living in small towns. Not that she was thinking about what that would be like.

Oh, she had to stop this. That was her MO, wasn't it? She'd strung herself along with hope about her career, a calling—or, in this case, a man. She'd sunk tears and time and energy into it, and in the end the whole thing would turn out completely different from her vision. She didn't feel like sharing more of her feelings with Davy, but she had to be brutally honest with herself. She cared about him and his misguided dedication to doing the right thing. Her heart squeezed when she saw his stupid floppy hair falling over one bright eye. She loved his gentleness, his chest, his hands, the fact that he looked at her like she was fascinating and exciting, as if he could see something in her that he'd discovered.

Of all the times to have inconvenient feelings, of all the people to have inconvenient feelings for.

She couldn't stay with him. He'd already told her! But instead of acting like a mature human being *because he was right, dammit,* she'd gotten angry with him. He'd still been trying to send her away before Rudy showed up.

Then she'd gone and defended him too fiercely, as if her feelings weren't already smeared all over her sleeve, like she'd reached over the table for someone else's food. She hadn't listened to him to stay back at the house because she wanted to be with him. And now she'd told him everything—had even possibly used the L-word—on the boat back to the mainland.

Zoey could never face him again. She certainly didn't want to enjoy more of his hospitality unless it was in a pit in the ground where she could cover herself in leaves and hibernate for the rest of eternity. Not that she knew where this inn was. But she wasn't supposed to leave town, and she got the feeling she couldn't afford anything else around here, either.

She would try to find somewhere to hide and charge her phone. She'd call Li-leng and they'd come up with money and figure it out.

"Excuse me, is there a public library here?"

"Down the block, to the left. It closes in an hour, though. And oh," the waitress called as Zoey paid her bill, "beware of mountain lions. There were a few sightings on the outskirts of town last week."

No need to tell Zoey that twice. After hearing Baby's roar, she'd had enough cougars to last a lifetime.

Zoey decided to hide in the stacks for a little while, like a coward, in a place that would at least be comforting, maybe even email Li-leng. As soon as she found out if Constable Dutta was okay and he was able to clear Davy's name, she was going to get back to Vancouver, back to figure out the shambles she'd made of her life, and put this whole episode behind her.

CHAPTER 15

TALKS, DINNERS, AND OTHER DISASTERS

Zoey was missing. Davy had been to the inn only to find she hadn't checked in. She wasn't answering her phone or her text messages. If she'd wandered out of town and into the woods, who knew what she might have encountered. A mountain lion? A bear? How could a tiny woman get lost in a small town so damn quickly?

He paced his room and fretted. It was the wrong kind of space for striding up and down. Papasan chairs, a creaky bed, and the smell of incense hung in the air. In the back of his mind, it occurred to him that maybe this wasn't the best look for a bed-and-breakfast in a swanky tourist area, and maybe it explained why there weren't any guests. But he didn't run it. It wasn't his business.

Besides, he needed to think of a plan to find Zoey. If she were here, he'd ask her to come up with one—no, she'd already be doing that.

Davy wasn't about to go to the police because, okay, it had only been a couple of hours since he'd last seen her. And he probably wasn't a favorite at the station.

But Zoey was in a strange town. Alone. She didn't even have her bike and he wasn't sure how much money she had.

He was just going to have to trust that she was all right. She was smart and tough. She was a practically a doctor, for God's sake. She probably wanted space from him, anyway. He had to try to respect that, no matter how much he needed to talk to her, no matter how much he wanted to have her around all the time.

He'd gotten spoiled, being able to touch her, glance over at her, wake up next to her.

A knock sounded at his bedroom door, and he leaped for it.

It wasn't Zoey.

"Davy! You want some tea?"

Georgette was his old babysitter and sometimes she still acted like it. She dressed like the elderly white hippie she was. He always associated her with the jangle of bracelets, and wildly patterned caftans. Today's was orange, green, and yellow, and she'd tied her hair back in a thick braid that hung down her back.

George set an inky brew on the rattan table and crossed her arms. Her bangles tinkled with the depth of her concern.

"No thanks."

"You seem tense. It's not good for you to get anxious. You need any—?" She brought thumb and index finger together up to her lips.

"No. Thanks."

He loved her, but sometimes he found her frustrating and forgetful.

"If you're sure, kiddo."

"I don't even take aspirin, George. No drugs of any kind anymore."

"Oh, right." George's face fell for a moment. "But listen, Davy. You've been on the phone the whole time. You've been distracted. And *pacing.* I can hear you stalking back and forth above me. You seem stressed about this girl who was about to show up. You want to talk to me? Open up heart to heart? Hash it out, so to speak?"

"I'm just worried she's lost her way around town, that's all."

George hooted. "How's she going to lose her way around here?"

That was true.

Zoey was definitely avoiding him.

"I'm fine. I get distracted. I pace. It happens."

"But not usually."

Except for that time when he'd lost himself. But George seemed to sometimes forget about their difficult years together, instead opting to remember him as a sunny little boy. Sometimes that deliberate forgetfulness made her say things that made him wince.

"Listen, if she makes your shoulders look like boulders, is she worth it?"

"Of course she is."

"You're in love with this woman!"

Davy didn't say anything. He didn't have to. George clapped her hands.

"My boy's in love!" she said to the room.

She dabbed her eyes. "Now remind me how you know her again?"

It was funny how he found himself regressing to being a surly teen. Davy told himself that George was trying to help. She'd always been kind to him, even when he'd destroyed her car, her garage, and changed her life. She'd showed him how to be good to animals, and she knew a bunch of old folk songs, and they'd sung harmonies together. She'd even taught him a little guitar. But she had that annoying habit of wanting to give advice when she had no idea what she was talking about.

Still. He had to get a hold of himself. "If you have any idea of who we could call. Maybe some of your friends might have seen—"

Davy bit his lip. He hadn't told George that he'd just been at the police station. "You should know," he said uneasily, "that an officer was shot with a tranquilizer gun while on my property."

"Fuck the police!" George said with glee. "What were they trying to do?"

"George, I don't want anyone to get into any more hot water right now."

"You! In trouble? You wouldn't hurt a fly."

There it was again. The forgetfulness.

"You wouldn't *eat* a fly," George continued. "I'm going to organize a protest! Call up all my friends, storm the barricades."

"Georgette Lavalle, do not do that! I haven't been charged with anything. I'm fine. And once Constable Dutta wakes up, he's going to tell them what really happened. But if you could ask some of your friends to keep an eye out for a young East Asian woman, about five foot three—?"

Georgina narrowed her eyes. She wasn't about to be deterred. "What happened with the police? Is it that woman? Did she flee the scene of a crime? Is that why she's missing? You do have to be careful with your heart. You're too naive."

That hurt a little because it was probably true.

But George continued, "Did she make you kill her elderly husband and frame you? Does she smoke cigarettes and trail around in slinky bathrobes? Is she making you take the fall?"

"No. Nothing like that. It's that Rudy Durrell—"

"That guy! Pig! Landlord! If he's her husband, he deserves to die."

"I'm a landlord."

"We own this place together."

"Just ask your friends to keep an eye out for her, okay? Zoey Fong."

George rolled her eyes at him. "You're no fun anymore."

"I am aware," he called after her as she clomped out, leaving Davy to wonder just how many hours George spent watching old movies. He should check in on her more often. But he'd tried so hard not to interfere with everyone or get involved. Instead of feeling free of responsibility, he felt like he'd shirked it and now George, who was already a little freaky, got…more imaginative over the years.

Of *course* he had to worry.

He went downstairs grumbling. On top of gnashing his teeth about what trouble Rudy Durrell was going to make and making sure the old inn didn't fall apart around them, he had to be sure George didn't start a terrible rumor while helping look for Zoey.

This was why he lived on an island most of the time.

"What about your work at the lab?"

Zoey was wedged in a corner of the library talking quietly to Li-leng. An elderly man in a baseball cap and pants hiked to under his armpits was reading the paper, but judging by the way his chair kept inching toward her, he was attempting to eavesdrop on her conversation.

Zoey was trying to keep her voice down, but dammit. Here was Li-leng—Li-leng, of all people, the one who hadn't worked on her diss since January and who quit jobs like they were bad boyfriends—reminding Zoey that she was supposed to be at the lab, with her slide.

She patted the envelope, still secure in her sports bra, as if to make up for all the neglect.

The action wasn't lost on her nosy neighbor. Or Li-leng. "I heard a crinkle. You're patting your bra to make sure it's still there, aren't you?"

"I'm not."

She glared at her neighbor because she couldn't aim her death rays at Li-leng. "There's been a change of plans." Or of The Plan. But Zoey didn't want to go into it here. "Anyway, my supervisor is still away—" Was he? What day was it even? "And my lab mate, Alec, probably is keeping track of things."

"More like keeping track of how many days you've unexpectedly been away."

For a moment, Zoey forgot that she was considering quitting. A spurt of panic hit her: Could all the hard work (watching her lab mates' experiments, and cleaning, and babysitting mugs), all that striving for perfection, be gone because she'd been careless?

That was the problem with trying to be perfect. You made one mistake, and it followed you more doggedly than any good.

But she wasn't doing that anymore. Besides, now that she had time to think about it, the standards she'd set for herself had been impossible.

"I'm owed time off."

"Aren't you always telling me science doesn't work that way? The experiments still have to be watched. And even if you're owed, you still forgot to call in for it and have it approved."

"I sent an email to my supervisor."

Who probably wouldn't get it until today or tomorrow because he was at that conference and would have liked to have had it cleared beforehand.

"It was an emergency. I'm on important lab business. Besides, I'm usually so dependable. Everyone says so. I can't help it if there was a storm, and I got stuck."

Li-leng laughed. "Got stuck, or did he stick it to you?"

Zoey's cheeks heated. "Stop."

"And now you're going to be staying in a quaint B&B in a small town with *him*."

"It's not like that."

Her voice was a little loud, probably from the force of all that denial.

The elderly man scooted a little closer.

"I'm sorry," Li-leng was saying. "It's just, it's so refreshing to see you get frazzled over love."

"It's not love."

"Okay, sexy times."

"It's not because of that. Ugh. Why not just call it sex? Sex. It's just sex."

She looked up to meet the curious eyes of her neighbor again.

She turned away. "Plus I won't have it with him anymore. It's over. There's nothing."

Li-leng's voice turned sharp. "Does he not see how awesome you are?"

Zoey had to gulp back a sob. That was Li-leng, always pointing out Zoey's bullshit, until she needed defending. Then there was no fiercer champion. "He does like me. It's not that, either. You can give me a pep talk when I figure out how to get myself home. I can't stay with him, and I left my bike on the island, so that's out."

"Ugh, no. You shouldn't bike hundreds of kilometers home alone and without any real gear anyway. Let me buy you a bus ticket."

"No," Zoey said quickly. "Don't buy anything. Can I even get a bus directly back?"

"Let's see."

Zoey wondered how her friend was checking everything with one hand burned. Her voice was distracted when she got back. "It looks a little complicated, to tell you the truth. Even though the Sunshine Coast is part of the mainland you have to take a ferry. If you can stay put in Narrow Falls a little longer, maybe I can borrow a friend's car this weekend, get it on the ferry, and come pick you up."

"I can't find a room to stay by myself. I can't afford it. Even in the off season you can tell this is one of those kinds of towns that has, like, big lodges made with huge hunks of timber and humongous windows that look out to forest and ocean views. It's for the kind of people who dress in designer yoga wear all the time and come here to cleanse their spirits."

"Well, there aren't any youth hostels as far as I can tell. And really, you're a little old for that—"

"Thanks. What about a motel?"

"Even a cheap motel out of town is going to add up by the weekend."

When Li-leng was practical, things were truly bad.

"I have some money saved up. We can put the other things on credit cards," Li-leng said. She added more softly, "Was he mean to you? Is that why you can't stay with him? Did he hurt you?"

Zoey closed her eyes. "No, Li-leng. That was the worst part. He's trying to be kind, to let me find my own path."

She was not going to cry in the public library. She'd already done that enough times in her life.

"He's a jerk. He has bad taste. He shouldn't strand you there."

"That's the thing, he's not trying to strand me. He wants me to have somewhere to stay. He said we should have separate rooms. He's so...considerate."

Her heart hurt a little.

"I thought you said he was handsome but not bright, right? Careless because he had too much money."

"I was too quick to judge. There are different kinds of intelligence."

"Right, he's a more hands-on type. How does it feel to fuck a boy bander?"

"Stop."

There was a scrape and a shuffle.

Zoey turned to see her elderly neighbor fleeing. Oh well, at least he wasn't trying to eavesdrop anymore.

Li-leng said, "Sorry. I'm a little jealous. But I'm going to try and get my friend with a car to drive us both down, and we'll come get you. But in the meantime, I want you to stay safe. And if you feel like Davy isn't a threat—"

"He isn't. Not that way, I mean."

"Maybe swallow your pride and stay at the nice bed-and-breakfast with him."

"But—"

"You don't have to do anything with him. You don't have to talk to him. You don't owe him. But you don't know anyone in town. Your first introduction to the place is you had to talk to the police. I know it's emotionally weird and painful, but the first thing is always to be physically safe."

It felt strangely easy to be comforted and reassured by Li-leng. Especially because she really wanted to stay with Davy. It would be so much easier.

"I could try harder to find somewhere to stay—that I can afford," Zoey said.

Not that she had exactly budgeted for this.

"You don't always have to do the harder thing just because it's harder," Li-leng sighed.

"I don't do that."

"Says the woman who's gone through med school and is still in it for a doctorate. Just accept this thing from a person who seems to care about you, all right?"

"I'm not anything special to him, Li-leng. He takes care of everyone. And everything. Brings his grandma pastries that he doesn't eat himself. Takes in a wild animal. Even sheltered me when I crashed into his life and altered his plans."

She changed the subject when she heard her voice getting too...fond. She had to get control of this conversation back. "What about you? How are you managing with that hand?"

"Don't I seem fine?"

She did. But Zoey wanted to keep her on the line anyway. "I should get back to Vancouver. I can take the bus. Buses. I worry about you."

Li-leng laughed. "I'm okay. It feels bad, but I take my pain medication. And unlike you, I'm not afraid to ask for help."

"What are you talking about? This whole phone call has been about me asking for all sorts of things. Rides, bus tickets."

"No, I offered all those things, and you rejected them. This thing has been about you feeling bad that you're hung up on someone who you might have to ask for help. You like to be the one who gives people things, but you hate having to admit you need anything at all. So as long as the main danger is that you get in deeper with the kind, hot, rich guy who was starved for sex with you and have to stay with him in a really nice inn, then I'll aim for the weekend to come get you. And we should be okay. Okay?"

Zoey opened her mouth and shut it. She was *fine* asking for help.

Maybe. What she didn't need was this kind of insight in her life right when she actually was in a position where she had to listen to her roommate for a change.

"I wonder if the B&B has huge, soft beds," Li-leng said before hanging up.

It felt like Zoey could hear her friend's laughter even after the call ended.

She was going to have to do it. She was going to have to, ugh, talk to Davy and accept help from him.

Again.

She might even enjoy it, *oh no.*

A message pinged on her phone. Another message from Davy.

This time she really had to respond. She took a deep breath. I'm okay. I'm at the library to recharge my phone.

A silence. Then the little dots started moving. OK, just checking. I sent the address.

And that was it.

He was casual. She could do that. Pretend it was all fine.

She took a deep breath and typed on her phone. Have the address now. Thanks. See you soon—

She backspaced. That seemed too eager. See you in a little bit.

No, take out the *little*. See you in a bit.

She slumped back.

One more message appeared.

I was worried about you.

She stared at it. Then sighed.

Why did he have to be this way? All…vulnerable and good and soft and honest.

She was going to have to tell him to toughen up.

She sighed, unplugged her charger, and headed out of the library.

"Okay, here's what I found out," George said, bursting out into the yard where Davy was chopping up some firewood.

While waiting for Zoey, he'd fixed the back door, and hammered down a loose board on the porch. The place was in worse shape than he remembered.

Zoey still wasn't back, but at least she'd answered his text.

"They say your girl was at the library talking with her 'friend.' Maybe an accomplice. She's planning on leaving town as soon as possible. And apparently she's also involved with a rock star."

He blinked.

"George, have you shared all this information with someone other than me?"

George shuffled her feet.

Davy stared her down.

"Okay, I texted Angela and she tweeted it. It went viral, if I do say so myself. At least two retweets."

Davy pressed his lips together. "George, you're not really helping us here by starting wild rumors."

George waved her arms wildly. "I didn't start any of *those* ones. And besides, this'll work to confuse the police."

"I don't have anything to hide from the police. If anything, I want things to be clear. I want the truth to come out. I didn't do anything. If the RCMP or anyone else in this town end up hurting Zoey, you and I will be responsible."

George looked defiant, the old shit-stirrer.

"Tell Angela to take it down, please."

"Do I have to?"

"George, I'm asking you to help me."

"No, you're asking me to help this woman who you like and who really doesn't sound like she's good enough for you."

"She's—Zoey is beautiful and smart, and she tries very hard to take care of everyone—sometimes irritatingly so. She was there when I had one of my anxiety attacks, George, and…she helped me. No judgment. And when Rudy Durrell decided to call the cops on me because he got injured while trespassing at my house she defended me. She is not this—this film noir character you seem to think she is."

George blinked.

Her face cleared. "Fine. I'll call, try to do some damage control. And take down the TikTok I made."

She zoomed out of the yard, eager to start on her new project.

He really had a talent for attracting grumpy older women.

His phone rang. "You're not going to believe this," Zoey said, "but I did get a little lost."

She sounded so annoyed with herself. He almost laughed, out of relief, out of the knowledge that she'd probably wandered around Narrow Falls for at least a half an hour before finally breaking down and calling him.

"Can you describe where you are?"

"Well, I'm on one of the side streets. There's a big patch of what looks like a jungle."

"Oh, yeah, that's the front yard. George likes to keep it a little wild."

He hoped it was only casual interest coming out in his voice, and not the utter and frantic relief he felt that she was arriving safely back in his domain.

But she wasn't Baby. She wasn't a damaged bird. He couldn't keep her and soothe her and feed her forever. He couldn't even ask her to do that, because she might agree.

He couldn't do that to her.

"I don't see a house. I see a path, but I don't want to walk down it if it's private property. We've already had enough of that kind of thing today."

"Let me come around from the back."

He started walking, and in a few seconds, she emerged out of the trees and grass. She was here, and safe, and glowing in the sunlight, and frowning and whole enough to be surly and herself. He added *Cut down the overgrowth in the front* to his mental list.

But thank goodness she was here. He wanted to hustle her around and hide her from George and everyone else. He wanted to hide himself.

It would probably be easy enough in this tangle of bramble.

He put his hands out, saw her looking at them, and stuffed them behind himself in his pockets.

It was ridiculous to want to hold someone he'd last seen only a couple of hours ago.

"Well, I guess I took the right path," she said, her voice sounding gruff.

He nodded. He was going to be ridiculous. "Can I hug you?"

"Yeah."

She stumbled toward him, and he held her. He didn't know how else to describe it: his body loved hers. The scent of her hair made the air smell better, he could finally feel his heartbeat when she pressed her arms around his rib cage. When she talked, he could feel the blood singing through his veins in accompaniment.

"How does anyone ever find this place?" she said. "You can hardly see the house and it doesn't even have a sign. No one in town had ever heard of it."

Another twinge of guilt assuaged by the fact that she was grumbling in his ear. He closed his eyes.

"George manages. I think she advertises the wildness of it. Also, I think technically she has people make their own breakfast."

"So it's basically a bed." She pulled away a little. "There are beds, right?"

She was delicious and round, and of course he wanted to take her to that bed.

He cleared his throat. "It's got a few. You don't have to—I mean, I'd like to, but I'm not expecting—"

She drew away completely this time. "Yes, I got that loud and clear."

"Zoey, I want—"

"There you are!" George interrupted.

She strode around the side through the tall grass of the yard, bracelets jangling, her long skirt sweeping dried leaves and twigs behind her. "You must be the girl Davy's gone on."

Davy winced.

But that didn't stop George. Nothing stopped George. "I'm Georgette, the manager of the Innlet! You're just as beautiful as Davy said. So delicate. Like a doll. I just want to pinch your—"

Zoey held up her palm. "Don't."

George dropped her hand. "Well!"

Davy cleared his throat. It made him a little uncomfortable, but he had to say it. "George, not everyone likes to be touched."

"Especially pinched," Zoey added.

"But how do we express love if not through touch?"

"I don't know you. So let's leave love aside for now."

George huffed. "Well, I love everyone."

It was pretty clear to Davy that she did not love Zoey—so far. But there was hope! Davy let it drop.

"George, I need to talk with Zoey about a few things, so you can finish making those phone calls you were supposed to make."

"Fine," George sulked.

"I'm not the warm, likable heroine she wants me to be," Zoey observed as George stomped back to the house.

"No, but that's okay."

"You're not going to say, *She'll come around*? Or try to play peacemaker."

"It's my natural urge," Davy admitted, "but my sister hated it when George pinched her cheeks, too. And it's hard for me not to try to make peace with it when you've been told your whole life you're supposed to be nice to older people."

"It's a mess, isn't it?"

They were wary, but at least they were smiling together

again. "Zoey," Davy said again, because he liked saying her name. Because it meant she was nearby.

Why couldn't he ask her to stay with him again?

Because they'd only known each other four days, and because she was going places in life. She needed intellectual stimulation. And he was going...back to a remote island.

But Zoey had closed her eyes. "When you say my name like that, it makes me feel like—"

He was so close to her. "Like what, Zoey?"

She opened her eyes. "Never mind. It's very kind of you to let me have a room here. You're always kind to everyone, aren't you?"

There was something about the way she said that, as if she admired him, but was still unhappy about it.

"I try?" he said, struggling to figure out what she was trying to tell him. He'd been bombarded with too many feelings today, especially his own. His natural urge was to attempt to make everyone smile, and it was stressing him out that there was no way to manage that under the circumstances.

This was why he needed to stay alone.

"I don't know what I'm saying," Zoey muttered half to herself.

It was a relief, because he couldn't quite follow her, either.

"Kids," George yelled from the porch. "Come in for dinner. You must be hungry."

"She pinches cheeks and calls us kids?"

Davy sighed. "I'm sorry everything's so..." he said. It was too overwhelming to think about.

Another ghost of a smile came over her lips. He let himself have a tiny measure of pleasure out of it. "I thought I said I didn't want to hear *sorry* from you anymore."

"I think you need to hear it again for what you may be about to eat."

★ ★ ★

"Foraging," Zoey said, her voice sounding a little weak, even to her.

It wasn't that the food was bad, as Davy had warned her. Or that it wasn't presented nicely.

It was that Zoey was a little afraid of it.

She stared at her plate. It was full of mushrooms. Ordinarily, she liked them, but ordinarily she also didn't have a death wish.

Zoey was hungry. The diner pancakes had been so long ago, and she'd spent a long time wandering through Narrow Falls.

She briefly considered grabbing a leaf from the wildflower centerpiece and eating that, but she was sitting at what seemed an enormous distance from Davy, with George in the middle, watching her, and there was no way to be unobtrusive.

Had she really expected a romantic dinner while she sat with Davy and his former babysitter?

Maybe she *had* been hoping for that. It was a stupid hope. She'd had many dinners with him. Some had been sexy and fun. And wonderful.

Instead, she took a big swig of water, eyed the mushrooms, and attempted not to remember what it was like to watch someone have their stomach pumped.

"I'm trying to be a more adventurous cook," George was saying. She had changed into a festive caftan of blue shot with silver thread that Zoey envied if she were honest with herself. Zoey was wearing the clothes she'd arrived at Davy's island in. Even though she'd washed them, she felt grubby and underdressed.

She was the mushroom here.

"The world is full of ingredients," George was saying. "The dessert I'm serving, for instance, is spiked with pepper."

The woman was trying. Davy was right about that. Zoey just wished George didn't have to attempt quite so much right now. But maybe there were a few more courses left. Hopefully they hadn't been dug up from the wild backyard.

"Are there any other special spices or home-uh-grown seasonings in the other dishes?" Zoey asked, pushing a little around on her plate.

"Nothing complicated usually."

It wasn't quite a no.

"I was thinking I could practice more so that we could make money touting this place as a foodie destination," George added, turning to Davy. Her voice was so hopeful. "I envision it as sort of like spa cooking—with good whole ingredients—but more rugged and earthy."

She turned to Zoey. "Give me your honest opinion. As an outsider. Davy already loves my cooking, so he's biased."

She patted Davy's hand.

At least he had the grace to look guilty.

He shoveled another forkful of mushroom into his mouth and Zoey hoped this day wouldn't end with a drive to the nearest hospital. Who knew where that could be in a town this size.

Zoey cleared her throat. "Everything has looked great so far, and it's good to hear you're experimenting with flavors and ingredients. I'm not an expert, but uh, I don't know if I'm prepared to eat foraged foods, though."

George glowered at her.

"It's a good start, George," Davy jumped in before George could begin flinging the mushrooms at Zoey. "Be prepared to give a talk about the local ingredients to guests, though. Maybe you might need backup dishes for people who might be cautious."

George beamed at Davy and jumped up to clear the plates.

She shot down Zoey's offer to help with a look more poisonous than the mushrooms.

"I don't think she likes me," Zoey said.

"You'll grow on her."

"Like a fungus?"

He snorted and put down his water, and she had to giggle. It was almost normal and nice to be around him. Well, except for the giggling. She didn't usually do that.

But, of course, she started thinking again, and Davy must have sensed it because he said, "Hey, what's the matter? Are you all right? I don't think George would try to poison you, at least not at first."

Zoey tried to keep her voice light. This was what she wanted, wasn't it? To be normal around him? "She has a waiting period?"

"At least a couple of weeks. Plus poison isn't her style."

She watched him as he got up and sat in the spot George had occupied.

Zoey couldn't help it. Every time Davy came near, she wanted to just let her eyes fall closed. He could do anything to her then—she'd let him do anything to her. Touch the delicate skin of her wrist, lean in to bite her, kiss her.

She wanted it too much.

She kept her eyes open and took a calming mouthful of water instead. "She strikes me as more of a hatchet person."

Davy watched her alertly, too. But his voice was rueful. "You strike me as similar. Maybe more of a hammer."

His voice seemed fond. But no, she had to be stern. "That's flattering."

"A sexy hammer."

Definitely fond. She could not be taken in by it.

"What does that even mean?"

Her question came out breathy.

His voice crinkled with laughter. "I don't know why I imagined you and George might get along."

She sighed and looked down, wishing there was wine—but

the kind with professional labels and a screw top and not made of dandelions and sealed with a homemade cork or a pine cone or whatever George might use. "You always see the best in people, Davy."

"Why are you saying it that way? As if that makes you sad?"

"Because I'm petty and jealous, I guess," she said. "I don't even know if those are the right words. Because I wish I were really special."

To you.

Oh, she knew he was right. She couldn't go live on the island with him. How could she even want that? She needed to be challenged, but maybe not as challenged as she was in her program. She needed her friends. Well, mostly Li-leng. Besides, she hardly knew the man.

Except. She understood the important parts of him.

Davy started shaking his head. "How can you believe that about yourself? The day I met you changed everything for me."

Zoey was suddenly too scared to continue with this conversation. It was too close to what she had been thinking. She tried a joke. "Sure, I've made things different. Like almost getting arrested with you for assaulting a police officer despite the fact that we didn't do it?"

"That's on Rudy," he said seriously. "I'm thinking now that he would have tried something even if you hadn't been there. It would have been worse without you. You defended me from the start, you questioned Rudy and cast doubt on everything he said. You put him in his place. But more importantly, you helped me see I deserved to be defended. I—I was surprised at how willing I may have been to let Rudy make me feel like I was wrong not just then, but for years. But you didn't do that, and it makes me understand that maybe I haven't always let people look out for me."

He turned toward her, and Zoey was surprised to see a sheen

of tears over his eyes. Or maybe the tears were hers. She swallowed. "Davy, you're loved. Maybe you live too far away from everyone to see it. But you're loved."

By me. But she'd already said it before. It wasn't as if she were ready or able to do anything about it.

But she could do one thing.

She was about to reach for his hand when George barreled in again.

She set down a plate of brownies and glared at Zoey.

"Dessert," she said.

She looked defiantly at Zoey. "Nothing foraged. Everyone says my brownies are delicious."

"I didn't mean to be—"

George took the largest rectangle of brownie, which was teetering on top of the pile, and slid it onto a plate in front of Zoey.

Despite what Davy said, this was probably definitely poisoned.

It smelled good, though.

"I should have asked if you're allergic to nuts," George said.

"I'm n—"

George cut her off. "Anyway. I'm off to bed."

"Please stay," Zoey said. "These seem wonderful."

"I don't want to interrupt the love fest in here."

George glared at Davy. "For the record, I'm happy to defend you whenever you need it. From Rudy, from the police, and especially from your father. I love you no matter what."

Davy hung his head. "George, I didn't mean—"

"God knows you're like a son to me."

She stomped out before he could reply. Zoey heard the back door slam.

Davy watched George leave, then turned to Zoey.

They both stared at the brownies.

"I think these are going to taste like guilt," Davy said, moving his chair closer to hers.

"She's always going to be in your corner, too. If you let her. Maybe you feel bad for not realizing how much she loves you, but you don't have to feel guilty about asking for help."

Davy dropped his head and pressed his hands to his eyes. Then he straightened his shoulders as if coming to a conclusion about himself. Then he looked up at her and, without breaking his gaze, reached over and broke off a piece of brownie from her plate and put it in his mouth, then offered a piece to her.

Zoey took the piece cautiously and nibbled. It was chocolaty and delicious. Maybe she should have believed more in George's cooking. Maybe they all needed more faith.

"Zoey," he said softly.

Her heart rate sped up. "Zoey," and this time when he said her name, his voice was low and rich. "We have to talk."

"You keep saying you want to talk," she whispered. "But I don't want to talk." Then for the first time in what seemed like years, she reached out and grabbed what she really wanted.

CHAPTER 16

VARIOUS COMMOTIONS

Zoey had taken a fistful of Davy's shirt and was towing him toward her with surprisingly strength.

He tried to slow his mind down to think about what she was saying, even as his body kindled at the sight of her flushed cheeks and her brilliant, intent eyes, even as he saw the lines of her body as she breathed in and out.

"I was so worried about you today," he stammered as she began kissing his neck.

What did it mean that he didn't like being apart from her for even a couple of hours?

They were alone in the house. The kitchen lights were out, and George had gone to her cottage. Davy supposed she'd left dishes in the sink. He'd take care of them later, like he always did.

"I think…" He didn't want to think. He wanted to feel the entire lush weight of her on him, to know that she was there. He wanted to be surrounded by her.

They leaned into each other at the same time, the old dining room chairs creaking in alarm at their sudden movements.

"Zoey," he said.

"Don't say that," she said, her fingers sliding across his chest. "I can't control myself when you say that."

"Zoey," he said again, smiling as he kissed her and pulled her onto his lap.

"You're exasperating," she said, gripping his hair hard.

"I'm sorry." He pushed his hand under her T-shirt and moved it up to feel her full breast. But it seemed...crinkly?

"I thought I told you not to say that to me, either."

"I won't, but what is this I'm feeling?"

Love was making his fingers detect odd things?

"It's the slide. Put it down and go back to what you were doing."

He slid it out and slapped the envelope down on the table and turned his attention back to her nipple and his thumb. She gasped, almost in outrage, and twisted on his lap, her hips and thighs unable to stop moving against him.

He pulled the tight bra up so that his hand had more room under her shirt. "Is it weird to be jealous of a slide that gets all your attention and got to live here?"

Zoey didn't answer. She was sucking his neck hard, harder every time he brushed her nipple, every time he stroked up her skin. With his other hand, he unzipped her shorts and pushed his fingers into her. She bit him, and the quake that went through his body as he tried to restrain his own liquid desire made her grind down more firmly into him.

Fuck.

The chair creaked ominously, the spindly legs thumping and lifting on the rug as they struggled with and against each other. Zoey had managed to unbutton his fly now, and as she reached inside, his knee flew up and banged on the dining room table.

Forks and dishes crashed against each other.

"We should probably go to—"

"No."

Zoey reached down, pulled with a long, firm, sure hand, and squeezed. "Do you have condoms?"

"Yes. I bought some in town."

He started reaching into his back pocket, but she grabbed them from him, the strip of plastic crackling in her hands. She tore open the first packet and threw the rest down. She stood and stripped off her shorts and underwear and slowly bent and breathed over him before slowly, languorously rolling it on him.

She paused and looked up at him, and he thought he would burst out of his skin. He gripped the seat of the chair and felt the straggly bits of plywood on the undersides crumble in his grip.

It was almost like being trapped in place, his shirt pulled up his belly, his jeans splayed open, his cock cased in pristine latex as if it had survived a great destruction.

She was still kneeling, stroking him, her face tender, yet a little cruel as she watched him, because she knew. She knew exactly how intensely he needed more, how his very bones stretched his skin so much they threatened to burst. *She knew him now,* knew how far she could take him.

Davy's grip on the chair tightened, and it creaked under him again as he shifted from trying to restrain himself.

Zoey stood abruptly, her movements decisive as she moved over him, grasped him, and took him inside her. The small part of his brain that wasn't blossoming in an agony of pleasure, the part of him that could think, wanted to laugh about how direct she was, even in her movements, even in the way she surged up and down against him.

He let go of the chair now and pulled her shirt off finally, so that he'd be able to watch the jounce of her breasts, lick her right there, where the sweat trickled between them. He grasped the underside of her thighs, helping her help him.

That knot that had been tight in his chest ever since the morning began to loosen. Despite the seriousness of this moment, despite the desperation, he almost wanted to smile. The corners of his mouth even began to pull up—it wasn't quite there, but it was something.

She clasped herself around him now as he bucked up into her, holding tight even as her body shielded him, a grinding sob coming from her throat. He groaned, too. It was too fast, too much. He had to do something for her.

He raised one slippery hand and pushed it between them, trying to feel his way to her clit through the hot cave created by their bodies.

Another hiss from her. She bit his shoulder and a growl came out of his throat.

He could feel the heavy liquid pulse inside him hammering with increasing pressure, wanting to explode. She was arching, her eyes going dark and almost angry, and then they were both past caring. His body surged into hers wildly and she slammed down on him with equal fierceness. And then, for one moment, he was on the perilous edge, a groan coming from him, from her. Then they were both in pieces, just limbs, light, sweat, and tangled hair.

"Are you all right?" he gasped.

"Stop asking me that," she said, collapsing against his chest. But judging by her smile, her heart didn't seem to be in it.

They'd knocked over a nearby chair in their fury, and it had taken a few forks with it, too. Or so he thought. Maybe the cutlery had fallen.

He was going to have a few bruises.

Zoey grunted, and looked down at him, still a little dazed.

234 | OPAL WEI

But she shook herself off slowly and looked around at the ruins of the dining room, as she rolled herself off of him.

"I don't know what came over me," she said.

Overwhelming lust? Uncontrollable desire? Maybe that love she'd mentioned?

It was sad how hopeful he was, sitting here among the ruins of dinner. Even now, after that bruising, blissful, and strangely emotional session—he didn't know anything anymore—he wanted more of her fierceness, her force. He always wanted more.

He sat up and reached for her and pulled her down on his lap again. The chair creaked ominously.

"This is a mess," she said, her voice grumpy yet oddly delighted. "We made such a goddamn freaking mess."

And she threw her limbs out in delight, knocking a stray fork across the room.

She was smiling.

"I can be a new person."

"Not too new."

"I don't have to be worried all the time."

"Of course you don't."

He wasn't sure what she was talking about, but he liked that she was happy. He'd made her happy. He got them both up, tied the condom, and started a trash pile.

She leaned against him as he worked, pillowing her head with her arms. "I can just have sex whenever I want," she said.

He swallowed painfully. Would that be with him? It couldn't be, not if he stayed on the island. His chest tightened.

"I can be fun! And spontaneous."

He closed his eyes and tried to focus on Zoey. "You've always been that way to me. From the minute you made me hold your bag at the lab door, the minute you slammed out of the cab to get my slide and showed up at the dock and insisted you come to the island. You're fearless, and—and emotionally brave."

He, on the other hand, was not.

"I can be emotionally brave," Zoey said with enough emphasis that Davy knew she was trying to convince herself.

She turned from him, her ass bare. He couldn't help staring up at her. "I should go to the bathroom so I don't get a UTI or something. And then I need to talk to my sister. I have to explain everything to her. But you and me, we aren't done here. We need to talk."

He wanted to agree with her—he'd been wanting to talk ever since they got off the boat and onto the mainland, but he kept getting distracted.

Zoey bent to grab her discarded clothing, which afforded him another view of the flex of her thighs, and she went off. He sighed, stood up, restored himself as best he could, washed his hands, and cleaned up some of the mess they'd made.

They'd just had dining-room-shattering sex. He should be completely serene and happy now. But instead, he felt restless and worried, not just about the fate of his wildlife preserve, but about Zoey going out there being wild and wonderful and still as smart and motivated before, but without him.

He was just putting away the dishes, when George burst in through the back door, wearing a kimono and a pair of boots. "Davy," she said, "you've got to leave! I just heard they're going to try to arrest you."

The commotion made Zoey return from the bathroom. George appeared to be flying around the kitchen, the sleeves of her robe flapping, making her look like a confused bat. Davy was watching her, waiting for her to calm down.

"What's happening?"

Zoey turned to Davy. "She didn't find out about the naked in the dining room, did she?"

"You have to leave now!" George said. "The cops can't catch you! I was listening to the scanner. They're coming to get you!"

"Why would they be coming to get Davy?"

Davy said, "They questioned me about Constable Dutta's injury."

"What? They seriously believe you had something to do with it, even after we both explained what happened with Rudy? That's ridiculous. I'm an eyewitness to the fact that he wasn't the one who tried to wrestle the tranq gun away."

"They don't trust you because they think you're his moll," George said.

"I'm his what?"

"His moll. His gangster girlfriend. You'd be willing to lie to save him from the clink. The pokey!"

"I—"

Davy said, "She watches a lot of old movies."

Zoey turned. "Never mind that! You are not in trouble. You aren't guilty of anything. It's Rudy Durrell's word against mine and yours."

"Unless Constable Dutta woke up and told them it was me who tried to get the tranquilizer gun. And it's my gun. It would be his word and Rudy's against mine."

"But you didn't do it! Stop going with the worst-case scenario. That's my job!"

"I'm going to pack an escape bag for you!" George announced.

She whirled around and grabbed a reusable bag from the hook.

"I'm going to turn myself in," Davy said. "I should go to the station."

"What about a lawyer? Did you call one?"

"I can call one there. Isn't that what they always say on those shows?"

"No. You don't even know they're going to bring charges."

"They're definitely going to bring charges!" George screeched. She dumped a small wheel of cheese in the bag.

"You have to do this right. You call a lawyer right now. You don't wait until the police come knocking."

"I wouldn't even know where to find one."

"Did you have someone arrange for the sale of this house? Did you have permits and things?" Zoey asked.

"Mariela Peterson," George said.

"But she's probably asleep. It's late. Doesn't she have children?" Davy said.

"Call her!" George and Zoey said together.

Davy pulled out his phone and thumbed through slowly. Zoey felt the impatience build up like steam behind her eyeballs. She loved this man. She felt like it was safe to admit this now that she was probably going to have to kill him for stressing her out.

"Hi. Hi, Mariela, I'm sorry to call so late but—"

Neither George nor Zoey bothered to pretend they weren't listening.

"Oh, so you've already heard—" said Davy.

George and Zoey glanced at each other briefly.

"No, she's not a gangster's moll!" Davy said.

"She's asking about you," George said, nudging Zoey.

"Yes, I got that."

"And no, I'm not trying to make the town into a wild animal sanctuary. Mariela, you know that. I definitely don't own a Siberian tiger. That's illegal. I don't even have to consult you to know that."

"Does everyone in this town make up wild rumors?" Zoey asked out loud.

"That, and we stream a lot of shows."

Davy was pacing, his head down.

"Are you sure she's a good lawyer? Is she going to be able to represent him well if...?"

Zoey hoped Constable Dutta was all right, but if he'd been the one responsible for all of this, then Zoey was going to make his life hell.

She should never have offered him tea and cookies.

"Mariela's okay. And even if she doesn't know how to do this kind of lawyering, she'll be able to get someone for Davy who will. He's a good boy. I was his babysitter for a few years, you know, when he and his sister first came to Canada. His parents were never around and his grandma hadn't arrived yet. Not that she knows anything about kids."

"I didn't get that impression from her, either."

George laughed and it sounded like a sob. "He's a good boy."

"I know."

"Always polite. Always thinking of other people."

"I know."

"They should never have let him join that band."

"I know."

"Not that anyone could have stopped him."

George put down the wheel of cheese and grabbed Zoey's hand. "You aren't going to let anything happen to him, are you?"

"I'm going to do my best not to."

"I don't expect you two to clean up after me!"

Davy's voice came out unexpectedly sharp.

"That's not what we meant, Davy," George said pleadingly.

She hadn't let go of her grasp of Zoey's hand. Zoey shook it gently and brought their joined hands up to show Davy, and said, "Davy. Please don't make any impulsive decisions. Just... think about the long term and all you've worked for."

She swallowed. "I know it seems bad from what the rumor mill seems to be saying, but nothing has happened for sure yet. No one has actually accused you. Think of Baby. She needs you not just to feed her, but to advocate for her. What would happen if that—that guy took over everything. Consider that."

George stirred uneasily.

Davy paced. "That's true," he said shortly. "We can't let him. But—" He speared his hands through his hair in frustration. "What are we going to do?"

He turned to Zoey. "I'm no good at planning."

"That's what you say, but you supervised a build on an island! Maybe your plans and the things you did need fine-tuning, but nothing ever works out exactly as it's supposed to. Look at me. I make goals and work and carry things out all the time, and I haven't accomplished the thing I set out to do. And I'll be okay. Let's sit a minute. George will help."

"Yes, I will."

"With George's local knowledge and contacts, and with everything else we've got, if we all stay calm, and put our heads together, with all the things that we know about what's happening we should be able to figure out a few different plans."

"I'll get a whiteboard!" George said gleefully, and she ran off.

"Zoey, if anything happens to me, I want you to know—"

"No," said Zoey. "You promised you would not talk like that."

"I promised I'd stop apologizing."

"Well, I'm making you promise more. I'm asking more of you. I don't give a shit if you think things you touch get screwed up. I'm telling you they don't. You aren't going to act like this is goodbye, because it isn't until I say so!"

Unexpectedly he smiled like the old Davy. "You're going to boss them until they make it right."

"I am."

He took a step toward her and put his lips to her ear. "You're going to tell them what's what."

Her voice came out breathy. "I will."

"I trust you completely."

It was the sexiest thing anyone had ever said to her.

Zoey squeezed her eyes shut. She had to stick to the plan, only this time The Plan was to make sure Davy was okay forever and ever. She was not going to get distracted by the man himself. No matter how good it felt to have him kissing her neck.

They were going to fight this. No one was going to get arrested except Rudy. She was going to come up with something foolproof... In a minute.

Too bad her being bossy seemed to excite Davy so much. She stretched herself into his kiss and he lifted her onto the counter, knocking off George's abandoned cheese wheel. It went rolling off to God knows where.

But just as Zoey was about to take off Davy's shirt, there was a knock at the door.

CHAPTER 17

GEORGE THE DRAGON

With the frustrated sex hormones still floating in his bloodstream, it was hard for Davy to be anxious. Even with the RCMP at his door, all Davy could think about was how soon he could get rid of them so that he could go back to what he and Zoey had been doing.

But before Sergeant Green could say a word, George burst into the room. "You can't have my Davy!" she screeched. "He didn't do anything wrong."

Sergeant Green put up a placating hand. "Ms. Lavalle. We're not here to do that."

Ignoring her, George had barreled to the front, putting herself between Davy and the police.

"He would never do anything to harm another being. In fact, I have watched this boy tear himself to pieces over the mistakes he made when he was a kid. He used to be so funny and easygoing. A smile for everyone. But now look at him."

He'd been about to intervene, but that brought him up short. Davy had been faking cheer so well when he had to. Or so he thought.

Davy's ardor cooled off even more when George continued her roll. "He takes responsibility for things that aren't even his fault. He was going to turn himself over to you even though he's not guilty, because deep down he feels like he has to atone for everything."

Zoey made a noise beside him and put her hand to her mouth. Was she laughing or crying? Davy was starting to get a little angry and the sexual frustration didn't help. He appreciated George was trying to defend him, but he didn't need the woman to tell the police every single detail of his life.

He felt Zoey take his arm.

"Let her do this," she mouthed.

He tried to unbend a little at her words, but he didn't like where this was going.

George was pacing the room now and waving. "I can tell you he didn't hurt that constable of yours because he's fashioned his whole life so that he doesn't have to hurt anyone or anything anymore."

"Ms. Lavalle. If you'd let us explain."

"George."

The word fell from Davy's lips like a warning. But for what, he didn't know. All he understood was that he wanted her to stop talking.

But George, as always, had other ideas. "I know your father probably told you to go to that island there and make sure you didn't hurt the family any more than you did—"

He'd actually told Davy not to ruin their reputation, but same difference.

"But your dad is a jerk. He's probably done more than anyone to make your condition worse over the years than anything you've ever done. Just by telling you you're wrong and bad and bad for other people every time he talks to you."

"Did he say that?" Zoey asked softly and dangerously.

Davy's throat was working.

This was…humiliating. He was a grown man.

George had no right to air all of this shit in front of everyone. But she just kept going.

"Davy, I don't miss the old house. I like my life here. Sure, I was mad when you trashed the garage, and we had to sell. I'd lived in that place for nearly thirty years. I was already old. I didn't know what my life could be without it. I was scared. But look at me here. I've made new friends. I've learned new things. I'm excited about the foraging idea. I'm thriving."

She didn't look like she was thriving at the moment. Her face was pale, and she was sweating. Davy took a deep breath to steady himself. But that old destructive anger in Davy stirred. He tried to clamp it down, but all the high emotions he'd gone through all day started to overwhelm him. How dare George stand here and expose his failings to everyone.

"I wanted you to retire," he said, keeping his voice calm.

It didn't fool Zoey, though. Because she squeezed his arm again.

George might have sensed his anger too because she snapped, "I don't want to be wrapped in cotton. You might like that for yourself, but it won't work for me."

"What is that supposed to mean?"

"No friends, no real connections. Because you're so afraid of hurting other people. Or maybe getting hurt yourself." George turned to the police. "I don't want his mental health to suffer anymore."

"Stop it! Stop!"

He wanted to stamp his feet and put his hands over his ears. "George, no one asked you to talk. Now they all know that I've got mental health issues, and they probably think I did it."

Zoey started talking and so did the police. But George's face twisted. "Davy, I wanted to help."

"I know you don't have much in your life," Davy said. George gave a gasp, but he went on, "But that doesn't mean you get to just act impulsively and give in to every one of your feelings, and just hope for the best. This is not helping. You're making it worse!"

Davy turned to walk away. Screw the police. Screw George. Screw everyone. He was going to retreat to his island right now. As for Zoey, if she wanted to wreck her life by follow-ing him, that was up to her, but he wasn't going to talk about this anymore.

He was halfway to the kitchen when he heard Sergeant Green say, "We're not coming to arrest Mr. Hsieh."

Davy paused. Well, that was good news at least. He still needed some air.

There was a flurry of running and stomping that he was ready to ignore. Still, something kept him from going out into the night. He was paused at the back door when he heard Zoey's voice, a new tone in it, ringing with authority. "We need to get her to a hospital."

He spun around and sprinted back to see George being low-ered gently to the ground. She was clutching her chest, her face gray. Zoey hung over her, murmuring and doing what looked like a quick assessment.

Sergeant Green had run off to pull the cruiser round. Zoey looked up and right at Davy, her eyes piercing right through all the heavy, red feeling that had been swirling around him. She said clearly, "Get over here right now. We need your help."

God he was in love with this woman.

But he didn't have more time to think about it. Zoey had turned back to her patient. And in a minute, he was helping to carry George out to the waiting police car.

★ ★ ★

This was Zoey's second time in an emergency clinic in the last four or five days. It was beginning to feel a little like home.

If home smelled like disinfectant and had glaring white walls.

Davy was glaring right back at them, so he fit in, too.

Then, as if he'd lost the staring contest with the wall, he slumped. "The last thing I said to George was so…"

Davy put his face in his hands.

Zoey held him. "Are you doing okay?"

"I'm just so…angry," he murmured after a minute.

"At George?"

"Yes? No? At everything? At myself? But I'm scared that she doesn't know how much I love her. No one in my life will know because I keep them away."

He was looking right at her. But the words weren't for her. Were they? She swallowed and said, "Davy, she knows. She knows you're always here for her, even when you're far away, even if you're walking away."

"She wouldn't be in the ER if it weren't for me."

"No. You didn't make her collapse. You didn't give her that pain. She'd still be at the emergency clinic because you would've gotten her here on time."

It was funny to be the calm, reassuring one who was taking things in stride. Oh sure, in medical school she'd studied how to deal with these things, but what if she didn't know what she was doing even as everyone looked to her for guidance, logic, knowledge, skill?

No wonder she hadn't wanted to actually practice medicine.

But now, it didn't seem so terrifying. She'd handled it— no, the police and Davy and she had all worked together. She didn't have to do it alone.

For once, she had no idea what was going to happen to her life, but she knew then she didn't want to figure it out by herself. Didn't *have* to.

Davy said, "What I just said to George, it was like the talk my dad gave to me when he came to visit me in the rehab clinic. *Why didn't you think before you acted? Why didn't you think of your family and what this all would do to us?* He said it in Mandarin, then in English, as if he didn't think I'd understand if he just told me one way."

"Your voice changed when you spoke to George. It became more—I don't know, like most of the time, when you talk I feel like it comes from here."

She put his hand on his chest, and it was hard to ignore the hard thud of his heart. "But when you said that to George, it came out of your—"

"Nose. My dad talks out of his nose," Davy said. "He's always searching for something. Always sniffing for blood."

"Oh."

"Yeah."

She'd known his father was terrible. This made it worse.

Thank goodness Davy had George. Even though Zoey knew it was ridiculous, she felt unaccountably guilty for not being able to get along with the woman at first.

Her heart was in the right place. She was trying, and she'd been the one person who'd loved and taken care of Davy. She was tough, though, and Zoey didn't think she'd had a heart attack, although with the pain on her left side, it had been better to be sure. Zoey had a feeling the woman would be all right.

"Come here," Davy said quietly. He rolled up his hoodie and put it on the bench in the waiting area.

Zoey huffed a little as she sat heavily on it. Since when had she become so old? The bench didn't seem wide enough to hold her butt, but as she settled against Davy, she felt better.

He didn't have a particularly soft body, but his shoulder was firm and comforting, especially when he pulled her in closer.

"I'll go check with the nurses again in a few minutes."

"I'll phone Li-leng," she said. "Not that she can do anything."

Davy paused. "You could go home, back to the inn. I'll stay here and make sure things go all right."

"I don't want to leave you, Davy."

"But—"

"You're always sending me away for my own good. And I'm tired of it."

She could feel Davy let out a long breath. "This isn't exactly how I pictured the rest of the evening going when we were in the dining room."

Nothing was how she'd pictured it this morning when she woke up on Davy's island. Or even a week ago when she was back in Vancouver in her lab. But somehow, despite the fact that she was in a small-town emergency clinic now, and her supervisor was going to kick her out of her program if she didn't quit first, and the bench was maybe the hardest piece of wood that ever was hewn from a log, she found her eyelids getting heavy. And despite it all, Davy made a fine pillow.

Davy grunted under her. "You're muttering to yourself."

His voice sounded amused.

"I always do that when I'm falling asleep. I get outraged because I'm tired."

"I know."

It was the last thing she heard before she drifted off.

Davy's grandmother was here, and it was his worst nightmare.

Davy had fallen asleep too, after the nurses had confirmed whatever George had didn't appear life threatening. Despite the fact that he was worried and angry, he felt strangely content with Zoey curled up against his side. It was hard to understand, because he was sure he'd never experienced a mix of frustration and stress and love like this before.

All those songs he'd written before about being in love had been wrong. Sure, he'd jotted down lyrics about sleepless nights, and *baby, you don't understand me*.

Most of his compositions nowadays were about yogurt drinks and, if he was lucky, luxury cars.

Those at least made sense. And the love songs? They were because either someone found someone hot, or someone did something wrong, and pain followed.

But what he was feeling as he drifted between sleep and waking wasn't so straightforward. Because he wasn't sure who was wrong, and he wasn't sure this was pain so much as it was a feeling of helplessness at the fact he'd felt like he'd failed George again, and that Zoey had to take care of everyone. He was beginning to realize that a part of this was his brain chemistry being a jerk, and it was something he was going to have to work on. But his grandmother arriving, that was a manifestation of his biggest fear. Because he didn't want her to be ashamed of him again.

Even if, as Zoey pointed out, it wasn't his fault.

It had been a long day.

Too bad he couldn't talk to Zoey about this more, though. He was pretty sure her enormous intellect could hold all these complicated feelings and elements in it. Then again, he couldn't exactly talk to her about her if she was the subject of those complicated thoughts.

Or could he?

She sighed and snuggled closer, burying her nose in his chest and grabbing his shirt in her greedy knuckles. Another overwhelming surge of love swelled through him, his anger and worry a small buoy bobbing along the top.

She snuffled a little in her sleep, her body a warm, open-ended parenthesis.

God, being around her was better than the crashing swell of an orchestra, the heavy beat of a drum.

But now his grandmother was here, ordering him in Mandarin to wake up.

He had barely a moment to rub his eyes before he was caught in the full glare of his A-mà.

Oh, she was furious.

Well, so was he, he realized.

And Zoey was, too. She was already on her feet. "Li-leng, what are you doing here? Did you bring *her*?"

"You should congratulate me for being sensible for a change," the tiny woman who must be Li-leng said. "You gave me her address, and she had a car and money. And you're in a hospital! Although from the way it looks, we interrupted your spooning session."

"I'm not in the hospital! I was asleep! We were waiting to hear about George. Plus, I'm fine! Don't I look fine to you?"

"You have a crease on your cheek, probably from lying on a boy bander all night. Boy band crease."

Davy wasn't sure he liked this Li-leng. But as he tried to figure out why Zoey's roommate was here with his grandmother, he noticed that A-mà's gaze was fixed not on Zoey's animated face but on a point beyond—on George, who was being wheeled out of the room by a nurse.

Damn.

Davy sprang up.

"Ms. Lavalle is fine," said the nurse. "She had acute indigestion. But I'd advise her not to eat so many mushrooms if they disagree with her."

He glanced at George. It hadn't been a heart attack or a

stroke. Zoey was right. He hadn't made her collapse. It was the mushrooms.

He went to her, knelt, and took her fingers. George gave him a grimace and a half smile. He was forgiven.

But that was the only quiet moment in the room. Li-leng was throwing up her hands and saying she'd hoped Zoey would be grateful she'd brought a car. A-mà kept her eyes on George and Davy.

Davy sighed and stood up. "Let's all go back to the B&B and continue fighting there," he said. He grabbed the sweatshirt and started pushing George's wheelchair, effectively herding everyone out the doors. "A-mà, is that your car? Did you drive?"

"Of course not," she said in Mandarin. "I would never be able to drive these country roads and onto that ferry. That young woman did. She knew where to go. She lied and told me you were in jail. I brought cash. But at the police station they said you were here."

"I'm walking home," George said. "The rest of you can ride in that thing."

Zoey said, "You're in a wheelchair."

"That's just for show."

"I won't ride in the same car as *her*," A-mà said, though it wasn't clear who she meant at this point since she was glaring at everyone.

Zoey took charge. "Then Li-leng and I will walk with you while Davy drives them home."

A-mà eyed her narrowly. "I'll ride."

A-mà made a show of handing him the keys. Davy swallowed his frustration and helped George into the back seat, where she'd be more comfortable. "This is the small town you've been hiding yourself in," A-mà observed in Mandarin as he came to give her his arm.

"I'm mostly on the island. But this place has what I need."

She sniffed.

"He's doing a good job," Zoey said before turning around and walking off with her friend.

God, he loved her.

Davy got his A-mà into the passenger side and started the car.

She said, "So good a job that I have to be woken in the middle of the night to drive across the province with a strange girl with bandaged hands to meet my grandson at the hospital again."

"You didn't have to come. I wasn't sick or in jail, A-mà. I'm not sure why you came."

A hesitation. "I wasn't sure the message hadn't gotten garbled."

He noticed his grandmother's hands gripped her bag white-knuckled as she said it. Then released slowly. Had she been worried that *he* was in the hospital?

He glanced in the back where George kept her eyes closed. She did that when A-mà chose to talk in Mandarin in front of them, knowing that she was probably the subject of conversation.

He said reluctantly, "You should know the police visited the house."

"Why?"

He shrugged. If they'd wanted to take him away, they hadn't done anything about it. "There was an accident on my property. But… I was trying to help. And if they don't understand that, then…we'll come up with a plan."

God, Zoey was starting to rub off on him.

"If they don't understand, I'll make them sorry," A-mà said.

Davy looked at his grandmother in surprise. "The police are that way," she declared. "Always blaming. Always wanting to arrest people whenever they feel like it. Everyone said

Canada was better. They respect people here. Ai-ya, people are the same everywhere and police especially are the same everywhere."

They turned up the street to George's house. Once again, he winced at the forbidding trees and tall grasses, the overgrown driveway, the general air of abandonment. The huge windows of the front room were obscured from sunlight, and the porch was in disarray. He wanted to live like a hermit but that didn't mean George did. And maybe *he* didn't want to be so remote anymore, either.

He needed to help to maintain the grounds, especially if George had all these ideas for attracting guests. But at least the house was big enough. There would be enough clean rooms for everyone if someone shared, but he doubted A-mà would like it if he stayed with Zoey.

Even as he thought it, a part of him protested. He'd slept on an unforgiving bench and his old bones were still grumbling at him. He used to be able to perform backflips for God's sake! But he'd closed his eyes and managed to fall asleep because Zoey'd been there, warm and reassuring even when she accidentally poked him with her sharp shoulders. Especially when she did that.

He didn't want to be away from her.

The car edged slowly up the long drive to the house. A-mà looked askance at the overgrown garden. "An island isn't enough? When you get to town you live in the woods, too?"

"It's mostly George who lives here, A-mà."

"George."

She said it flatly, her accent making it two drawn-out syllables. *Geooh-geh.*

The woman in the back had no visible reaction. Either she was really tired and wasn't listening to them, or she'd taken his careless words tonight to heart. He would apologize again, this time out loud.

Then, as soon as he got a moment, he was going to call his contractor and a landscaper. He'd make sure George's cottage was in good shape, too.

It wasn't until they got inside the house and he'd gotten George settled that A-mà turned to Davy. "Now," she said, "you're going to tell me why you didn't come to me about this mess earlier."

CHAPTER 18

THE CONSOLATIONS OF BROWNIES

Zoey had lost the slide.

Again.

It was much later in the day. The nap she'd taken had given Zoey a false sense of optimism. Now she was pitching the clothes she'd worn last night into the washing machine when she realized there was an important part missing.

She sat down on the floor in front of the washing machine, the cup of detergent still in her hand.

Where had she put the thing? It had been in her bra. She patted her boobs in case it was still nestled against her bosom, but no crinkly paper sound greeted her.

She'd had it at the library, and she'd kept it until—

Oh.

She raced into the dining room and, setting the cup down, spilled some of the sticky detergent on the dining room table.

The floor had been swept clean. All the dishes were done, the silverware put away. She checked the drawers, the side table. She even looked under some of the remaining chairs.

Her envelope was not there.

Zoey closed her eyes and opened them.

She took the cup of detergent and went back to the laundry room and set the machine.

Her breath seemed very shallow.

She'd been fine last night. But the events of the last few days were starting to hit her. George had gotten sick. They'd spent the night in an emergency clinic. Zoey had had more brushes with the law in the last twenty-four hours than any others combined. She was quitting her program, and she had no more plan. She was in love, and she wasn't sure Davy loved her back. Not that there was anything anyone could do about it.

And she'd lost that connection she had to her former life. The slide was gone.

Again.

Zoey went to the kitchen and pulled out the compost.

It had been emptied.

She looked through the recycling. Also empty. She tried to take a deep breath. Then she went out the back kitchen door to scream.

"Something wrong?" Li-leng popped out of the tall grass, making Zoey cry out again.

"I lost the slide," Zoey said dully.

Li-leng started to laugh.

"I'm so glad you're able to laugh in the face of my complete and utter self-destruction."

"It's just that you usually act like you're so together."

Zoey took a deep breath. "I'm not. Despite how I seem— to you, to the person who knows me probably best of all. I'm really not."

Li-leng rolled her eyes. "I know. That's why I'm enjoying this. It's hilarious seeing you so completely undone by love and circumstance and your own inability to keep your bra on around Davy X."

"His name isn't Davy X," Zoey said with a dignity she didn't feel. "And if you'll excuse me, I'm going to find out where the garbage may have ended up."

"Are you really going to climb a compost pile to find this thing?" Li-leng asked.

Zoey blinked once, then twice.

"You already know you don't need the slide, don't you? There are copies."

"But—"

She wiped her eyes on her sleeve.

"Is this because of Davy?" Li-leng asked after a moment.

"A little. Yes, because of stupid handsome Davy."

"Who isn't so stupid."

"No, he's not. The jerk."

"Does he know how you feel?"

"Yes. Embarrassingly, yes."

"Are you sure he doesn't feel the same way? Because the way he—"

"The way he looks at me? The way he listens to every word I say? The way he holds me at night on the bench in a hospital? What do I do with love? What can I do with this? Love isn't a job. Love doesn't give me a degree. Love won't give me a place to live."

"Davy would."

"I'm not so sure about that. And would I want that? Long term?"

Li-leng thought for a moment. "Look, no matter what happens with him, you don't have to go back to the way things were. You don't have to try to do any of the things you do now. You don't have to work all the time, or eat a vegetable with every meal, or pick up after everyone else, or keep all the cups or whatever—"

"Mugs."

"You don't have to keep all the fucking mugs or stay in this program that's making you miserable."

"But I already put so much time and money into it. I can't be a quitter."

"It's your *life*, Zoey. Don't quit on that, because if you do, you choose a plan over your happiness. Yeah, you invested time and money in becoming a perfect student. But if you don't want to do it, you shouldn't have to make yourself do it for the rest of your existence. You're a planner. Have you imagined what the rest of your days will be like if you keep doing what you've been doing exactly the way you've been doing it?"

A pause.

Zoey found she'd sunk down into the overgrown lawn and was gripping handfuls of grass as if someone were threatening to pull her away from here right at this moment. She didn't want to go back to the lab and sticky-note-stealing Alec, back to smelling faintly of chemicals and sterile air. The truth was, she couldn't even imagine having to go back to the tiny apartment she shared with Li-leng, to the constant smoke alarms, to her small room and her cold bed.

Then Li-leng said, "This is probably a bad time to bring this up, but I think you should know that I'm staying here. I had a chance to talk with George, and she said it would be okay. I want to help her fix the place up so it will really be a functional bed-and-breakfast. I'll pay up the rent on our old place for the month, but you'll have to start looking for another roommate."

"But what about your things? Your dissertation? Your... your hand."

"It was a minor burn, and I felt okay enough to drive. When I go back to get my books and clothes, I'll see the doctor again. And I can always call you."

"This is very sudden."

"You departing on a bike for a remote island with a former pop star was very sudden," her friend noted dryly.

"So, you're quitting? Just like that?"

"Don't you wish you could do it?"

"I am doing it. I—"

She wasn't, though, was she? Why was she still searching for the slide? Especially now. She eyed the compost heap that she'd thought briefly of climbing.

"If I got the slide back," Zoey said slowly, "then I'd still have my options open. I could go back to the lab and act like I hadn't planned to quit."

She could pretend that she wouldn't be hurt if Davy rejected her.

"So you thought it was an open ticket back to your old miserable life? An escape hatch?"

"I like backup plans," Zoey said defensively.

"What would make it impossible to turn back?" Li-leng asked, her eyes gleaming.

Zoey gazed thoughtfully at the compost pile for a minute. A fly buzzed lazily around it. Then she said with great dignity, "I'm going back into the house. I have a phone call to make to my sister."

Once inside, and out of Li-leng's hearing, Zoey made an annoyed *Gaahhhh*. She kicked a cabinet door, which fell askew—well, even more askew. Then she spent some time swearing and trying to fix the thing she'd broken.

She hated when Li-leng was right.

But she had to calm down before she talked to her sister. She brewed tea and found some of George's brownies. She didn't care if they were made from boulders and scat foraged in the backyard. Zoey hadn't eaten since last night—not that she'd consumed much then, either. She needed fortification for the conversation ahead. Not that she thought Mimi would be angry. They didn't talk about those awful years very much. Or at least Zoey didn't. Mimi could casually chat about the patient in the bed next to hers who liked drawing superheroes, or her favorite doctor. But after all these years, Zoey still couldn't manage to bring it up in casual conversation.

She stuffed a huge chunk of brownie in her mouth while she cut up some apples. Her cheeks were as full as a gerbil's when she turned around and found herself face-to-face with Davy's A-mà, who had somehow glided in without a sound.

Zoey, on the other hand, made a honk that was disturbingly like a goose.

"I heard some strange noises. And a bang," A-mà said. She didn't even pretend to look away from Zoey and her predicament. "Are you always this noisy?"

Zoey swallowed the boulder of brownie that was lodged in her throat and coughed a little. A-mà didn't even pretend to glance away politely. She watched dispassionately.

"I was about to…bring you a tray. Why don't we sit down at the table?"

A-mà deigned to sit.

There was a short silence.

A-mà regarded her with expectation.

Zoey tried to make conversation. "Did you have a good car ride here?"

"Of course I didn't have a good journey," A-mà said. "Your one-handed roommate drives these country roads like a Taipei cabbie. Then we had to put the car on a boat because even though this isn't an island it's as difficult as one. I was worried to death about my grandson because I thought he was in trouble. Again."

"He was fine!"

"He's not all right. He hasn't been for years, and his father made it worse."

Zoey blinked. She finally saw A-mà's fury—and fear—for what it was. She said gently, "Davy's doing well for himself. He's writing music. He's trying to achieve some good in the world."

"By feeding a tiger."

"Cougar."

"What's the difference? He'll be the tiger food in the end. Doing good. That's his whole problem. This whole generation of yours with your bellies full and your eyes still full of tears. You're just like him, too. An almost-doctor who lives with a roommate and who has to take the bus."

She took a sip of tea and grimaced.

Li-leng had been talking during the road trip it seemed. Oh well. Davy's grandmother had her values. They'd probably been forged through the kind of hardship that Zoey could barely understand, but they were heavy and immovable.

Zoey had hers, too. She hadn't realized how much she'd lost touch with what she really wanted until she'd flung herself on that boat with Davy.

But Zoey understood A-mà's belligerence now. She was worried about her grandson, and she dealt with it by getting angry and destructive.

A little like Davy had been.

Davy's grandmother was reaching for a brownie. She still had that look of disgust on her face. "George made those," Zoey said, unable to resist poking the cougar.

The old woman froze with the dessert halfway to her mouth.

"George is experimenting."

Zoey grabbed her own brownie and took another huge bite. She was starving. She was going to eat every crumb of this stupid thing and enjoy it. She knew she wasn't going to change this woman's mind about her. Zoey didn't have to justify herself to someone who would never like or understand her. But

she could have compassion for another person who was trying in her own way.

Wasn't that a freeing thought?

Even if things hadn't worked out with research, even if they
didn't with Davy, Zoey had choices. One of her choices was to
not take what Davy's A-mà said about her to heart.

She almost started giggling.

It must have shown up in Zoey's face. "Are you laughing
at me?" A-mà said. "You think it's funny for me to come all
the way up here in the middle of the night and be forced to
eat this—this *baking*?"

It was way she said the word *baking*—in English—that did it.

Zoey started laughing. Her mouth was stuffed with food,
and she was probably going to die choking in front of this elegant old woman who, even if she could do the Heimlich ma-
neuver, probably wouldn't because it would mean she'd have
to touch Zoey's weak, overly sympathetic body.

"If you'll excuse me," Zoey finally gasped, "I have to call
my sister."

"I don't know what you see in her," A-mà began again.

Now that he'd had some sleep, Davy had been trying to escape to town so that he could talk to his lawyer, Mariela. And
maybe go to the hardware store to hire a landscaper and pick
up some equipment and start fixing things himself.

"I drive all the way here in the middle of the night to find
you were not even in trouble."

It sounded like his grandmother would have preferred he
was.

"You were cuddling with *her*, her cheek on your chest,
your hand in her hair. She makes all sorts of strange noises and
tries to give me tea and—and this chocolate dessert, as if this
is her house and her kitchen and she can open up the pantry

and it's hers. And she serves me in her kitchen. As if I'm not important."

"Well, technically it's George's house and mine."

"*George.*" She spit the name out again. "Another one who's using you. She picked you up from school for, what, two years, and gave you snacks, and now you have to buy her a house?"

"You hired her," Davy said mildly.

His grandma looked away.

Davy continued. "She helped me with my homework when I was a kid. She came to the office when I got sick at school and the nurse couldn't get a hold of you or my parents. Long after we stopped paying her, she was my emergency contact. George took me in after rehab. She's not a perfect person, but neither am I. It's because of her I've got a plan for the future."

His grandmother snorted. "She cared for you. I paid the bill. Now we're even."

"Not really."

"Well, you don't have to support her anymore. You give everything of yours away to people who are nice to you."

"She had money for a down payment, and I helped with the rest. We're partners. So what if I did take care of her? What is the worst thing about that?"

They'd paused in front of the grand staircase in the front hall. But now, Davy saw his grandmother glance at the stairs and her hand tightened.

If she hadn't been tired, she would never have let even one of her hairs quiver. In fact, even as they paused, she stood straighter. Bracing herself.

She didn't like the stairs, but she wasn't going to admit this to him. She never wanted to appear vulnerable. "Let's move you to the bedroom down here. It's through this door."

She said nothing.

He put his arm under hers and guided her into the space. She sat down heavily on the bed, something she'd normally never do unless she'd changed into her lounging clothing.

"A-mà, are you all right?"

She waved him off impatiently. "I'm fine. Stop asking me that. Why do you always ask me that?"

"You and Zoey are more alike than you imagine."

"Don't compare me to that girl."

She said it without any rancor.

"I'll get your things from upstairs and put your pills next to your nightstand. There's bottled water over there, but I'll get you a carafe of boiled, cooled water later."

"First you're fighting, then you're fussing," she said, waving him away.

"I think you're the one who's fighting here. I've never been much for yelling and screaming."

She shook her head. "No. You like to please people. Which is why you stay away from them. It's too overwhelming for you. That's why you have those episodes. I stay away from people, too, and I'm fine."

Davy paused. He'd never considered that possibility before.

"A-mà," he asked carefully, "is that why you shut yourself away at the house in Burnaby? Do you get panic attacks?"

"Of course. Doesn't everyone?"

"No. But they can be made manageable."

"I do fine on my own. Alone."

Davy breathed in deep. Suddenly things were a lot clearer. "I thought I did, too."

CHAPTER 19

A CHAT, A CHANCE, AND A CHANGE

Zoey's sister, Mimi, was breathing heavily when she answered her phone. "I'm sorry I forgot to text you back. School's been bananas!"

After another gulp of air, she added dutifully, "But I miss you, too."

"It's fine. Never mind. Are you all right? Where are you? What are you doing? Why are you panting?"

A pause. "I was just out for a run."

Zoey relaxed. "Good. That's fine."

"Of course it's fine."

Zoey could almost hear the rolling of Mimi's eyes. Her sister was still such a *teen*. Zoey paced the creaky floor of her room at the B&B. It was funny how when she hadn't talked to her sister in a while, Mimi became younger, more child-like, more vulnerable in Zoey's mind. It was easy for Zoey to revert to the concerned and (*slightly!*) bossy older sister she had been when they were kids.

But it didn't have to be that way anymore.

"I've been thinking about you a lot lately."

"Oh?" Mimi sounded wary.

Zoey had to laugh at that, even as her heart squeezed. "I'm not going to tell you to quit your creative writing program if that's what you're worried about."

"I might drop it anyway."

"Wait, what? Just like that?"

She made it sound so easy.

"It's not really what I expected. Besides, I still have time to figure it out. I'm still young, unlike you."

"I'm plenty young enough to quit!" Zoey said, her voice rising with indignation. "I have a whole life ahead of me."

"Whoa," Mimi said laughingly. "Sounds like I hit a nerve."

"It's just... I—" Zoey stopped and took a deep breath. Her hand tightened on the phone. "I've decided to drop out of my program, too. I don't think I want to be a cancer researcher. I'm so unhappy with how I'm doing. I wanted it to be different. I hope you're not disappointed in me."

Mimi sounded bewildered. "Why would I be disappointed? It's your life. If you want to be a...?"

They both stopped.

"Ah," said Mimi. "Okay. I sometimes wondered if it had anything to do with when I was sick."

"Mimi, you had to know."

"We never talked about it. And I didn't ask you for this, Zoey."

"I know, honey."

"It's my life. I don't want to be anyone's *inspiration*. That's gross. I mean, I guess I knew in a way, but if you've been sticking with it because of some misguided notion of taking care of me *even though I'm fine*—"

"I'm not. Or at least I'm going to try not to anymore."

"You and Mom and Dad treat me like I'm so fragile."

Zoey closed her eyes. "I know. I'm sorry. You're nineteen, and you're amazing. It's just hard to forget."

"This is a you problem. Not a me problem."

"Yeah."

Another pause. Zoey heard her sister taking a swallow of water.

She hoped Mimi was wearing sunscreen if she was running outside.

Probably best keep that thought to herself at this moment, though.

"So what are you going to do now?" Mimi asked in a more normal tone.

"I don't know."

She wanted to stay with Davy, but that wasn't a goal.

"You could always go into practice."

"I'd have to do my clerkship and residency. I don't even know what's out there for someone like me."

Mimi started to laugh, and Zoey's heart squeezed again. She wasn't usually the one to make Mimi laugh, and she regretted that. "What's so funny?"

"It's just, you're usually the one who's five steps ahead of everyone. It's kind of great that you've abandoned that, and you don't know what you're doing for a change. You're so grumpy about it."

"I'm not. I'm fine."

She was not fine. But she couldn't tell her sister that.

Or could she? "Mimi, that's a lie. I'm so not fine that I almost dove into a compost pile an hour ago."

"What?"

She'd wanted to make Mimi laugh. Instead, she heard it: the concerned-sister voice. Mimi must've listened to it come out of Zoey's mouth a thousand times. She winced at how it sounded. "I thought I could still salvage my career. I needed to find this slide I'd lost, and that I told myself I'd get into trouble for letting out of my hands."

"I don't get it."

"The slide. It was a cytological specimen from an osteo-blastic osteosarcoma."

"The kind of cancer I had."

Zoey had no idea how Mimi could say it so calmly.

"I lost it this weekend, and I went on a whole journey to get it back. But I found out I didn't need it after all. I never needed it."

Mimi waited a moment before she said anything. "Well, if you do find the specimen of that horrible thing again, I hope you step on it and grind it under your heel. Then walk away."

"Mimi."

"Kick that slide's ass."

"That...doesn't make sense."

"I know."

"You want me to destroy it for you?"

"No. From now on if you do anything, do it for you."

Davy hadn't meant to eavesdrop. But he'd been out looking for Zoey and had gotten distracted trying to cut down some of the tall grass in the back. He'd taken his shirt off for the moment and stopped to stare at the outbuildings near the woods when he'd overheard Li-leng's piping voice.

"So, what did she say?" Li-leng was asking.

"She was annoyed with me for putting her in that position."

Zoey's tone was quiet, sad. He put down his shears.

"What are you going to do, then?"

A pause.

Zoey asked, "Are you really staying here? With George?"

"Definitely."

Zoey's voice was hesitant. "Do you think I could do the

same? I want to but I don't know if…other people would like that."

Davy strode out. "No," he said. "*No*. Don't go with George. Stay with me. Please, Zoey."

Zoey popped right up, her hair adorably disheveled. She stared at him.

Or maybe at his chest.

A few feet away Li-leng rose languidly on her elbows and gave his shirtless torso a smirk. "I could be tactful and go," said Li-leng, "but I so want to hear this conversation."

The sun was bright, but Zoey's glare, directed at her roommate, was incandescent. "Go and find some non-poisonous mushrooms for dinner," she said in that irritable voice that Davy loved.

He laughed and pulled his tee back on. Li-leng rolled her eyes, hoisted herself up, and walked back toward the main house. "I should go and sic Davy's A-mà on you both now that we're BFFs from our road trip."

Davy did not miss Zoey's shudder.

"Your grandmother hates me," Zoey said.

"I'm not sure she likes anyone, if that's any consolation."

"She loves you."

"But she doesn't seem to *like* me."

He sat down in the spot Li-leng had abandoned. He took a deep breath, suddenly nervous that she hadn't told him yes. A gust of wind rustled through the grasses as if trying to cover up the silence between them.

"I talked to Mariela at her law office," he said. "She has records of all the letters and permits I applied for. So even if Rudy wants to raise a stink about Baby, she doesn't think he has grounds."

"Oh!" she said. "That's a relief."

Her voice was warm. A rich chord of relief strummed

through him. "Mariela was really eager to tell me about all the rumors circulating about us, so you can probably expect some strange looks when you go into town. One had us being undercover journalists from a travel magazine hoping to write a great story about Narrow Falls that makes it the hottest tourist destination on the Sunshine Coast sort of piece."

"Small towns," Zoey said.

She did not sound like she liked the idea of living in one. He was messing this up. He wiped his hands on his jeans. "It doesn't clear up the other stuff with the police. But I hope Constable Dutta comes through and remembers what happened."

He saw Zoey's hand flex. "He'd better," she growled.

In a calmer voice, she said, "I'm sure he will. There were probably some complications from being shot in the foot like that, but he seems young and healthy, and you *will* be cleared."

She was on his side. He knew she always would be. The dark notes of her most authoritative voice always thrilled him. He had to try to get this right. He cleared his throat. "So I have a plan to run by you."

"Maybe you shouldn't consult me on those since I'm not great at making them."

"It's not set in stone. I'm hoping you'll contribute. A lot."

He sat down beside her, close enough that he could feel the warmth coming from her arms. Her skin was golden, and he wanted to smooth his hand along its softness. But first he had to do this. "I was thinking of moving to the mainland. Here, to Narrow Falls. I can fix up the guesthouse George lives in and the main house, too. I've had experience overseeing green construction at this point. I can work from here."

"Davy, you've invested so much in making a home on the island."

"I'm ready for a new kind of home."

"You almost brought your piano."

"I didn't, though. I changed my mind, and I can keep changing it when I see another opportunity."

She lifted her eyes to his. "But what about Baby?"

"She's safe, she can still hunt in her way. She'd be happier without any human beings there. Even without the beeves, she'd be okay. There are small animals she usually catches. I can figure out what kinds of other animals can benefit from a sanctuary from here as well as there. All those zoo animals who don't want to be on display anymore can come to Davy's Island. Plus, it's easier to drive to the universities and harass experts from the mainland.

"But the main thing is, I want to have a chance at a relationship with you. With the people I love. I don't want to hide away anymore. I want to be here to build and fix things. I want to argue with you. I want to find out if your backpack really is full of keys, if you prefer fresh artichokes over canned ones—"

"Yes."

"I want to see all the pajamas you own. I want to take them all off of you. I want to debate which movies we should see, and have you convince me that your choice is better. I want to change my mind with you."

Zoey stared at a blade of grass. "I want this, too. But it sounds like you're giving up a lot. For me. And I don't even know what I am anymore."

"We can have time to figure that out."

She finally looked up. "I'm scared, Davy. I can't keep track of one single slide. My best friend is moving out of the apartment that I hate, and I'm terrified because I'll have to leave it anyway because I can't afford to rent it by myself. I keep subtracting and subtracting and subtracting things from my life and my path seems to get narrower until it's like I'm walking on a tightrope, and I can't look down or around me. I have nothing for *you*, Davy. That's what bothers me about this whole thing."

"But I don't want anything from you other than to learn more about you."

Maybe it was impossible. Maybe it was a lie. He wanted everything from her, but he wanted to give her his all, too. He knelt in front of her. He took her beautiful, sun-warmed face in his hands and held her velvety cheeks and stroked them with his thumbs, and it was like feeling music under his fingers.

As if echoing his thoughts, she said, "I want this so much and I'm scared."

Her eyes had fluttered shut at his touch, but with a seeming effort, she opened them again and...they widened.

God, she really was terrified.

"Davy," she whispered in a choked voice.

"I love you," he said, because she should know it even if she was frightened of the future. Maybe his love could be a handle, a perch, something to steady her.

"Okay, same. But Davy!" she said urgently.

Not the response he'd expected. But she was complicated. He'd go with it. "What is it?"

"You didn't by chance bring Baby with you, did you?"

"Uh, no."

"Is the Sunshine Coast known for cougars?"

A chill ran down his spine. He straightened. "Yeah. They sometimes attack dogs in the area. Not often, though."

She trembled and drew even nearer. "I think there's a cougar back there. Behind us. And I'm not about to check up close, but this one probably has all its claws."

CHAPTER 20

CONFESSIONS IN A SHED

Davy didn't even pause. He threw himself toward her, and somehow trundled both of them to the shed near the compost pile, slammed them inside. Before Zoey could catch her breath, he'd started piling bins and tools and boxes in front of the door.

"Make some noise," he said. "Bang on the walls of this thing. It's metal. It'll be loud. Cougars hate that. I'll call the house and tell everyone to lock their doors. I'll phone the conservation hotline. And I might have to call the police so they can put out an alert for Narrow Falls and the surrounding areas. That will be awkward."

"I can't believe you had the conservation hotline on speed dial," Zoey said.

"What?" Davy shouted.

He'd already started rattling some screws in a jar.

"Good you have the conservation hotline number!" she yelled.

She might be as loud as she could in every way she could, too. Except for some reason, it was making her want to laugh hysterically now.

He loved her. The Handsome was in love with her and he wanted to give up everything to be with her, and his reasoning was completely impractical and impulsive, which was why she loved him. Her emotions should have been tired from all the swooping and plummeting they'd done in the last hour, day, week. But all she could feel was energy bubbling up everywhere.

She was probably going to be eaten by a big not-Baby cat in the wilds of the Sunshine Coast, so nothing mattered anymore. Not the slide. Not The Plan. Not her fear.

Davy was barking orders into the phone as she clanged on the walls with a piece of wood she'd found.

"Davy!" she yelled.

"Are you okay?"

"Stop asking me that! Davy, I have to tell you something!"

She ran the wood against the corrugated edges of the shed, almost delighted with how awful it all sounded. "If I die—"

"Zoey, that's not going to happen. The walls of this thing are thin, but I don't think a cougar's going to bother."

"Let me finish," she yelled, and it felt great to put her whole body into the shout. "Davy, if I die in here, I want you to know you are a Good. Wonderful. Person."

She punctuated each of her last words with a hit against the wall.

"The sex was the best—" she put her whole arm into that one and oops, she may have left a dent in the shed wall "—I've ever had in my entire life."

Davy covered his phone with one hand, then looked at it. Then he yelled, "There's a cougar wandering in town. And also, I have to talk to Zoey. I'll have to call you back, Officer."

He turned, his whole focus zeroing in on her. The pounding noises they were making came in sync.

"I didn't want to face the fact that I have choices, but I do. I can go back to medicine. I don't have to keep that door closed just because I did it back then. The Plan made me think I didn't have choices. No, *I* made myself think I didn't have choices. It feels foolish and humble changing my mind, but we can make a new plan together, and it doesn't have to be set in stone. I don't have to live so scared all the time that I need a map."

She paused to take a breath. "Although I am sort of scared now."

"Zoey, we're in a metal shed screaming at each other because a cougar might attack us. I think you're entitled to a little fear!"

"But Davy, I don't want to die without trying to find happiness. There are always going to be people who don't like me, who want to hold me back, things and moments that make me have doubts about myself. But if I lose this chance to find out what I really love, and if I lose this chance to be with a person I love, then I'd be stupid. And I hate—" *clang!* "—BEING—" *clang!* "—STUPID!"

She screamed the last bit at the top of her lungs.

Davy dropped his jar of screws. "Zoey," he whispered.

She banged harder on the side of the shed to make up for his inattention to their predicament—her fault entirely, even though she was trying to avoid apportioning blame because there had been enough of *that*. Davy pulled her into his arms and, luckily, she managed to keep her leg thumping against the wall while he kissed her.

Oh, it was like joy and fireworks. Everything in his smile came out in the bright burst of his kiss. She could feel the vibrations of him against her teeth, every luxurious swipe of his tongue against hers tripping sparks behind her eyes, down her back, and deep down between her legs.

Davy broke the kiss. "Zoey, I love you. I want to help you do whatever you want to do with your life. I know it doesn't seem like I can accomplish a lot—"

"Stop that!"

She emphasized that with a huge kick to the side of the shed. "You can do anything you put your mind to. Your walking into my lab on Friday was the best thing that ever happened to me, and everything that followed has made me realize that I've been too afraid to live. You make me feel alive, Davy. You make me value my life."

Davy kissed her again and for a few moments, everything was quiet.

This time, it was her turn to break them apart. "At the same time," she yelled, renewing her noise with much vigor, "I mean it when I say I don't want to die now, so if you could call the conservation hotline again and see what's holding them up, that would be great!"

Both his and Zoey's enthusiasm for making noise was starting to flag, although between worry for Zoey's safety and calling the house to make sure everyone was all right, Davy had managed to get in as much kissing as possible. *Carpe diem*, after all. *Carpe* the-woman-who-was-too-good-for-him-even-though-she'd-hate-that-he-said-that-*em*. If they ever got out of this, he would look up the Latin and make it his motto, maybe get it tattooed on his arm, just like all the nonsensical Chinese characters he saw on biceps and shoulders out there.

He was so preoccupied with this full slate of thoughts and actions—and noises—that he almost didn't catch the rapping at the door of the shed.

"Wait, did you hear—?" he said.

"We've established that cougars don't knock," Zoey said uncertainly.

"It's the RCMP!" someone called out. "Are you all right in there?"

"We're fine!" Zoey yelled first.

It took a minute for them to realize that they could stop making their clamor. Suddenly the silence was very...silent. "We barricaded the door," Zoey said. "Give us a couple minutes."

Davy didn't go for elegance. He was ready to come out and start his new life with Zoey. He started throwing tools and boxes aside until he saw Zoey trying to stack his things a little better. Then he was more careful.

They were sweating and a little breathless by the time they threw open the doors.

But, oh, it was the best feeling in the world to be stepping out hand in hand with Zoey into the sunlight and the fresh air and to see everyone who had gathered together, all the people who wanted them to be safe and—in their own ways, and sometimes at cross-purposes—happy.

There was Li-leng, whose eyes sparkled when she saw them together. She let out a whoop when they emerged, and Zoey laughed. Sitting on a stump was his grandmother, looking somewhat annoyed—well, at least it was a little dialed down from her usual ferocious expression. Standing beside her was a confused but beaming George. Maybe it was a rare show of solidarity.

Davy smiled at the RCMP, too. Because he was happy. The last face was Constable Dutta, whom Davy almost didn't recognize because the man wasn't in uniform. He was the only one who looked relieved to see them.

"Constable!" Zoey said, going forward, and towing Davy with him. "You're all right!"

"Yes. I am. I'm feeling much better thanks to your efforts."

Constable Dutta blushed at Zoey's radiant smile.

But after that first hiccup of embarrassment, the man braced himself and held out his hand to Zoey and repeated, "Ms. Fong. Thank you. I mean it. I wanted to thank you for giving me the necessary medical attention, and for making sure I got to a hospital when the incident I'm not at liberty to discuss occurred. However, rest assured, Mr. Hsieh will be cleared of any wrongdoing."

He directed a quick look at Sergeant Green.

"I hope you're still on leave," Zoey said. "I thought at the time you might have had a reaction to the tranquilizer, and your foot is clearly still bothering you."

She indicated the crutch that the constable was holding.

"Oh...this."

Back to being embarrassed again. The constable scratched the back of his neck.

There was a brief silence.

Davy wasn't sure what was going on, but Zoey said, "The cougar is gone, I'm guessing? If you're all out here."

Li-leng rolled her eyes at her friend, but Zoey's question seemed to snap Sergeant Major Green back to realizing she was out here for a job and not just an uncomfortable garden party. "Maybe this will teach you to keep dangerous animals off your property, Mr. Hsieh," she said with a touch of asperity.

"First of all, Davy had no control over this mountain lion. The big cat out here was not Baby and as a member of the community you should know there are cougars around here," Zoey said. "Second, Mr. Hsieh, as you probably already know, did all the necessary paperwork and notified all the proper authorities about the cougar he has been trying to keep safe on the island."

Her voice rang out into the meadow. Maybe he and Zoey should've been standing out here the whole time. He could have let Zoey harangue the big cat with confidence, and he would have stood back and simply admired her.

"It's not like cougars are endangered," the sergeant major muttered. "Especially around here."

"Just because something doesn't seem like it's in danger doesn't mean it's not important."

Green narrowed her eyes and opened her mouth—a sure sign that an argument was pending—then she glanced at Constable Dutta and shut her mouth again. She cleared her throat. "Well, ah, wildlife officials told us you should be safe now. Constable Dutta insisted on coming out to see you to thank Ms. Fong—"

"And you, Mr. Hsieh," the constable interrupted. "For trying to come to my aid when I had to deal with Mr. Durrell."

Green looked stolid again and, if anything, she stood up straighter. Davy supposed she was probably uncomfortable with her underling interrupting her to tell her prime suspect he'd been definitively cleared. Well, let her feel awkward. She'd made him and Zoey—and George—plenty uncomfortable the last few days.

"Has the man who accused my grandson been charged?" A-mà asked in her clear, careful English.

"We're not at liberty to discuss a matter that is still under investigation," Sergeant Major Green said.

Davy gripped Zoey's hand tighter and beamed at them all. "Hey, I'm just glad you're up and about, Constable Dutta," Davy said.

It was so easy to be happy and magnanimous now that the sun was shining, and he was holding Zoey's hand and she loved him, and there was no threat from a mountain lion.

"So, I guess we can all head to the house, unless there's anything else."

George helped A-mà up, and the officers started walking. Zoey hung back with Davy and a smirking Li-leng.

"What?" Zoey asked. "Why is everyone looking at me and Davy this way? Or avoiding looking at us."

"You came out hand in hand, flushed and glowing after a

lot of banging in the shed. It sounded like you were having sex," Li-leng said.

"We were trying to keep the cougar away!"

Li-leng clapped her unburnt hand on Zoey's back.

"Is that what you kids are calling it these days? Whatever works. I'm happy for you."

CHAPTER 21

THE LOST AND FOUND

Later in their room, Zoey sat straight up, knocking Davy in the chin with her knee.

"The slide!" she said.

She scrabbled at the bedsheets as if she'd be able to find the cursed white envelope right there among the patchouli-scented linens.

"Should I be worried that you dislodged me to talk about the slide when I was about to go down on you?" Davy said, flopping to the side.

He was breathing hard.

"Mimi told me to destroy it if I ever found it again, and well, now I feel like I should complete the ritual. For closure."

Davy crawled up to be closer to her. "We can go look for it."

"No, it's late. We can't tunnel into a compost pile with flashlights in the middle of the night to dig around for a slide."

But no, common sense was going to rule this time. This wasn't her responsibility. She didn't have to finish this job. God knew, the slide hadn't been on her for most of the week. "We are definitely not doing that," she said, thumping the pillow for emphasis.

"But it's obviously bothering you. So why don't I promise to look, starting here."

He rolled up to kiss her stomach, then the undersides of her breasts. She let out a long breath as he touched her skin with his tongue.

"Uh, that's not where it'll be."

"But in your bra is the last place you remember it being, right?"

His fingers traced around her chest, two circles like a horny kid's drawing. He dotted her nipples with his thumb. Except that what she felt was nothing like an immature person's longing.

"I can be thorough sometimes," he said, his voice silky.

She buried her hands in his hair, pulling him closer. "I get swept up in you," she said. "Every time."

"And you don't like that?" he asked, looking up at her.

He smoothed his hand down her stomach to soothe her, but his eyes were the smallest bit worried.

"I get scared," she admitted. "For a moment. Because all of this is new to me. Being in love. Feeling free. It's like letting go of a handrail and leaning over a precipice to truly enjoy the view of what's in front of me. It takes getting used to."

Davy nodded and looked down, moving his hand lower to tease her between her thighs. "So you don't want the slide because you want your position back? You don't want to keep that in your back pocket?"

She shivered. "No, I want what's ahead. For us."

Zoey kissed the top of his bent head. "You don't have to worry that I'm going to have regrets when I realize now that all I wanted to do was quit. I jumped at the chance to run away with the slightest of reasons. I didn't have to follow you around town all day. I didn't have to scramble on a boat with you. I didn't have to put off looking through your crates—which really, you have to organize—for days and hours. I told myself I was trying to save my career by chasing after the slide, but what I really wanted to do was go after you. Follow my joy."

Davy did glance up then. "So, I could've put the thing in the mail all along?"

She was glad to see the worry gone from his eyes, replaced with a little crinkle of mischief in his brow. His finger tweaked her, and she gasped. "Yes. Stop that—no, keep doing that."

Zoey could feel herself getting distracted again. She wanted to let go. Wanted to feel his mouth all over her skin. She wanted him to suck with delight on her belly button, turn her over and lick his way up the curves of her ass, sometimes pausing to exclaim over her, to caress her until she quivered. She wanted him to kiss that spot between her shoulders that she couldn't reach, that she never really got to see. There were spots on her body that he already knew better than she ever would.

She wanted him to surprise her. And he always did, even when he did exactly as he was told.

But one little worry still niggled.

"It has nothing to do with you, you know. The fact that I think of the slide, the fact that I do like to finish things, get things resolved. It's just how I am. Sometimes I'm going to worry this way."

It was his turn to kiss her and soothe her. "And sometimes I'm going to have anxiety, and it's not going to be your fault."

"But I still don't know—"

He reached up and kissed her mouth, which made her stop talking. He kissed her nose. "I like this," he said.

He kissed her shoulder. "I like this. And I like this. And this."

With each flick of his tongue, each brush of his lips across her cheek and hair and collarbone, she felt herself slipping lower and lower until she was lying down on the bed once again, rolling over on top of him, and kissing him and biting him, wet and greedy and sloppy.

She grabbed a fistful of his hair, which she loved, and rubbed her cheeks on his stubble, reveling in the scratchy texture, the thereness of him. She put her lips against his tender mouth and felt him laugh under her and felt herself laugh into him.

Davy's body felt right to her. His strong shoulders, the carved-out chest—others might have seen it, but she was the one who got the mature version of it. She was the one who got to hug its warmth to her and press her ear against it so that she could hear the thumping of his heart underneath. She touched herself as she made her way down his body, kissing along his sides, so hard yet so ticklish, down his hairy thighs, stopping to scour the hair under her hands. He groaned as she teased him but let her take her time. Then finally she twisted to the nightstand to grab a condom, and both their hands tangled greedily to take it out, to smooth it over him.

She hadn't known how ready she was for this, but somehow in the journey down his body she found herself open and yearning. She was wet and panting with an exertion she hadn't known she'd made. He watched her, playing with her hair, her breasts and nipples, seemingly careless as she poised herself over him,

Her first slide down onto his cock was almost exhilarating and strange. The stretch of her muscles and tissues, the feeling of *him* so alive and insistent in her space. Maybe it always would be, and yet, her body wanted it again and again, warming to it, becoming fluid and stronger around him as she rode him.

Her body never felt freer, free to move as she wanted, to laugh and grunt and scream. She touched him everywhere her greedy hands could reach, grabbed and held his biceps even as they strained to boost and lower her body. She thrust her breasts shamelessly into his mouth, demanding his tongue and teeth on her nipples. With a smile on his face, he, of course, complied.

Later, much later the next day, in fact, Zoey was in her room packing up. There wasn't much. She'd come with a backpack with some gym clothes—and her bike, which Davy would fetch from the island later.

She, Davy, Li-leng, and Davy's A-mà were going to drive the car to the ferry to get them back to Vancouver. Zoey was going to drop off her letter saying she was withdrawing from the MD/PhD program, pack up her things from the lab and the house, and she and Li-leng would turn over the keys to the landlord. Then she, Davy, and Li-leng planned to come back here.

She didn't have a plan, but she had all the time in the world to come up with one.

For the first time in a while, she thought of her future without the sinking terror she'd felt when she got on her bike to cycle to the lab, without the panic in her lungs and heart every time she talked to her supervisor about her experiments, without the heaviness as she imagined years and years more in the lab with Post-it purloiner Alec and her gaggle of sad, ugly mugs.

Oh, and she was definitely throwing those out. Maybe that would be the first thing she did.

As she folded her laundry—she *was* glad that she was going to be able to put on some other clothing soon—she glanced at the top of the dresser.

A familiar white envelope lay on top.

She dropped the pile of clean clothing on the floor.

"Oh my God," she whispered to the empty room.

Her hands trembled as she reached out. If she touched it, would it disappear? No. The ceiling would fall on top of her.

No, the house would collapse around her but this room would stay intact, but she'd forget about the envelope as she went to save others, and she wouldn't remember until everyone was accounted for and mad at her because she'd brought this curse down upon them.

Maybe that was a little bit of magical thinking.

She grasped the envelope with trembling fingers, but her grip was so strong she had to tell herself to relinquish it in order to be able to peer inside.

The slide, small and transparent, winked at her in the sunlight of the room.

She kicked her clothing aside and left her room for the kitchen.

"Where did this come from?" she asked George wildly.

George looked up from over the sink where she was cleaning mushrooms. Zoey didn't even comment on them. She waited for George to reply.

"Oh, that? I suspected it was yours. I found it in the dining room."

"It's been in my room the whole time?" Zoey's voice rose.

"Well, you'd know it was there if you spent any time in it last night."

"George! I was looking for my slide. I was asking about it. I tore the house apart the other day and questioned you about it—"

"You *are* a little intense. But I guess if Davy likes that sort of thing, then I'm going to have to get used to it."

"I almost dove into a compost heap looking for my slide, George. Why didn't you tell me you'd found it?"

George blinked at her. "Your slide? I know what a slide is. That isn't a slide. That's an envelope with a piece of glass in it."

Zoey opened her mouth and shut it.

She was going to kill George. She was going to make George

eat one of those damn mushrooms and then she was going to have to drive her to emergency services to have her stomach pumped because she couldn't have this on her conscience.

She was going to— "Thank you, George. I really appreciate this. I was worried about it."

Zoey took a deep breath. She thought about dropping the slide and grinding it under her heel, as Mimi had wanted. But that was Mimi—not her. Zoey couldn't reshape her life for the sake of her sister or her idea of her sister anymore. She had to do what felt right for her. Instead, she took the slide to the study, labeled the envelope, and stuck it in a bubble mailer with her supervisor's address like anyone could have done all along. Then she left the kitchen to go find Davy and tell him the good news.

CHAPTER 22

A BABYLOGUE OF SORTS

A-mà was refusing to get off the boat. Which was a change from a few hours ago when she had refused to get on it.

"We're going to be late, A-mà," Zoey said.

"It's a party for a big cat. A big cat doesn't care about time."

But she stood up and stepped carefully off the ramp carrying her cane. She was followed by George and Li-leng and even Davy's older sister, Nina, who seemed even more skeptical than A-mà for all her silence.

Then again, for Nina, showing up to something of Davy's was already a spectacular and unprecedented show of support. He'd take that nod from his somewhat distant older sister.

As soon as they all settled on dry land, Davy felt the electric zing of nerves. This was normal anxiety, he reminded himself. They'd been planning the ceremony for months. But after it was all over this wouldn't have to be his show anymore.

Davy's family and friends were all there for the ribbon-cutting ceremony for the Hsieh Wildlife Sanctuary and Animal Rehabilitation Center.

A few interested people from town were invited. A local

news crew had even accepted the invitation to come out, as had the provincial minister for forests, land, and natural resource operations, who was chatting with the mayor.

Rudy Durrell was not there. The government had ended up seizing his land and his stakes in town when it was discovered after his scuffle with the RCMP that he hadn't been paying all his taxes. Rudy's island was now up for auction. Davy was almost tempted to bid on it, but Zoey had told him that he should concentrate on trying to organize what he already had instead of going in for a new project.

She was probably just afraid that he'd adopt more big cats.

It felt strange to have so many people on the island milling and loitering and laughing about in the small area in front of the house. He'd been so alone here, and he'd told himself he was content, but with Zoey around, everything was brighter, newer, shinier.

Although it was true that there were a lot of new developments on the island. The house had largely been refashioned into an animal clinic and a meeting area for the center's wildlife rehabilitation workers. He'd left some beds in place, however, in case staff got stranded on the island for inclement weather.

He had to smile a little at that memory.

As if knowing what was in his mind, Zoey stepped closer to him and leaned her breast into his arm. Beyond the curve of her cheek, he could see her smiling, too.

Sometimes, he couldn't believe she had moved from Vancouver for him. But, she'd explained, it was a pragmatic choice. First of all, she had wanted to practice medicine, and after her residency, the government had offered her forgiveness for some of her loans for working in a remote area. And second, their friends were with them.

He couldn't believe he'd ever wanted to be alone.

Davy and Zoey had ended up moving into the secluded

guesthouse behind the refurbished B&B. George brought her things into the main house, where she could cook and hold court. In the mornings, Davy walked Zoey into town to her clinic and then wandered back to spend time in the studio that he'd built to replace the shed they'd banged up. With Zoey's support, he'd overcome his aversion to taking even prescription drugs and found a balance of counseling and anti-anxiety meds that worked for him. His composing work had picked up, too. One of his songs for a commercial had ended up attracting the attention of a producer who'd asked him to score a fantasy C-drama with flying swords and high intrigue. He'd also written a simple ballad that one of the actors sang to tease the heroine, which had ended up getting remixed and parodied in the show's growing international fandom.

Li-leng, of course, delighted in sending him all the versions she encountered.

Someone found a chair for A-mà. Davy went up to the microphone and introduced the staff to the audience and made way for the minister of forestry and wildlife.

Clearly bored, A-mà leaned over to Zoey and Davy during the minister's speech. "When are you getting married?" she asked. Because now was as good a time as any to continue *that* particular conversation.

"She likes me now," Zoey told Davy.

A-mà said, "I don't. I've settled for you."

"Love you, too, A-mà."

It was Davy's turn at the mic soon enough.

He strode up with his guitar.

"Oh yes!" Li-leng screeched from somewhere in the small crowd. "Take off your shirt, Davy X."

Zoey was glaring at her former roommate, but Davy laughed and the rest of the audience cheered. "You probably don't want to hear any speech I could give. So I've written a song to mark the occasion."

He'd kept it simple. It was the first time he'd performed in front of more than five people in years, and he felt surprisingly comfortable in front of this group of faces that he loved. Well, he didn't love the minister of forestry and wildlife, but he tried to exude some warmth toward her nonetheless.

Maybe it was because Davy knew they weren't out for him to fail. They wanted this to work. A whole community, a whole town wanted good things him, for the animals, for this cause.

He found Zoey's bright face in the crowd and poured out the song for her. Because, of course, even though he'd managed to fit wildlife and conservation and rehabilitation and a list of animals in the lyrics, it was for her. They were all for her. Even the jokey song-now-meme about swords and heroines was for her. Maybe that one especially. He looked into her eyes and poured his voice, his heart in her direction.

Zoey took his A-mà's hand. George dabbed at her face with a tissue. They all looked so *proud* of him. It radiated from them. He could practically feel the warmth. He had to look down at his guitar for a moment and keep his eyes on his fingers because he was tearing up.

That was why at first he didn't notice the gasps from the crowd, and even the small scream.

"Davy!" Zoey shouted.

He looked right up at her, at his love, and sang to her louder. Her eyes shone. Were those unshed tears, too? She was going to hate that he'd seen that.

But then she stood and pointed behind him, and he half turned and caught a glimpse of *her.*

Baby.

The cougar was sunning herself on the roof of the house,

her belly up, her eyes closed. It seemed like she was enjoying the warm weather, the crowd, the music. He almost started laughing. This was why his solar panels always stopped working. This was why she'd sounded so close so many times. The big cat had somehow figured out how to get across the fence, and she'd been climbing the roof.

But when he turned back to the audience, he noticed that most of them had started retreating toward the boats. First among them was the minister of wildlife and forestry, who was apparently not a fan of the animals under her jurisdiction.

Ah well, the show must go on—but when it was over, it was over. He ended his song to the distracted applause of the few, foolhardy people who remained nearby.

What could he say to that? Upstaged by his own cougar. At least the ceremony hadn't taken too long.

"It appears we have a special guest," he said into the mic. "This is one of our elderly rescues, Baby. We'd like to ask that you all remain calm. Our staff are on alert, and your boats are ready for departure."

"Baby?" his grandmother said loudly in English. Zoey and his sister, Nina, were helping his grandmother from her chair, but A-mà was still talking. "This was not the kind of baby I was hoping for from you."

Zoey snorted.

Davy grinned and went over to lend a hand. "I thought you'd be used to disappointment by now," he said.

Zoey shook her head, and tucked herself into his chest, exactly where she belonged, taking a small moment of shelter before the next storm. "Never disappointment. Always the unexpected."

★ ★ ★ ★ ★

AUTHOR NOTE

Readers, I took liberties with British Columbia coastal geography. One cannot charter a private vessel from the Burrard Civic Marina in Vancouver to one's own private island. (Driving from the Vancouver area to the Sunshine Coast overnight with a burned hand is also not recommended.) Also, while I have only done cursory research on cougar behavior, everything indicates that one should not keep them under any circumstances. Canada geese are also best left alone.

ACKNOWLEDGMENTS

What a time we've been living through! Thank you so much for all the support and encouragement over the years. The emails, tweets, posts, messages, replies to newsletters—it adds up to a lot of love, and it means more than I can say. I am lucky to have you.

Big thanks to Alissa Davis, whose comments are always generous, insightful, and wise. Kerri Buckley, Stephanie Doig, Katixa Espinoza, and the team at Carina are a pleasure to work with. And thanks very much to my copy editors, the Harlequin Art Department, and the publicity and marketing people who make my books look good.

I've received a lot of pep talks/life talks over the years. Kate, Emma, Jenny, Jackie, Amber, you probably don't know how much even a short conversation with you helped. Sharone and Hayley, my film-buff friends, your enthusiasm when I described this project has kept me going.

I am indebted to Cindy Lee/Lucy Khoo, cancer researcher

and romance writer, who made many invaluable observations and suggestions. All errors are very much my own.

Thank you to Tara Gelsomino, who really believed in this book.

Finally, thanks to my opinionated extended family. To my husband and daughter, you are the joy in my life.